DEATH TRACK

SALLY RIGBY

TOP
DRAWER
PRESS

Edited by Emma Mitchell of @ Creating Perfection.

Cover Design by Stuart Bache of Books Covered

GET ANOTHER BOOK FOR FREE!

To instantly receive the free novella, **The Night Shift**, featuring Whitney when she was a Detective Sergeant, ten years ago, sign up for Sally Rigby's free author newsletter at www.sallyrigby.com

Chapter One

Detective Chief Inspector Whitney Walker sucked in a breath and let off six successive shots at the target facing her. It was impossible to see how accurate she'd been from where she stood, but she was confident she hadn't missed.

'Cease fire,' the instructor shouted at the ten officers lined up in the individual booths of the shooting range.

She'd spent the last three days on a firearms training course, and today was their final assessment. She had a good eye when shooting, and even though she rarely used it in her job, she made sure to keep up to date.

She was hoping to finish early so she could get in an extra visit to her mum and brother, Rob, both of whom had recently moved into care facilities following her mum's dementia diagnosis several months ago, which meant she couldn't look after her brother who had brain damage and was unable to fend for himself. Whitney resented having to move them, but her job made being a full-time carer impossible. The guilt was horrendous, but she knew they were in the right places.

1

'Don't move while I check your targets,' Ray, their trainer, yelled.

She pulled out her phone to see if she'd missed any messages, as her phone had been on silent. There was one from her Detective Sergeant, Matt Price. *Please call. Urgent.*

Damn. It had to be serious if he was messaging. He'd never been one to overdramatise or panic.

'I'll be back in a minute,' she said to Jeff, the guy in the next booth, as she hurried past him and made her way out of the range.

She pushed open the side door leading to the training centre's car park, and once outside, she called Matt.

'It's me,' she said when he answered.

'Sorry to bother you, guv. A teenage boy's been found dead on a train. Knife attack.'

'Shit. Do we know what happened?' Her body tensed. A murdered kid. It didn't get worse than that.

'No. All we know at this stage is he was found on the Newcastle to Lenchester train. I'm on my way to the station now. I wanted to let you know straight away.'

A knife attack on a teen was going to attract media attention, and as much as she trusted her DS, this wasn't something she would allow him to handle alone.

'I'll meet you there. I'm about forty minutes away.' Leaving the training before the end wasn't ideal, but there was no alternative.

'Are you sure? What about the course?'

'Leave it with me.'

She ended the call and returned to the range, heading straight to where Ray was examining the targets. 'I've just had a call from one of my officers. I've got an emergency to deal with,' she said as he glanced up from the pile of targets he was examining.

'You haven't finished the assessment. Don't you have people who can work on it for you?'

'Normally, yes. Not this time.' She debated telling him about the murder, then decided against it. It wasn't relevant, and she really didn't have time.

'I can't pass you unless you complete all the course components.' The trainer shook his head.

'Can I come back and take the remainder another time?'

If she didn't, she knew her immediate boss, Detective Superintendent Jamieson, would come down on her for wasting police resources. These courses were expensive, and he hadn't wanted her to go in the first place. He believed that, as a DCI, she should be more involved with the metrics and algorithms of twenty-first century policing, rather than what was happening at a grass roots level. She disagreed. Which wasn't surprising, as there was little on which they saw eye to eye.

'Give me a call and we'll see what we can arrange,' Ray said.

'Thanks. I appreciate it.' She flashed him a smile.

Why did criminals seem to sense when she had personal plans? She not only had to leave the course, which she was loving, but she had to cancel her family visits, with no idea when she'd be able to rearrange them. Murders took precedence over everything else.

Chapter Two

Sunday, 9 June

Whitney drove down the side road leading to the rear of Lenchester's railway station. She parked in one of the empty taxi rank spaces. Officers had been strategically placed at all the entrances, not allowing anyone in. Closing the station on a Sunday shouldn't be too much of a problem, and she was sure they could arrange bus transport back to the city from the next station on the line. Tomorrow would be a nightmare for commuters and traffic, though, if it remained closed. But until she'd assessed the scene, she couldn't make a decision on how they were going to deal with it.

There was a cordon around one of the trains, and a police officer was standing on duty.

'Morning, Beth. How's it going?' she asked the constable.

'Everything's in order, guv. I was first officer attending. DS Price is here, speaking to the Station Manager, and the pathologist is on the train.'

'Have the British Transport Police been here?' She

4

didn't want the BTP involved, however much they wanted to be. This was her investigation.

'Not to my knowledge, guv.'

'Good.'

Whitney checked all the relevant steps had been taken to secure and protect the scene from unnecessary evidence contamination, then scanned the log to see who'd been allowed into the scene, signed it herself, and walked towards the train. As she got closer, she saw Matt talking to a grey-haired man in a suit. When Matt saw her, he came over. He still had a slight limp from the gunshot wound he'd received a few months ago when he was acting as a decoy in a sting operation to catch a vigilante seeking revenge on men who groomed young girls on the internet.

'Sorry to drag you away,' he said.

'No problem. Tell me what you know.'

'This is the journey's end, so the conductor was checking everyone had got off, when he found the body. It was the fast train from Newcastle, stopping at Leeds, Coventry, Banbury, and terminating here.'

'Any witnesses?'

'None, so far. By the time the train arrived at Lenchester, there weren't many people on board.'

'Are any of them still here?'

'Unfortunately, not. The body wasn't found until everyone had left the train. The victim was in the last carriage to be inspected.'

Coincidence? Or well planned?

'We'll put a call out for passengers to get in touch,' she said. 'What about the conductor?'

'Stanley Crabtree. He's in the manager's office at the moment. In shock.'

'I'll need to speak to him.'

'He knows that. I've asked him not to leave until after we've interviewed him.'

She nodded. The conductor may have been the last person to see the boy alive. He could be a person of interest, too. They'd need to background check him, a-sap.

'Which pathologist is here?'

'Dr Dexter.'

Thank goodness for that. Claire Dexter was the best there was. She might have an awkward manner, but Whitney didn't care. She was in a class of her own, and in cases like this it was imperative to have the best.

'SOCO?' she asked, hoping he'd organised for the scene of crimes officers to attend.

'They're on their way.'

'Good. Take me to the body, then we'll speak to Crabtree.'

They walked along the platform to the last carriage. After pulling plastic booties over their feet and putting on disposable gloves, they stepped onto the train. It was old and had blocks of discoloured plastic seats with faded blue-and-green striped upholstery, all facing the same way. As they walked through, they came to two cream tables with seating for up to four people.

'This way,' Matt said as they headed to the rear.

'A perfect spot to kill someone, as there's no chance of anyone wandering through the train,' she muttered to herself.

'Stay where you are.' The booming voice of Dr Claire Dexter brought them to an abrupt halt.

In front of them was the Lenchester pathologist, whose looks belied her true personality. Smaller than Whitney's five feet four inches, and rounder than the detective's slight built, she had short red hair, which always looked like it could do with a comb, and she wore the most bizarre clothes imaginable. Always loud, and never matching. Peeping out from the neck opening of her protective suit was the collar of a bright orange shirt with purple spots. A pair of red and green enamel parrot-shaped earrings dangled from her ears.

'Hello, Claire. What have we got?' she asked.

'It's not pretty. Young boy. Stabbed in the heart region. Let me finish taking photos and you can come over.'

Whitney swallowed hard. *What the hell had happened?*

'Rigor?'

'Not yet. But that's hardly surprising seeing as he's on a train and the murder only happened a short while ago.' There was no mistaking the sarcasm in Claire's tone. Some things never changed.

'I hadn't thought of that.' She impatiently moved from foot to foot while the pathologist carried on taking photographs in the confined area.

'You can come over now,' Claire said as she stepped back from the double seat where the victim was situated, leaving room for them to move forward.

Whitney headed over, with Matt following. The boy was leaning against the window, his face white and jaw relaxed. A smattering of freckles across his nose were a stark contrast to his pallor. It was as though they'd been painted on. To all intents and purposes, it looked like he was asleep, until her eyes fixed on the dried blood on the front of the grey sweatshirt he was wearing. She shuddered. He was just a kid. Fourteen, if that.

There was a maroon and black rucksack on the seat beside him. 'Have you photographed that?' she asked, pointing to it.

'Yes. It's all yours,' Claire said as she put away her camera and packed up her case.

Whitney took hold of the rucksack and unzipped it,

hoping to find some identification. Inside there was an iPad, a food container holding a half-eaten ham sandwich, an empty crisp packet, and the wrapper from a bar of chocolate. At the bottom was a dark-brown leather wallet. She opened it, and in one of the slots found a photo ID card from Westfield Independent School, in Banbury. The name on the ID was Hugo Holmes-Reed. She glanced at the card, at the smiling face, and then at the victim. There was no mistaking the likeness. It was definitely him.

'Hugo Holmes-Reed.' She shook her head and looked through the rest of the wallet. Inside was a train ticket with today's date. 'It looks like he got on at Coventry and was going to Banbury. He must have been going back to school, as he has an ID for Westfield.'

She'd heard of the school but didn't know much about it, apart from it being independent.

'A Westfield boy. Good school,' Claire said, nodding.

'You know it?'

'Of course. One of the top ten schools in the country. My brother went there.'

Whitney shook her head. Of course he did. And no doubt the forensic psychologist, Dr Cavendish, who she worked with sometimes, would know the school, too. Whitney had suddenly surrounded herself with posh people. And it was just plain weird. That aside, this was the sort of case on which she could use George's professional capabilities. Except she couldn't call her now, as she was spending the weekend with her parents. Most inconvenient.

'We need to contact his family. Hopefully his address will be in here.' She went through the remainder of the wallet, but it wasn't there. She then searched through the rest of his backpack but still no address, though she did find a mobile phone, which she dropped into an evidence bag. She'd take it back to the station for her resident research guru, the young Detective Constable Ellie Naylor, to check. She was trained in extracting information from mobile phones, which saved them enormous amounts of time, as it meant they didn't have to send phones to the digital forensics unit and wait for their analysis. She'd also get Ellie to do a quick background check on the conductor.

'Matt, contact the school and get the victim's address.'

'Yes, guv.' He walked to the other end of the carriage.

She glanced out of the window and noticed Jenny and Colin, two members of the forensics team, walking down the platform.

'SOCO's here,' she said. 'We'd better get out of the way and let them do their work.'

'How come I don't get the same treatment?' Claire said, locking eyes with her and arching an eyebrow.

'You love me being here. Who would you moan at, if I wasn't?' Whitney quipped.

'If you say so,' the pathologist replied, rolling her eyes.

'When will you have something for me?' she asked Claire.

'You expect me to dignify that with a response?' the woman said, shaking her head.

'I'm not asking for an exact time. I know it depends on what you find. But I was hoping for something approximate, like tomorrow morning, maybe.' She knew Claire wouldn't give her anything concrete, but she asked anyway, just in case. Usually, she'd ask a question and Claire would refuse to answer.

'Some time tomorrow, yes. I'm not committing myself to a time. I'll be in touch when I'm ready.' The pathologist dismissed her with a flick of the hand, picked up her equipment, and squeezed past her and Matt, who was heading back towards Whitney.

'Did you contact the school?' she asked.

'Yes. They gave me his address in Coventry.'

'Let's speak to Crabtree, and then we'll head out to see his parents.'

They left the train and went into the red-brick building housing the ticket office, waiting room, and station offices. When they arrived at the room labelled "Station Manager", Matt knocked and a man answered the door.

'Mr Hughes, this is DCI Walker,' Matt said, nodding in Whitney's direction. 'We're here to speak to Stanley. Is he still with you?'

'Yes. Come in.' He held open the door and they walked through.

'We'd like to speak to him alone,' Whitney said as the manager was about to close the door.

'Okay. When can we open the station again? Having it shut is playing havoc with our timetables.'

She understood where he was coming from, but it hardly showed respect for the body of the young victim. That aside, she couldn't answer his question until SOCO had done their work and her officers had started investigating. She also wanted to hear from Claire before a final decision was made.

'Not today. We'll be in touch to let you know.'

'Can we at least move the train into one of the sidings? It makes it easier for trains passing through,' he said, his tone impatient.

'Once forensics have finished then, yes, it can be moved.'

Moving the train would help preserve the crime scene and stop people going on board.

'Thank you,' he said as he opened the door and left the room.

She walked over to where the conductor was seated at a round table with Matt.

'I'm DCI Walker, from Lenchester CID,' she said, holding out her warrant card. She sat on an empty chair next to her officer. 'Please could you take me through exactly what happened.'

The conductor audibly sucked in a long breath. 'I've never seen anything like it. We come across all sorts in this job. I've seen someone dead after a heart attack. I've seen bloody fights. But, a young kid. I'm telling you; this will haunt me until I die. It—'

'Mr Crabtree,' Whitney said, gently, interrupting him. 'I understand how awful it must have been. Why don't you start from where the journey commenced? Take your time and tell me exactly how it all went.'

'Sorry. It was just so … so …' He held up his hand. 'The details. I get it. You want the details.'

'Thank you.' Whitney nodded encouragingly.

'The Newcastle to Lenchester train on a Sunday is usually only a quarter full, if that. Today was no exception. I checked the tickets of everyone on board when we left Newcastle, and then each time new people got on. It's a fast train and there are only four stops: Leeds, Coventry, Banbury, and Lenchester. Nothing seemed strange.'

'Do you remember checking the victim's ticket?' she asked.

'Yes. He got on at Coventry.'

'Can you remember who else got on at that station?'

He paused for a moment. 'Five people got off and four got on. The young boy, and a woman with two children.'

'Can you remember who got on and off at Banbury?'

The murderer could have got off the train there. Or did he wait until Lenchester? Either would be possible.

'Actually, no. I didn't see. I was talking with the driver.'

Damn. 'Do you remember who else was in the carriage with our victim?'

'He was alone when I checked his ticket. There were people in there when we left Newcastle, but they got off at Leeds and Coventry.'

'How many people?'

'Three. A young couple in their twenties, who got off at Leeds, and an elderly woman on her own, who left the train at Coventry.'

'What about in the other carriages?'

'This train only has six cars on a Sunday. There were people in all of them. The last one, where the boy was, isn't one that usually fills up. Most people prefer to sit in the others.'

'Why's that?'

'It happens on all trains. The first two or three carriages are the most popular, then the fourth, fifth, and so on until the last one. I think it's because people are anxious to find a seat as soon as possible, so they can settle. On quiet trains there are rarely many people in the last carriage.'

Did the murderer know that? It was something they needed to consider during the investigation.

'Leading up to when you found the body, did you notice anything out of the ordinary?'

'No.' He shook his head. 'Once the train had emptied, I did my usual check of all the carriages to make sure everyone was off and to pick up any lost property. When I got to the last carriage, I almost didn't see him, as he was slouched down against the window and hidden behind the headrest of the seat in front. When I did notice him, I thought he'd fallen asleep. I went to wake him, but before calling out I spotted the blood on his top. I then noticed his half-opened eyes ... lifeless ... and then I realised he was dead.'

'What did you do next?'

'Ran to get Mr Hughes. He took charge and phoned for you lot.'

She glanced at the clock on the wall. It was already three, and they needed to get to the victim's family. It was an hour's drive away, and she didn't want to ask the Coventry police to handle it. She owed it to the family to be the one to break the news, as she'd seen Hugo. She also needed to arrange for a formal identification of the body.

'Thank you for your help, Mr Crabtree. Do you live locally?'

'Yes. I live in Lenchester.'

'I'd like you to go to the station and make a formal statement. We also need your fingerprints so we can eliminate you from our enquiries.'

'Do you want me to go now?'

'If you can. I'll radio on ahead and someone will be expecting you.'

The conductor left, and Whitney called the police station, making arrangements for him to be dealt with when he arrived.

'Let's go,' she said to Matt once she'd ended the call. 'We need to speak to this poor kid's family.'

Chapter Three

Sunday, 9 June

Dr Georgina Cavendish sat back in the chair at the expensive restaurant her parents had insisted on visiting for their twice-yearly lunch. She enjoyed good food, but this particular restaurant was more pretention than excellent cuisine. Even on a Sunday afternoon it was full of Oxford's glitterati, and reservations had to be made months in advance. Unless you were her father, of course, who had successfully operated on the owner's son, saving his life, which meant he could eat there whenever he wanted.

'I know the Vice Chancellor of your university. Would you like me to have a word about you failing to get the post you applied for?' Her mother sat opposite, making her usual Vivienne Westwood statement in a terracotta pleated skirt and white pinstripe shirt with lace trim.

'No thank you, Mother,' she said, picking up her glass and taking a sip of the excellent Smith Woodhouse Vintage Port her father had ordered with their dessert.

'Why ever not? I've told you many times, it's not what you know but who you know in this life.'

'I'm happy staying as a senior lecturer.'

Her mother glanced at her father, who was staying uncharacteristically silent.

'Really?' her mother said.

'I wasn't at first, especially when I found out who was offered the position. However, I've since realised it was for the best, as it means I can continue working with the local police, as well as undertaking my research and supporting the students.' Why did she feel like she was making excuses, even though it was the truth? She'd been angry at first, having never been turned down for anything in the past. But she meant what she'd said. She had the best of both worlds, and wouldn't change it.

'And why is that a preferred option from being an Associate Professor?' her father asked.

'I enjoy putting theory into practice. I work with a good team of police officers, especially DCI Walker.'

'Georgina, I fail to see how working with police officers can be as fulfilling as what you do at the university. Admittedly, being an academic can't be compared with surgery or international law, but it's a good career option for someone of your ability,' her father responded.

Did he ever listen to himself? Well, she wouldn't give him the satisfaction of knowing his attitude affected her.

'It's extremely fulfilling. What's better than using my knowledge to help prevent murderers from getting away with their crimes?'

'Well, at least one of my children is high-flying,' her father said, not answering her question.

George tensed. He was referring to her younger brother, who was also a surgeon. She'd planned to do the same, but her medical career hadn't lasted long, thanks to her aversion to blood. She'd then briefly considered law, following in her mother's footsteps, but decided against it once she'd discovered forensic psychology.

'Edward, stop being so negative towards the girl. She's doing the best she can,' her mother said. If only her words didn't come across as being patronising.

'Maybe she should settle down and have a family,' her father said.

It was like they'd forgotten she was sitting there.

'Well, she can hardly do that now she's split from that delightful young man she was seeing. I was so hoping for some grandchildren.'

They were referring to Stephen, who she'd been seeing for a while last year. It didn't turn out well. But that wouldn't matter to them. He came from an exceptionally privileged family, who were distantly related to aristocracy. They'd have forgiven him almost anything to have those connections.

'Mother, the delightful young man to whom you refer, cheated on me. Not only that, he'd had a vasectomy, so he was never going to have any more children.'

'Who are you going to bring to your brother's wedding?' her mother asked, seeming oblivious to her comment.

Not only was her brother an eminent surgeon, but he'd found a suitable partner. A paediatrician with a family who had all the right credentials, too.

George hadn't met her future sister-in-law, but she knew exactly how she'd be. To quote Whitney Walker, *she'd be posh and typically stiff-upper-lip English*. Exactly how Whitney categorised George. They'd moved past that stereotype and were now friends.

'I'm sure I'll find someone to bring,' George said.

'Hmmm,' her mother said. 'I'm not sure *finding someone*

is entirely appropriate. Your partner has to be suitable for such an occasion.'

'Trust me, Mother. I do know how to behave, and the person I bring won't show the family up.' She surreptitiously glanced at her watch, willing the lunch to be over.

'What research are you undertaking at the moment?' her mother asked.

'I'm writing a paper on working with the police as a forensic psychologist, and how it aided in the arrest of the twins who carried out the Campus Murders. You would have seen the case reported in the media.'

'Sounds fascinating,' her mother said.

'I fail to see how's that going to contribute to the field,' her father stated in his usual overbearing manner.

She could always count on him for the put down.

'Well, for a start it—'

'May I take your plates?' a waiter asked, interrupting her as he approached their table and leaned in to retrieve the plate in front of her father.

'Leave it,' he snapped, his tone icy. 'We're in the middle of a conversation.'

'Certainly, sir.' The waiter stepped back and stood a few feet from them.

'Was there any need to speak to him like that?' George said through gritted teeth, angered by her father's behaviour.

'I will not tolerate rudeness.'

George leaned back in her chair, thankful she only had to meet up with her parents twice a year. It was more than enough. Her father was so full of his own self-importance, he failed miserably to be empathetic to those around him in any way, shape, or form. Not that she excelled on the empathy front. She knew that. But she wasn't bombastic and rude.

Her mother, on the other hand, let most of this pass her by. Considering she was a highly sought-after international human rights lawyer, when it came to family, she was off on another planet.

'Edward, he was only trying to do his job,' her mother said.

'And as I've said before, Fleur, it's not acceptable for someone to interrupt without a by your leave.' He turned his head to where the waiter was standing and clicked his fingers. 'Now you may take the plates.'

As the waiter came forward, George took a look. He was around her age, mid-thirties, tall with curly blond hair. As she was checking him out, he glanced up and his blue eyes locked with hers. He gave an almost imperceptible wink, and she averted her gaze, embarrassed at being caught out.

After he'd left, she turned to her mother. 'What case are you working on at the moment?'

'I can't tell you too much about it, because it's confidential. But let's just say I'm hoping we can extricate a young woman from the Middle East and bring her over here.'

'I look forward to hearing all about it when you're able to tell us more,' she said.

'You'll probably see it in the media before we next meet.'

And of course, her mother wouldn't ever think of telephoning to keep her up to date. Sometimes George felt she was out with virtual strangers.

'What about you, Father? Any new cases with famous people?'

'None I can talk about. Especially as you've now started consorting with people who might not realise the importance of keeping one's council.'

'I'm certainly not going to tell everybody the ins and outs of your private patient list. And irrespective of that, I trust the people I work with on the force. If you'll excuse me, I'm going to the loo.' She took the white linen napkin from her lap, placed it on the chair, and left the table.

She was annoyed with herself for getting angry. It never happened, other than when she was with her parents. She skirted around the tables. The restaurant was still full, despite it being late into the afternoon. As she headed down the corridor leading to the ladies' loo, she accidentally walked into someone.

'Sorry.' She glanced up and saw it was the waiter.

'Don't be. It was my fault,' he said, a soft Irish lilt to his voice.

'You don't have to show deference to me, I'm not my father.' An embarrassed laugh escaped her lips, taking her by surprise.

'I'm glad to hear it.'

'He doesn't mean it,' she said, feeling duty-bound to make an excuse for her father's behaviour.

'I get it. I'm just a waiter and should know my place.'

He had her father nailed.

'No, of course he doesn't think that.' She caught his eye and noticed it twinkling. 'Yes. That is his view. But it's not mine.'

'That's good to know. I'm Ross.' He held out his hand.

'George,' she said as she shook it, surprised at how his hand enveloped hers, making it seem small, which it most certainly wasn't.

'Pleased to meet you, George. I haven't seen you in the restaurant before.'

'I'm sure you can't remember every person who eats here.'

'If they looked like you, I would. You have an incredible jaw line.'

She frowned. Was that a compliment? It certainly wasn't one she'd heard before.

'Thank you. I won't keep you any longer. I don't want you to get into trouble.'

'That's very considerate of you.' He grinned. 'Would it be too presumptuous of me to ask if you'd like to have dinner with me sometime?'

Was he asking her out on a date? It sounded like it. She hadn't been on one since finishing with her ex, and there had already been enough said about him that lunchtime. Maybe she should go. First impressions of him were favourable. She glanced across to where her parents were seated and imagined their response if they found out she'd agreed to go out with their waiter. That swayed her. How could she say no?

'Yes, I'd love to.' She opened her bag, pulled out a business card, and handed it to him. 'Here are my contact details.'

He took hold of the card and stared at it. 'I look forward to it, *Dr George*.' He flashed a smile in her direction and headed back into the restaurant.

Chapter Four

Sunday, 9 June

'Come on. Let's get this over with,' Whitney said to Matt as they stood outside the large double-fronted Victorian house belonging to the parents of Hugo Holmes-Reed. She rung the bell, and the door was opened by a woman in her late thirties wearing running gear.

'Mrs Holmes-Reed?'

'Yes.'

'I'm DCI Walker from Lenchester CID and this is DS Price. May we come in?' She held out her warrant card.

'What's it about?' A worried look etched itself across the woman's face.

Having to tell a family their loved one was dead was bad enough, but when the victim was a child, it was on a whole different level. It never got easier, no matter how many times she had to deliver the news. She'd learned not to let her emotions show, even though at times it was hard not to break down and cry. But it wasn't her grief. She owed it to the victim's parents to remain in control. It wasn't easy, though, when she considered how her daughter, Tiffany, wasn't much older than Hugo.

'We'd rather discuss it inside, please.'

The woman opened the door and ushered them into a narrow hallway. 'What is it?' she repeated once they were inside.

'Is your husband in?' Whitney asked.

'He's in the sitting room. We've just got back from a run. I was just about to have a shower.'

'Perhaps we can go in there, so we can talk to both of you together.'

The woman led them into the room, where a man about the same age as his wife was sitting, drinking from a water bottle.

'It's the police. They want to speak to us,' Mrs Holmes-Reed said anxiously.

Her husband, a tall wiry man with closely cropped hair, jumped up from his seat, a guilty expression crossing his face. 'On a Sunday? Surely this could've waited. We can speak in my office, next week. I've already explained, I had no knowledge of the embezzled funds. It doesn't have to involve my wife.' He went to move towards the door.

'Mr Holmes-Reed, I'm not sure what you're talking about, but it isn't why we're here. Please, sit down.'

'I don't want to sit.' He glared at her.

'It's about your son, Hugo,' Whitney said, gently.

'Hugo? He's at school. I took him to the station myself, this afternoon.'

'I'm sorry to have to tell you, there was an incident on the train and—'

'An incident? Is he hurt? What happened? I told you he wasn't old enough to travel on the train by himself.' Mrs Holmes-Reed's voice cracked.

'He was attacked on the train. His injuries were too

severe for him to survive. I'm very sorry for your loss,' Whitney said, maintaining eye contact with the woman.

Mrs Holmes-Reed stared at her for several seconds, her face expressionless. Suddenly she let out a piercing, anguished scream. Her husband, who had turned deathly pale, rushed to her side and held her in his arms. He guided her to the sofa, and they sat down. Whitney and Matt sat opposite on single armchairs.

'Can you tell us what actually happened?' Mr Holmes-Reed's voice was stilted, like he was trying to stay in control.

'It's too early to say conclusively, but we are investigating,' she said.

'I want to see him,' he said.

'Of course. We will need you to make a formal identification of Hugo.'

'Why him?' Mrs Holmes-Reed moaned. 'I didn't want him to get the train, but he insisted. Why didn't you back me up and say no?' Her fists were clenched, and she thumped her husband on the chest.

'Stop, Vicky,' he said, gently removing her hands from him. 'It's not helping.'

'Mr Holmes-Reed, I'd like to ask you some questions, if you're up to it?' Whitney said, forcing herself not to be distracted by the palpable grief in the room.

'Yes,' he said, nodding.

'Did anyone know Hugo was going to catch the train back to school?'

'We only decided this morning. He might have sent a text to one of his friends. I don't know, he didn't say.'

'How often did he come home during term time?'

'Usually only at half-term, but he came back this weekend for his younger brother's birthday party yesterday.'

'Where is your other son?'

'He's with my parents. His grandparents. I dropped him around there after taking Hugo to the station.'

'Would you like us to contact them for you? They could stay with your wife while you come with us to make the identification,' Whitney suggested.

'I want to see him, too,' Mrs Holmes-Reed said. Tears stained her face, but she looked determined. 'I want to come with you, Alan.'

'Okay,' her husband said, taking her hands in his.

'We'll take my car and then go to my parents' house after.'

'I'm not letting you drive,' he said. 'You're not up to it.'

'Are you sure?' Whitney interrupted. 'We can take you both to Lenchester and bring you back here, later.'

Mr Holmes-Reed glanced at his wife. 'Thank you, but no. We'd rather be alone.'

'I understand. Before we go, please may we take a look at Hugo's bedroom?' Whitney asked.

'Why?' Mrs Holmes-Reed frowned.

'We'd like to check if there's anything out of the ordinary in there. Anything that can help us identify who has done this to your son.'

'I'll show you the way,' Mr Holmes-Reed said as he got up from the sofa.

He led them out of the sitting room, across the brown and white geometrically shaped floor-tiled hallway, and up the dark wooden stairs. He opened the first door on the right, and they walked into a large square bedroom with a bay window overlooking the road. On the walls were posters of Coventry City football team.

Mr Holmes-Reed leaned against the door frame, while Matt and Whitney pulled on disposable gloves and searched. There was a desk against the wall, but there was nothing on it other than two comics and some juggling balls. On the floor was a rumpled pair of jeans and a sweatshirt. It was a typical fourteen-year-old's bedroom. Whitney opened the wardrobe and saw a selection of clothes hanging, with a few items screwed up at the bottom.

'Did Hugo have any hobbies?' she asked.

'He loved his football, and whenever he was home, we'd go to watch Coventry play. He was in the school football team and also liked swimming and tennis.'

'So, he was very sporty,' she said.

Mr Holmes-Reed nodded and let out a low moan. 'I can't deal with this. What are we going to do? What?' Tears filled his eyes and rolled down his cheeks.

'Why don't you go downstairs to be with your wife,' Whitney suggested. 'We'll meet you back there. We won't be long.'

The man nodded and left them alone.

'God, I hate this job sometimes,' Matt said as he shook his head.

'I know,' she agreed. 'We walk into people's lives and change them forever. I don't know what I'd do if Tiffany was taken away from me.'

'Try not to think about it,' Matt said as he looked through Hugo's possessions.

After a thorough search there was nothing obvious that could help, so they went downstairs. Whitney's throat tightened at the sight. Mrs Holmes-Reed was crumpled up, while her husband, sitting next to her, was as stiff as a statue. Silence filled the room.

'Would you like me to make you both a cup of tea before we go?' she asked.

'No, thank you. We'd rather go and see Hugo,' Mr Holmes-Reed replied, his knuckles white against his knees.

'Okay. We'll leave now and you can follow in your car.'

She drove to the morgue, making sure to keep the parents in sight in her rear-view mirror. She'd phoned on ahead to alert the duty pathologist they were on their way. Unfortunately, it wasn't Claire, as she was in a meeting with the coroner.

The journey took just over an hour. She parked outside the morgue, which was adjacent to the hospital, and left Matt in the car. When Mr and Mrs Holmes-Reed joined her, they seemed calmer and more in control than earlier. Whitney knew it wouldn't last, as once they saw their son's body the reality of the situation would hit them.

'It's just through here,' Whitney said to the couple as they pushed open double doors and headed down the corridor.

As usual, the faint sickly sweet smell, disguised by the overpowering antiseptic odour, hit her, and she could see by their facial expressions, it had done the same to the couple. She opened the door to the morgue and turned right, into the small office where the pathologists worked.

Tim Haig, the duty pathologist, was sitting at one of the desks. He stood.

'Hello, Dr Haig. This is Mr and Mrs Holmes-Reed. They've come to identify Hugo.'

'I'm very sorry for your loss,' Tim Haig said. 'If you'd rather not see him, I can show you photographs, and you can identify him that way.'

Mr and Mrs Holmes-Reed looked at each other and were silent for what seemed like ages.

'I want to see him,' Mrs Holmes-Reed finally said, her voice a whisper.

'We want to see our son,' Mr Holmes-Reed agreed, nodding.

'As you wish,' Dr Haig said. 'You can view him through here.' He ushered them out of the office and into a small room with a window from which the main lab area could be viewed. There were three stainless steel tables, and on the one closest to the window, a body covered in a sheet was stretched out. Whitney took a step back so the couple could see.

'Are you ready?' Dr Haig asked.

'Yes,' Mr Holmes-Reed said, his fists clenched by his side.

The doctor left the room and walked into the lab. He pulled back the sheet, but only as far as the young boy's neck, which Whitney was grateful for. She didn't want them to see the stab wound.

Mrs Holmes-Reed gasped and grabbed hold of her husband's hand. He stood there staring, his jaw tight.

'Is this your son, Hugo?' Whitney asked.

'Yes,' Mr Holmes-Reed said, his voice raw and broken. 'Thank you.'

She nodded to the doctor, and he covered Hugo's face with the sheet.

'Let's sit in the office for a moment,' Whitney suggested. 'Any chance you can rustle up some tea or coffee?' she asked the doctor as they left the room.

'I'll get some out of the machine,' he said.

The couple sat on the office chairs.

'I'm so sorry you had to go through that,' she said.

'You better get the bastard who did this,' Mr Holmes-Reed said, his eyes bright with anger. 'If you don't, I will. I won't rest until we find out who took my boy. He...' His voice broke and he collapsed in on himself, violent sobs shaking his body.

His wife, who'd been silent, rushed over and pulled him into her arms, stroking his head, whispering soothing platitudes.

Whitney couldn't bear to watch, so she left them alone and went into the corridor.

'I'll get the fucker who did this, if it's the last thing I do,' she said to herself.

Chapter Five

Monday, 10 June

'Good morning. It's Claire,' the pathologist said as Whitney answered her phone.

'I didn't expect to hear from you so soon.' She glanced at her watch. It was only eight in the morning, and even though Claire worked long hours, early starts had never been her thing.

'I wanted to speak to you about something of interest on the body.'

'Go on.'

'I believe chloroform was used on the victim before he was stabbed,' the pathologist said.

'To subdue him?'

'That would be the most likely reason. I could tell from the smell once I was doing the autopsy. I've sent his bloods to toxicology, and that should confirm it. We're lucky we got to him quickly. Chloroform doesn't stay in the blood-stream for long.'

Newspaper headlines flashed in Whitney's mind. Chloroform. Knife attack. Train. A series of murders all over the country.

'Oh, no. Not us. Please not us,' she muttered.

'You know something?' Claire asked.

'If it's what I think it is, we're sitting on a time bomb. You heard of the Carriage Killer?'

'I know of those murders. Why do you think this is linked?'

'What isn't widely known is that chloroform was used in the attacks. I heard about it by chance. If it's Lenchester's turn, this is the first of four. I better go. I need to speak to George, PDQ. We're going to need her help on this one. We'll come and see you later this morning and discuss the rest of your findings, if that's okay with you?'

'It will have to be,' the pathologist said in her usual way before ending the call.

Whitney keyed in George's number, strumming her fingers on the desk while she waited for the psychologist to answer.

'Whitney. How are you?'

'Fine. How was the weekend with your parents?'

Although the psychologist didn't often confide in her, she did mention how arduous she found the time she spent with her folks. Whitney's relationship with her parents had always been loving and deep. She still missed her father, even though he'd been dead for over ten years. She pitied George for not having a close family.

Whitney didn't have many friends because she spent so much time at work, but George was special. It was thanks to her that towards the end of last year Whitney's daughter Tiffany was saved from being murdered by a pair of psychotic twins. No words could ever express her gratitude. She'd walk over hot coals for the woman.

'As to be expected, and not something I want to relive if it's all the same to you. Why are you calling?'

Whitney was used to George's abrupt manner and didn't take offence.

'A young teenage boy was stabbed to death while travelling on the train yesterday. The killer used chloroform to subdue him. If the offender is who I think it is, we need to act fast. There'll be other victims.'

'What else can you tell me?'

'No clues were left, apart from the chloroform, but that hasn't helped. If I'm right, after choosing an area, four murders will be carried out over a two-week period before the killer moves on. Lenchester is the fourth city to be targeted. How soon can you get here?'

'Give me a couple of hours. The students are on exam leave at the moment, but I do have a tutorial with one of my PhD students. Shall I see you at your office?'

'No. Meet me at the morgue. We'll speak to Claire together.'

She ended the call and went to the incident room next door. Her team was waiting. It was a large space and had around twenty officers working from there. She headed to Ellie's desk and handed her the evidence bag containing the victim's phone that she'd taken out of the storage room earlier.

'Take a look through this and see if our victim texted anybody while he was on the train. He might have seen something suspicious and told someone about it.'

'Yes, guv.'

Whitney walked over to the board at the back of the room and wrote *Hugo Holmes-Reed* in the centre.

'Listen up, everyone. I've just been speaking to Dr Dexter and she's given me some information that leads me to believe we're dealing with a serial killer.'

'Not the Carriage Killer, guv?' Frank, the oldest detective constable on her team, said.

'It looks like it, especially as chloroform was used. But we can't discount a copycat. I want all CCTV footage in and around Lenchester railway station checked.'

'Is there CCTV on the actual train?' Frank asked.

'You'll need to check. As far as I'm aware there isn't. It's just on the platforms. The train was one of the older ones.'

'Well, if it isn't, it should be.'

'Agreed, but that's not important at the moment. I also want you to get in touch with both Coventry and Banbury police forces and train stations, because it's likely the murder took place somewhere between those locations. The victim got on at Coventry and was due to get off the train at Banbury, where he goes to school, so we need to see footage for those areas.'

'He could have been murdered in Lenchester. If he'd been given chloroform before Banbury and it looked like he was asleep, no one would have noticed,' Matt suggested.

'Yes, that's another consideration. But why wait? Why not sedate and murder straight away? Dr Dexter may be able to give us the time of death, although I suspect it won't help us, as the locations are so close together. I want background checks on everyone who works at the station. Doug, if you can do that, starting with Stanley Crabtree, the conductor on the train and the one who found the body.'

'Yes, guv,' Doug said.

'Sue, I want you to get in touch with Westfield School and speak to the head teacher. Find out everything you can about our victim. We need to know if anything unusual happened there. Find out whether the victim was liked, who his friends were, and what the staff thought of him.

Speak to as many staff and students as you can. Take one of the PCs with you.'

'Yes, guv,' Sue said.

'Actually, Matt, you can go with,' she said, changing her mind, as she trusted Matt's light touch and knew he'd get the information they needed in what was going to be a fraught situation.

'I've heard of that school. Don't they wear straw boaters and act like something out of *Tom Brown's School Days*?' Frank said.

'I have no idea. But judging by the way he was dressed, I think it's just a normal school. Well, normal for posh people,' Whitney said.

'I'm surprised you've even heard of Thomas Hughes, Frank,' Doug said.

'Who?' the old detective asked.

'He wrote the book.'

'What book?'

'*Tom Brown's Schooldays*,' Doug said.

'I remember seeing it on the telly. You know I don't read books.'

'Guys, focus,' Whitney said.

'Yes, guv,' both detectives said in unison.

The team was close, and the banter between them good natured. But she still needed to pull them in line sometimes.

'Ellie, once you've examined the victim's phone, I want you to produce a list of people who were on the train. We need to interview them as soon as we can. The journey commenced in Newcastle.'

'I'll get in touch with the train operator and check credit card payments, so we can see how many tickets were bought and where from,' Ellie said.

'We need to ask members of the public to come

forward if they were on the train. It doesn't matter where they got on or off, they might have seen something, and we need to interview them. Right, let's move it. I need to see the Super to arrange a press conference.'

She left the incident room and made her way to Detective Superintendent Jamieson's office. Usually she liked to keep her distance from her boss, but in this instance, she had to get his permission to speak to the media.

She and Jamieson had a love-hate relationship. Actually, the more she thought about it, hate-hate was a better description. He was new to the force, in comparison to the number of years she'd put in. He'd come in through the Fast Track scheme and was keen to be promoted as soon as possible. She was keen for him to be promoted, too, but not for the same reasons.

When she reached his office the door was shut, and she could hear him speaking on the phone, his voice booming out, as usual. She waited until he'd finished and knocked.

'Come in,' he called.

He was seated behind a large reproduction antique desk, surrounded by his certificates of achievement on the wall. He might have gone to Oxford University, but she wasn't impressed. Perhaps she should put up on her office wall the gold medallion swimming award she'd earned at primary school, when she was ten.

'Good morning, sir. I need to talk to you about yesterday's murder.'

'I've only just heard about it, as I wasn't contactable yesterday.'

'Our victim is a fourteen-year-old boy, on his way back to boarding school after spending a weekend at home with his family. Having spoken to Dr Dexter, I believe it's linked to the carriage murders carried out over the last two years.'

'Carriage murders?' he said, frowning.

Seriously? He didn't know anything about these murders? There had been plenty of media coverage.

'Yes, sir. There have been twelve murders over the past two years. It's a pattern whereby the killer targets an area, kills four passengers on separate occasions, and then moves on to somewhere else. So far, the murderer has avoided capture.'

'Where have the murders taken place?'

'On trains running through Glasgow, Liverpool, and Bristol. The media is aware of something, but so far, we've been able to keep it from them. We need a press conference to let them know and to encourage people on the train to come forward.'

'I assume the Regional Force is part of the wider investigation,' Jamieson said.

'I believe so, as the murders have crossed county lines. But I don't know much about the RF's investigation, as it hasn't impinged on us up to now.'

'The first thing we must do is contact them and see how they can help us.'

'With all due respect, sir. We don't know for certain whether it is the Carriage Killer. It could be a copycat. We need to investigate ourselves first, before we consider handing the case over to anyone else.'

'Walker. I know you like to do things your way, but you're not an island. We need to speak to the Regional Force and prepare them for the possibility Lenchester is the next area. You can leave that to me. I'll let you know the results of my discussion.'

Witney's arms were rigid by her side. She hated him interfering. She was well aware they would need to speak to the RF and find out what they had. But this was the beginning of the enquiry, and it was her case. She wanted to have the facts straight before involving other forces. They'd come in and want to take over. She wasn't going to allow that.

'But, sir …'

'No buts, Walker. We're doing it my way.'

'What about the press conference?' she asked, struggling to remain calm.

'We can go ahead with that. I'll arrange it for later on today.'

'Thank you, sir. Then we can start gathering witnesses. If our investigation leads us to conclude this is the work of the Carriage Killer, we're on a tight timeline. I'll get in touch with the forces where the other murders took place and ask them to send over their files, just in case. Then we can compare notes and work out when to expect the next murders.'

'Keep me informed of anything you find out, and I'll email you the time of the press conference once it's organised. This is to be kept as our investigation. I don't want the BTP involved.'

'Yes, sir. They've already handed over the reins, given the severity of the case.'

She left his office, managing to hold it together until far enough away from him not to hear.

'For fuck's sake,' she said out loud, though there was no one close by. 'What is it with the man that he winds me up so much? He needs to stick to his paper pushing and leave the rest of us to do what we do best.'

Chapter Six

Monday, 10 June

George walked into the morgue and headed to the office, where she saw Claire sitting at her desk, staring at the computer screen.

'Morning, Claire. How are you?'

'What the fuck?' Claire said, slamming her hand against her chest. 'Don't creep up on me like that. You nearly gave me a heart attack. What are you doing here?'

'I've arranged to meet Whitney to speak to you about the murder victim.'

'Well, you're early.'

'She should be here any time soon.'

'You can wait here, providing you're quiet, as I'm trying to finish this report. Sit over there.' The pathologist pointed at one of the chairs on the other side of her office.

'Is it on the victim?'

'No, it's a funding application for some new equipment we need. It's like getting blood out of a stone. Anyone would think I was requesting a hot tub for my garden. My

37

job would be so much easier without all this administrative crap.'

'Funding applications are my speciality, if you want some help?' George offered.

'Thanks, but no thanks. It would take too long to explain everything to you. I'll do it myself, if you'll just be quiet for a moment.' She let out a frustrated sigh and ran her fingers through her short red hair until it was sticking out at all angles.

'I'll grab a coffee from the machine. Would you like one?'

'No,' Claire responded, without even looking up, as her fingers started to run across the keyboard.

George left the office and went into the corridor where the vending machine stood. She wasn't a fan of the coffee from here, but she hadn't had time for one earlier. As she was taking her cup, the double doors swung open and Whitney walked in.

'Get one for me, too, please,' the officer asked.

Whitney's addiction to caffeine was legendary. George had learned by experience you should never let her go more than a couple of hours without any, or she became extremely grumpy.

She got another coffee and handed it to her. 'Here you are.'

'Thanks. I need this.' Whitney took a sip and screwed up her face. 'Not that the coffee here is anything to write home about, but it will have to do. How are you doing?'

'I'm fine, thank you.'

Whitney stared at her, and George shifted awkwardly on the spot. She didn't like being scrutinised.

'Why are you staring at me?'

'There's something different about you, and I can't decide what it is.'

'That's ridiculous. I'm exactly the same person you saw the last time we met.'

'No. There's definitely something different. I just can't put my finger on it. It's as if you're more relaxed than usual. Yes, that's it. More relaxed and lighter, somehow.'

'Nonsense. I've barely spoken to you, so you can hardly discern anything. You have a very vivid imagination.'

'It's that sort of look you get when you begin something new. Something exciting,' Whitney persisted. 'Maybe you have a new boyfriend and haven't told me.'

A lucky guess. Whitney wasn't to know George had arranged to go on a date. Not that one planned date counted as a new boyfriend. Although she had to admit, she was looking forward to seeing Ross. He'd phoned within an hour of her leaving the restaurant, and they'd arranged to meet that evening in a pub ten miles away. Midway between Lenchester and Oxford, where he lived. She hadn't planned on mentioning it to Whitney. Should she?

'I don't know what you're talking about,' she said, deciding against telling her friend. There was nothing to tell. And if she did mention it, Whitney would go into detective mode and want to know the ins and outs of a guy she hardly knew anything about, other than he was a waiter and his name was Ross.

'Okay, have it your way. Come on, let's go and see Claire.'

'She was finishing up a report when I went in a few minutes ago. She might be free, now.'

They walked into the morgue. Claire was out of her office and standing by one of the tables. She turned her head as they entered.

'Over here,' she called.

When they reached the table, Claire pulled down the

overhead light, illuminating the body. She pulled back the sheet covering the young boy.

'What a waste of life,' George said, shaking her head.

'I know,' Whitney agreed. 'We have to catch the bastard who did this before they kill anyone else.'

'Good luck with that,' Claire said. 'If it's the murderer you think it is, catching him won't be easy. He's lasted this long without capture.'

'That doesn't mean we won't be the ones to succeed,' Whitney replied forcibly.

'You said *he*. Has it been ascertained the murderer is male?' George asked.

'Not that I know of,' Whitney said.

'I don't know for sure, but in most instances, this type of murder is committed by a male. It's expeditious to say *he* rather than *he/she* every time we discuss it,' Claire said.

'What have you discovered, so far, Claire?' George asked.

'Plenty. First, if you look at the wound, you can see how the blade was held flat, so it slid between the ribs. Your offender is definitely someone who has knowledge of the most efficient way to kill. It gives two opportunities. If it hits the heart, then death is likely to be instantaneous. If the lungs are wounded, they fill with blood. The victim, in effect, drowns in their own blood. In this instance, the knife went straight through the heart.'

Whitney swallowed hard. 'Fuck. That poor kid.'

'We can tell from the angle of the entry point the perpetrator was right-handed,' Claire added.

'So, the killer would have subdued the boy using the chloroform, and then stabbed him. But to get the exact entry point, would he have had to lift up his sweatshirt?' Whitney asked.

'Not necessarily,' Claire said.

'Can you tell if that's what happened in this instance?'

'Judging by the amount of blood on his clothes, and the tear where the wound entry was, I don't believe the victim's clothes were moved.'

'What about the chloroform? Couldn't that have killed him?' George asked.

'Yes, it certainly could. You're one step ahead of most people. It's not like they show in films or on TV, where a chloroform rag is used and it simply anaesthetises the victim. It can be fatal if too much is given, or if a chloroform-soaked cloth is placed too firmly over the face.'

'In which case, can we assume there was something symbolic in using the knife to kill the victim? Otherwise why not just kill with the chloroform? It would've made the murder much easier,' George said.

'That's your area of expertise, not mine,' Claire said.

'How long before the murder was the chloroform given?' Whitney asked.

'It depends on the dosage. A small amount would make a person tired and dizzy straight away and may cause a headache. A slightly stronger dose could render someone unconscious almost immediately.'

'And if that was the case, they wouldn't feel any pain while dying,' George said.

'So, what you're saying is, it's possible the murderer didn't want to cause any discomfort to the victim. He just wanted to kill?' Whitney said.

'Exactly,' George said. 'It indicates it wasn't anything particular about the victim that caused him to be chosen. It's the same as the previous murders where the victims weren't linked. Three cities. Twelve random people.'

'So why does he do it?' Whitney asked.

'It's the actual killings themselves which are important. The killer could be sending a message.'

'But what? And to whom?'

'Obviously, we can't get into his head, but the fact all murders are committed on trains must be considered. We need to know more about the other murders before we can draw further conclusions.'

'Agreed,' Whitney said.

'Then again, it could just be chloroform was used to prevent the victim from screaming,' George said.

'Not necessary. When someone's been stabbed in the lungs or heart they can't call out or scream,' Claire said.

'And if the killer knew what he was doing, as you mentioned, he'd certainly know that,' Whitney said.

'True. Plus, if he carried out the murders in empty carriages, it wouldn't matter if the victims screamed, because no one would have heard them,' George said.

'Do you still believe he was doing it so there was as little suffering as possible?' Whitney said, looking at George.

'It's certainly a possibility.'

'Any chance you two can continue this discussion elsewhere and leave the rest of us to get on with our work?' Claire said. 'I have nothing more to discuss with you until I have the results back from the lab.'

'Okay, Claire, we get it. You want to be left alone,' Whitney said.

'Hu-bloody-ray. Finally, you're beginning to understand,' the pathologist replied.

'Before we go, you haven't mentioned any trace evidence found,' Whitney said.

'There were some fibres around the mouth, which I believe came from the cloth used to sedate him. Other than that, nothing of any significance.'

'Thanks. Now, we're leaving,' Whitney said.

They left the morgue and walked along the corridor.

'Are we heading back to the incident room, or do we have time to go to the crime scene? I'd really like to see it,' George said.

'I thought you might. We'll go there now.'

After arriving at the railway station, they parked in the car park and made their way towards the building.

'Did you close the station yesterday?' George asked.

'Yes. They were allowed to re-open today. The train where the incident occurred is parked over there in the sidings.' Whitney pointed across the track. 'We'd better go inside and let the station manager know we're here.'

They walked into the station and up to the information desk. Although there were three people waiting in the queue, Whitney went to the front, holding out her warrant card.

'Please call Mr Hughes and let him know we'd like to speak to him.'

The person on the desk picked up the intercom. 'Mr Hughes, please come to the information desk. Mr Hughes to the information desk. Thank you.' The woman replaced the intercom. 'He shouldn't be long,' she said.

They moved to the side so the woman could continue dealing with the customers.

George glanced around the station. Although the red-brick building was old, inside it was modern. She rarely travelled by train these days, preferring to drive most places. She enjoyed driving; it was her stress release.

'DCI Walker,' a voice called.

George turned in the direction of the voice and saw an older man in a grey suit with a white shirt and red tie. His hair was cut short and thinning on top.

'Good morning, Mr Hughes,' Whitney said. 'This is Dr Cavendish; she's working with us on the case.' George nodded in his direction. 'We'd like to go onto the train. Is it locked?'

'It is. I'll let you on board. How's the investigation going? It hasn't been on the news yet, although I've had the press calling for information about the incident. As instructed, we haven't said anything. They didn't appear to know there had been a murder.'

'We're going to inform them later today. Thank you for keeping it quiet.'

They walked out of the building and turned left along one of the platforms, until reaching some stairs, which took them over the bridge to where the train was situated.

Mr Hughes unlocked the front carriage.

'We'll take it from here,' Whitney said.

'Do you need me to wait for you?' he asked.

'No, but we might have some questions after we've finished.'

Once he'd left, Whitney pulled down the handle and opened the door. They stepped into the carriage.

'This train's got to be way over thirty years old,' George said as she observed the worn seat coverings and the marks on the wall.

'I suspect the choice of an older train is deliberate.'

'It makes sense, as it's likely there's no CCTV in here, making it a lot harder for the perpetrator to be caught.'

'We need information about the other murders to see if it's true of those as well. The murder took place in the last carriage,' Whitney said.

As they walked through the train, each carriage was much the same as the first. Worn and old.

'I read somewhere the UK has the oldest trains in Europe. They really should update them. Though I suppose it's a cash problem,' George said.

'It shouldn't be, given the price of train tickets.'

When they got to the last carriage, there were signs of forensics having been there.

'Did SOCO turn up anything?' George asked.

'Not that we know of, yet. Obviously, there were hundreds of fingerprints, but I doubt any belonged to the murderer, as he would've worn gloves. How else could he have evaded capture for so long?'

'How many passengers were travelling in the carriage?' she asked.

'According to the conductor, it was a quiet day, particularly Banbury to Lenchester, the last leg. He noticed that, apart from the victim, only three other people were in here, and they got out before the victim got on. Not that it would've stopped anyone from coming into the carriage once he'd done his rounds.'

'As it was quiet, you'd have thought someone would have noticed a person strolling through the train and coming into here,' George said. 'Especially as they would have left through the door they used to come in.'

'Exactly,' Whitney said.

'Hang on, I want to check something.'

George went back to the previous carriage to check whether she could see anything, but thanks to the connecting doors, it was impossible to get a good look. She returned to Whitney, who was staring at the seat where the boy was found.

'What were you looking for?' Whitney asked.

'I wanted to see if the murderer could've seen the boy from the next carriage. He couldn't.'

'But that doesn't mean he wasn't in there,' Whitney said.

'True. And it would be the perfect place to lay in wait.'

'So, at the moment, we believe the murderer was probably sitting in the next carriage and then made his move, after checking out who was in here,' Whitney said.

'On which platform did the train come in?' George asked.

'Platform one.'

'Let's take a look and see if there's anything that might help us,' she suggested.

They walked back through the train and made their way over the bridge until they got to platform one.

George walked to the end of the platform, assuming that was where the last carriage would have ended up. 'Anyone on the platform could have seen the boy through the window, as he was on this side of the train.'

'Except no one would be this far down. Once people got off the train they would have turned right for the exit,' Whitney said.

'We need to check on what days the other murders were carried out. Presumably they wouldn't all be on a Sunday afternoon, as that would make it much easier for the police to catch the killer.'

'We'll also look at the passenger lists and compare them. I'm assuming the murderer would've staked out the line before deciding which route to go for. We need to get back to the incident room and see what the team have discovered. I haven't heard from Jamieson with the time of the press conference.'

After informing Mr Hughes they were leaving, they left the station.

'Are you spending the rest of the day with us, or do you have to get back to work?' Whitney asked.

'I've got a couple of hours, but then I must get back. Let's go. We've a lot to do, and judging by the timeline of the other killings, not long to do it.'

Chapter Seven

Monday, 10 June

Whitney pulled out a hand-mirror from her bag and quickly smeared on some lipstick. After running her fingers through her dark curly hair, which she'd worn loose that day, she slipped on her jacket. She was running late, and Jamieson would go off on one if she missed the start of the press conference. She picked up her bag, slung it over her shoulder, and hurried out of her office through the incident room. She glanced at those members of her team who were there and not out in the field.

'I'm just off to the press conference,' she said to no one in particular. 'I'll see you later for a briefing.'

She left the room and half-walked, half-ran down the corridor, going directly to the conference room. When she arrived, Jamieson was outside the room speaking Melissa, the PR officer.

'You're late,' Jamieson said, making a show of looking at his watch.

'Sorry, sir. Got caught up on a call.'

'Let's do this,' he said.

Melissa pushed open the door, and they were greeted by a cacophony of sound. Camera crews were at the back, the arms of their tall mics hovering high over the crowd, and reporters were sitting in front. Jamieson and Whitney sat at the table, and Melissa was seated to the left of them.

'Thank you for coming,' Melissa said. 'I'll hand you over to Detective Superintendent Jamieson.' She slid the mic towards him.

'Good afternoon. As many of you are aware, an incident took place at Lenchester railway station yesterday. A fourteen-year-old boy's body was found on the train. We are treating this as a suspicious death and would ask any members of the public who were on the train which left Newcastle at eight-thirty yesterday morning and arrived in Lenchester at one-ten in the afternoon, to make themselves known to us.'

'Questions?' Melissa asked, as she leaned towards the mic.

'How was the victim killed?' a reporter sitting in the front row asked.

'We can't disclose that until the pathologists have done their work and it's been reported to the coroner,' Jamieson said.

'What is the victim's name?' another reporter called out.

'We're not disclosing his name at the moment. We want to protect the family's privacy at this difficult time.'

'Could this be the work of the Carriage Killer?' someone called from the back of the room.

Whitney took a surreptitious glance in her boss's direction. The question wasn't unexpected, but they hadn't discussed what they were going to say. She assumed he wouldn't mention their suspicions, but she wasn't certain. In her opinion, he often acted irrationally and didn't think through the wider consequences of his actions. He'd no doubt disagree.

'We're not ruling out anything. However, we have several more lines of enquiry to pursue before we draw that conclusion.'

She supposed that was the best she could hope for.

'If it is the Carriage Killer, we should expect more murders,' the reporter added.

'Once we've done our investigation, we'll have more to tell you. But, at the moment, what we really need is for people to come forward if they believe they have any information regarding the incident. Especially if they were on the train at any point during the journey from Newcastle to Lenchester. Thank you for your time.'

Jamieson stood, and Whitney and Melissa did the same. They headed out of the conference room, and the PR officer walked on ahead.

'We'll go back to my office, and I'll update you on my discussions with the Regional Force,' he said.

'Yes, sir.'

Had he given them carte blanche to take over her investigation? Or was he going to let her do her job properly?

They walked in silence until they got back to his office. He took off his jacket and hung it on the coat stand in the corner of the room.

'Sit down.' He gestured to one of the chairs in front of his desk, and he walked around and sat on his. 'I've spoken to the Detective Super at the RF who's in charge at their end, and he's very interested in contributing to our investigation. They've already helped the other forces who have had similar murders.'

'Yet haven't managed to catch the perp,' Whitney said, arching an eyebrow.

'I've asked for copies of their files.'

Clearly, he wasn't going to acknowledge her comment.

'And when will we receive them?'

'Shortly. He wants to send a couple of his guys to work with us on the case.'

Whitney tensed. That was all they needed, some know-it-all cops who wanted to take over.

'Even though we've no idea whether it's the same killer. I'm surprised they want to waste their resources until we know for certain. Considering how strapped for cash every police force is at the moment.'

'Once I mentioned the use of chloroform, he seemed fairly certain we're dealing with the same perpetrator. I agree with him. The similarities are too great for it to be a coincidence.'

'I'm still not convinced they can help. I'd rather just have the files. Did they tell you anything of use?'

'He said to expect a second murder within a few days, a third a few days after that, and a fourth exactly two weeks after the first.'

'We could've worked that out for ourselves, based on what has happened in the past. I'm guessing it's because they have very little to go on.'

'Walker, you have to realise you're not a one-man-band.'

'I think you mean one-person-band, sir.' He was always going on about how she needed to be current. So should he.

'You know what I mean. If the RF is prepared to send two of their officers to help, then we should welcome the assistance.'

She was fighting a losing battle, but she wouldn't give up without him knowing her feelings on the matter.

'Just because they're the RF, doesn't make them any better than we are at our jobs.'

She hated the elitism implicit in any discussions surrounding the Regional Force. She'd worked with them on a case in the past, and it hadn't ended well. They might be the most far-reaching force in the country, but that didn't mean they were the best. Far from it.

'Walker, it's no longer up for discussion. You will work with them when they're here, for the good of the case. This is not all about you.'

'Yes, sir,' she said through gritted teeth. 'Do we know when they'll be arriving?'

'The Detective Super didn't know. The officers he wants to send are currently involved in another case, so it might not be until next week.'

At last, something she wanted to hear. She'd have solved it by then, without their interference.

'Okay.' She forced back the smug smile threatening to cross her face.

'And while I have you here, I understand you left the firearms training early yesterday, missing the afternoon session.'

It didn't take long for her absence to get back to her boss. Did the tutor have a hotline to him? What was it about those people? All they wanted to do was conspire to get her in trouble. It wasn't like she'd disappeared to meet a friend or go to the cinema. She did actually have something more pressing to deal with.

'The only reason I left was because I had a message regarding the murder. I accept we're taught to delegate, but this was one instance when I thought you'd want me to be there and take charge. Especially as we needed someone senior there to ensure we had no issues with the BTP trying to muscle in. Am I wrong?' she challenged.

'You should have sought my permission first.'

'You'd already told me you weren't contactable yesterday, so that wouldn't have been possible. I made the decision and stand by it. I have a good team, but when there's a young boy who's been murdered, that's where my priority lies. The only thing I missed was part of the final assessment, and I've arranged to do it another time.'

'That's really not the point, Walker. You have a history of ducking out of things you don't want to do. Under normal circumstances, you leaving wouldn't be an issue, but this is more of the same. In addition, I went out on a limb to get you a place on the course, as you well know. You can go now, as I have other things to do. I want you to get everything ready for when the RF officers arrive.' He dismissed her with a flick of his hand.

'Yes, sir.'

'And don't let me hear you've been anything other than cooperative. Otherwise, you'll have me to answer to. I need you to be on top of the investigation.'

Whitney seethed all the way back to the incident room. How dare he treat her like that? He was happy enough when she solved cases and he had the results he wanted. But he had to realise that getting results can conflict with conforming to the rules. Good policing sometimes involved going out on a limb, within the law of course, and she wasn't going to change the way she operated. She just had to pray he'd soon get promoted.

The incident room was buzzing when she got back, as most of the team had returned.

She went to the board. 'Listen up, everyone. I've just come from the press conference, which means we'll soon be receiving calls from the public. Make sure someone is by the phone at all times. Right, where are we so far? Ellie?'

'I've run the victim's phone through the self-service

kiosk and found he sent two texts to a friend saying what time he'd be arriving and confirming their plans for the evening. There was no mention of anything out of the ordinary on the train. I've also got lists of credit card payments from the different stations, for those who had bought tickets. What we don't know yet is whether the purchasers were the ones who actually got on board. In the case of the victim, his ticket was bought by his father, Mr Holmes-Reed. I'm going to contact all of the buyers.'

'Well done. Where are we with the CCTV footage, Frank?'

The older detective always enjoyed CCTV work. It meant he could stay in the warmth of the office and be close to the facilities.

'As you know, there's none on the actual train, so at the moment we're looking through footage from Lenchester station. People getting off the train, and those waiting on the platform. With the exception of an adult with two young children, all travellers getting off here were on their own. Once we track them down, we can interview them.'

'What about the other stations?'

'We're still waiting for the footage to be sent. They're going to email it to me,' Frank said.

'Let me know when it arrives. Sue, who did you speak to at the school?' she asked, directing her question to the officer sitting next to Ellie.

'Matt and I spoke to the head teacher, Hugo's house-master, and several of his friends. They were devastated but had nothing to add to the enquiry. He was a popular boy, good at sport, worked hard, and didn't cause any problems.'

'We asked them not to mention anything to the press, as we haven't yet released Hugo's name,' Matt added. 'But I don't know how long before it's public knowledge.'

'I agree, especially as at the press conference reporters were asking if it was the work of the Carriage Killer. They'd already made the link.' She shook her head. 'Doug, where are you on the background checks?'

'Nothing on Stanley Crabtree, guv. He's worked on the railway for twenty years. I've received a list of employees from the station manager, and I'm going through it now.'

'We also need background checks on the employees at all the stations on yesterday's route. Newcastle, Leeds, Coventry, and Banbury. You'll need help.' Her phone rang, and she pulled it out of her pocket. It was George. 'Okay, good job, everyone. We'll meet again in the morning.' She answered her phone and walked into her office, closing the door behind her. 'George?' She'd only left an hour ago, what did she want?

'Just thought I'd ring to see how the press conference went, before I go home.'

'Do you fancy a drink, and I can fill you in on everything so far? I could do with offloading, as Jamieson's being his usual self. What is it about that man? I've been trying so hard not to let him rub me up the wrong way.'

'I've told you before, it's all about mindset. You go into his office expecting the worst, and that's what you get.'

'Since when have you become my therapist?' She laughed.

'Someone has to, or you'll drive yourself mad.'

'So, what time for this drink? We could meet at the Crown and Anchor.' It was nice and quiet, and they wouldn't bump into anyone they knew.

'Sorry, I can't tonight. I've already made arrangements, which I can't cancel,' George said.

Damn. It looked like a night in on her own, unless she popped to the pub near the station. There would be plenty of people there to speak to. But not to confide in. 'Okay, no problem. Are you coming in tomorrow?'

'Yes. I can be with you all day.'

'Great. Where are you going tonight? Somewhere nice?'

'Umm ...' There was a pause. Why was George being to secretive?

'What do you mean "umm"? Don't you want to tell me?' Whitney asked, intrigued by the doctor's out of character behaviour.

'If I tell you, don't read anything into it.'

'I knew it. You're going out with someone, aren't you? I could tell before from the way you were acting. You've got yourself a new boyfriend.'

'He's not a new boyfriend, and I didn't tell you because I knew this was how you'd react. Jumping to unjustified conclusions.'

'Are you, or are you not, going on a date?'

'It depends on your definition of date.'

Whitney let out a sigh. 'Talking to you can be so difficult. Are you going out with a man? Someone you haven't been out with before?'

'Yes. I'm going out to dinner with someone I've met.'

'A date. So, I was right. What can you tell me about him? Does he work at the university?'

Knowing George seldom did anything other than work, go for drives in her car, or occasionally see arty films with subtitles, which Whitney didn't understand, she thought she was right in assuming he was a colleague. George didn't mind the lack of social life. She said she preferred it that way.

'No, it's not someone from work.'

'Well, who is it? You don't go anywhere to meet potential dates. It's not someone from here, is it?' Not that she could think of any single guy in the Lenchester police force George would be remotely interested in.

'No, it's not.'

'Why are you being so secretive? I don't understand.'

'Okay, I'll tell you. And maybe we can put this issue to rest. I'm seeing a man I met when I was out with my parents. He works at the restaurant where we had lunch yesterday.'

'A chef?' Whitney's cooking was ridiculously bad. She'd love to have someone cook for her.

Of course, George was excellent at cooking, as she was at everything.

'No, he's not a chef. He was our waiter.'

Whitney's jaw dropped. '*You're* going out with the waiter?'

She didn't see that one coming. Not that she had anything against waiters, but George was so smart, and such a high-powered academic, she couldn't imagine her with someone who had an ordinary job. She should stop being so stereotypical. Maybe this man was what George needed. Someone who was in the real world and not full of long words and pompousness.

'I know what you're thinking, but he seemed nice. My father was rude to him. That was one of the reasons I agreed to see him.'

'To get back at your dad? That's not like you at all.' The one thing about George was she didn't allow her emotions to get the better of her.

'I know, but sometimes my parents frustrate me so much it makes me want to do things I wouldn't normally do.'

'That makes you human.'

'Are you saying I'm not otherwise?'

'You know I'm not. Anyway, he must be nice, otherwise

you wouldn't have said yes, irrespective of what your father said to him.'

'I'll know more after this evening.'

'Where are you going?'

'Out for a pub meal.'

'I want to know everything about it when you come in tomorrow. This is the first date you've had since splitting up from what's-his-name.'

Whitney knew George hadn't been out with anyone since the ex. Mind you, she could talk, as she rarely dated. There just wasn't enough time in the day for her to do everything.

'Yes, this is my first date since Stephen. From what I've seen so far, Ross is very different.'

'I look forward to hearing every little detail tomorrow. Enjoy yourself, and I'll see you first thing in morning.'

Chapter Eight

Monday, 10 June

George pulled open the wardrobe door and stared at the row of clothes, all in order, ranging from smart to casual. What should she wear? Something dressy? Or would she be better in jeans and a shirt? It would have been good to ask Whitney, but it was too late now, as she had to leave to meet Ross in twenty minutes. She'd already done her make-up; nothing heavy, just light, natural coverage.

There was a frisson of excitement in her stomach, which was weird. She'd never experienced that before. Thinking back to Stephen, they had worked together, and it wasn't until many months after they'd first met that he asked her out to the theatre. It was a gradual thing, and the first time they'd gone out had seemed perfectly fine and easy to navigate.

It was the same with others she'd dated. She'd only ever gone out with people she'd known as a friend first, while at university and work, and there hadn't been many. She didn't like meeting new people, and didn't manage social situations well, often saying things which caused upset without even realising she'd done it.

Glancing at the rail of clothes again, she decided to go casual, and pulled out a pair of navy jeans and a pale pink-and-white striped shirt, which she paired with some flat, dark blue sandals.

After going into the garden for a calming cigarette, she cleaned her teeth and left the house. She drove out of the city, enjoying the scenery once she'd reached the country-side. The light evenings made it her favourite time of year. She arrived at the pub early so stayed in her car for ten minutes, as she'd no idea whether Ross was inside. He certainly hadn't come into the car park since she'd been there.

Feeling a little apprehensive, she stepped out of the car and made her way to the entrance.

'George.' She heard her name as soon as she was inside. She hadn't been there before, but it was a typical country pub and restaurant, with low beams and a convivial atmosphere.

Ross walked over to where she was standing. He looked different out of his uniform. She'd forgotten how tall he was. Definitely over six foot, which meant he wouldn't feel intimidated by her height, as many men did.

'Hello, Ross.' She held out her hand to shake his, and he looked at it and laughed.

'I don't think we need to be that formal,' he said, leaning in and kissing her on the cheek. 'I've booked us a table. The restaurant's through there.' He pointed to a room off the main bar.

Once in there, they were shown to a table. It was already busy, which she assumed meant they'd made a good choice of venue.

'Would you like to sit here?' Ross asked, pointing to the

chair facing outwards, so she could see what was going on. Stephen wouldn't have done that, as he always wanted to face the action. She hadn't minded, but the fact was he'd never given her a choice of where to sit. He'd just assumed she'd be fine where she'd ended up.

'Thank you,' she said.

'I'll get us a drink while we're waiting to be served. What would you like?'

'A beer would be good, especially if they have any real ale.' Should she have asked for wine? Something more appropriate. No. That was a ridiculous thought. She wasn't trying to impress.

His eyes widened. 'You like real ale?'

His reaction was so typical.

'It's my favourite.'

'Mine, too. Not many women drink it.'

'Agreed. Most people are surprised when they find out I like it.' She smiled at him. Perhaps it wasn't going to be too bad. At least they could talk about beer.

'Right, I'll go grab us a pint. I assume it's a pint you want.'

'Yes, please. But only one, as I'm driving.'

'Me, too.'

She scrutinised him as he headed towards the bar. He wasn't too skinny, which suited her, as she much preferred well-built men. She also loved the way his fair hair curled so attractively around his ears.

While sitting alone, she reflected on the case, hoping they'd be able to make some progress before a second murder occurred. She'd had a little time to research what had been reported about the earlier cases. It seemed the murderer had no specific type of victim. In fact, in terms of victimology, there was no pattern at all. It really was just happenstance the young boy had been chosen.

The fact the killer was prepared to murder a child made her sick to the stomach. Hugo was the youngest victim so far. The rest had been a mix, ranging from people in their twenties to people in their sixties and seventies. To murder a child took it to a different level.

Ross came back to the table holding two pints, and he placed one in front of her.

'No real ale, I'm afraid, but this is the next best thing. I thought you wouldn't mind.'

She took a sip. 'Hmmm. Not too bad.'

'So, Dr Georgina Cavendish. All I know about you is what I've learned from your business card. You're a senior lecturer at Lenchester University in the forensic psychology department. What else can you tell me?' He smiled, lighting up his clear, blue eyes.

She hated when people wanted to know all about her, as she never knew what to say or how much to tell them. Once they found out who her parents were, they inevitably made a judgement. In his favour, he'd already met her parents, but she didn't know whether he'd been told who they were. But seeing as the owner was such a huge fan of her father, she guessed that he probably had been.

'You go first, as you already know something about me. All I know about you is at the weekend you work as a waiter. Is that your full-time job?'

'I only work there sometimes, as a favour to the owner.'

He knew the owner, and the owner knew her father. That answered her question.

'How do you know him?'

'I know his wife better, as she bought a piece from me. She happened to find out I'd been trained in silver service while I was at university, so I help them out when they're short staffed.'

'A piece?' Did he make jewellery? Paint?

'I'm a sculptor.'

'Fascinating. Apart from the most famous examples, I'm not familiar with many sculptures. What led you into sculpting?'

'I started when I was at school. I also enjoyed art and couldn't make up my mind what to study. Eventually, I decided to go to Edinburgh University, as it had the best sculpting course.'

'And what sort of sculpting do you do?' she asked, assuming there were different types and feeling rather inadequate for not knowing more. Not a position she was used to being in.

'My work is what's known as figurative realism. Which means it depicts realistic figures. You might have heard of the sculpture *Boy* by the Australian, Ron Mueck. It's a five-metre depiction of a crouching boy.'

'Yes, I have. It's in Denmark, isn't it?' she said, relieved to have seen it, and now not feeling so out of her depth.

'Right.'

'Have you exhibited in any of the prestigious galleries?'

His face clouded over. 'Not for the want of trying.'

She could've kicked herself, as typically she'd said the wrong thing and touched a nerve. 'Do you have anything in local galleries?'

'I have an exhibition coming up in two months, in Oxford.'

'I'd like to see it,' she said. 'Tell me something else about you.' She wanted to keep the conversation off herself for as long as possible.

'Not a lot to tell. I come from a small village north of Dublin. My parents still live there. I have a younger sister who's a journalist in London. I'm thirty-six-years old, single, and never been married. And that's me.' He shrugged.

'What brought you to Oxford?'

'I followed a girl here after university. That didn't work out, but I stayed, as I liked it so much. Right. Enough about me, now it's your turn.' He flashed a disarming smile.

'Are you ready to order?' The waiter's intervention was timely.

'Can you give us a few moments? We haven't yet decided,' Ross said.

He handed George the menu, which she gratefully took, happy for the reprieve. She studied it in silence.

'I'll have one of the specials, please. Crumbed fish with home-made chunky fries and salad,' she said after a few minutes.

'I'll join you,' Ross said. He beckoned for the waiter to come over, and he took their order. 'Back to you,' Ross said, once they were alone.

She drew in a breath. 'Okay. I'm thirty-four, soon to be thirty-five. I'm a forensic psychologist, although my initial career choice was medicine, like my father.'

'I remember your father,' he said, raising an eyebrow.

'I'm sorry how he treated you. He's always the same, but that aside, he's a genius when it comes to surgery. One of the best in the country.' Why on earth had she felt the need to praise her father, as if his behaviour could be excused?

'So why didn't you pursue medicine?'

'I got accepted at med school, but it turned out I couldn't handle blood. The sight of it made me vomit.' It had taken several years before she'd been able to discuss it so dispassionately.

'That's a good enough reason.'

'But I'm glad, as I discovered forensic psychology,

which is my passion. I also spend a portion of my time with the Lenchester CID, helping them on murder cases.'

'Wouldn't that sometimes involve blood?'

'I've got it under control now. After many hours in a hypnotherapist's chair, I can handle most things blood related.'

'Tell me about your family.'

'I have a younger brother, who's following in my father's footsteps, and my mother's an international human rights lawyer.'

'A highflying family, that's for sure.'

'What about your parents?' she asked, wanting to pass the discussion back to him.

'My dad's an electrician and has worked for the same company for the last thirty years, and my mum is a doctor's receptionist.'

She could imagine her father's response if he knew that. He was such a snob. Her mother wasn't so bad, but he more than made up for her.

'Yet both you and your sister work in England.'

'There are more career opportunities here. I get back to Ireland as often as I can to see my parents, especially as they're not getting any younger.'

'That's good of you. I only see my parents twice a year: June, and December, for Christmas lunch.'

'That's very regimented.'

'It works for us, as we're all very busy.'

Not to mention she wouldn't want to see them any more than that. People might think that callous. She called it self-preservation.

'What about hobbies? Do you have any, other than real ale?' he asked.

'I don't have time for any, apart from doing jigsaws, and I do those as they help me think. They enable me to compartmentalise, especially when we're working on a case.' Could she sound any more boring? Why couldn't she be interesting, like Whitney? Did she really mean that? She didn't know. It wasn't something she'd considered in the past.

'What have you worked on recently?'

She wasn't meant to discuss a current case, and Whitney would be livid if she did. But she should be fine mentioning one from the past, especially as it would likely be published in her research. 'The most recent one involved men who'd had their genitals removed before being murdered as retribution for grooming young girls for sex.'

'I remember those murders. It seems to me they got what they deserved.'

'A lot of people would agree with you, but vigilantes can't be allowed to take matters into their own hands. We have a legal system for a reason, and nobody should be above it.'

'Are you working with the police at the moment?'

'I am, but I can't discuss the case.'

'What about your colleagues at the university? How do they feel about you working with the police? Especially as Lenchester University is well known for its affectations?'

How did he know that?

'They're happy in respect of the research outputs, but it did affect my promotion prospects. I was up for Associate Professor a few months ago but got passed over.' She could talk about it now without getting too annoyed. But it surprised her how easily she'd blurted it out, considering he was a virtual stranger.

'I'm sorry to hear that.'

'Don't be, it's water under the bridge. I'm happy doing what I do.'

'Let's change the subject,' he suggested. 'Favourite film of all time.'

She flashed him a smile, grateful to be moving on. 'That's easy. *La Dolce Vita*. Have you seen it?'

'Hasn't everyone? It's one of my favourites, too. I'd say it has more cultural influence than most current films. Even though it was released in 1960, it tells us a lot about celebrity and can be applied to life today.'

A film buff. That surprised her. Not many people enjoyed the types of films she did. She'd assumed he was going to be the same. If anything, he seemed more knowledgeable about them than she was.

'I couldn't agree more. What other films do you like?' she asked, feeling a lot more comfortable now the focus was off her.

'Art house films are my favourite. Have you seen *The Rules of the Game*?'

'No, but it's on my list.'

'I'm sure you'll enjoy it. It's about the idle rich in France. It doesn't only take an ironic look at their pretensions, it also shows the hypocrisy going on in Europe at the time. When it's next showing locally, I'll take you.'

Was he asking her on another date already?

For a while they sat in silence. But it wasn't uncomfortable. She already liked that he didn't feel the need to fill every moment with conversation.

After the meal arrived, Ross discussed his work and the processes involved in its production. It was fascinating. When she glanced at her watch it was already ten-thirty.

'I have to go. I've got a busy day tomorrow, and a half hour drive to get home. Thank you for a lovely evening.'

'It's my pleasure.'

When he returned from paying the bill, they walked

back through the pub, which wasn't as busy as it had been earlier, and out into the car park.

'Nice car.' He nodded appreciatively when they'd reached where she'd parked.

'Thanks. I love driving and fast cars.'

'A petrol head and real ale drinker. I think I've died and gone to heaven.' He laughed.

She wasn't quite sure what he meant but wasn't going to question him. 'Thank you, again, for a lovely evening.'

He leaned in and gently kissed her on the lips. It was like a bolt of electricity shot through her. She pulled back.

'I'm sorry. I didn't mean to upset you.' Guilt was etched across his face.

'You didn't. It just took me by surprise.'

'Can I see you again?' he asked.

Did she want to? Yes, she believed she did.

'You have my card. Give me a call.'

Chapter Nine

Tuesday, 11 June

Whitney was peering over Frank's shoulder looking at some CCTV footage, when the door opened and George walked in. She headed over to her.

'Good morning, George,' she said, unable to hide the smirk on her face. She was desperate to find out how the date had gone.

'How's it going?' George asked as they walked towards the board.

'We've got some witnesses coming in to be interviewed following the press conference. But what I really want to know is how it went last night.'

'There's nothing to tell. I went out for a meal with Ross, and we had a nice time.'

'Are you seeing him again?' She was frustrated at the woman's inability to spill the beans.

'He did ask me if I'd see him again, and I said yes.'

'That's great. So, you're dating.'

'No. I'm just seeing him again.'

'Come on, George. Admit it. Tell me what's he's like.'

'He's tall, with fair hair, and blue eyes.'

She shook her head. 'And that's it, is it? What does he do? Where does he live? How old is he? Give me the details.'

'I'll tell you later. This isn't the time. We're too busy.'

Whitney rolled her eyes. George could be such hard work sometimes. Even if she was right about them needing to get on with their work, it wouldn't have hurt if she could've gone into a little more detail.

'Okay. Let's start with the briefing. Attention, everyone. Get me up to speed on where we are.'

'I haven't yet got a complete list of people who paid for tickets using a credit card, as I'm waiting for the other stations to give me the details,' Ellie said. 'Also, some passengers paid cash, so I've asked the stations to send me their CCTV footage from the ticket offices. We have the times when the cash tickets were purchased, which will help when we look through it.'

'Good work. What about people who contacted us following the press conference?' She scanned the rest of the team.

'Only four people got in touch. One lives in Coventry, one lives in Banbury, and two are from Lenchester. We'll be interviewing them today,' Matt said.

'Doug, where are we on the background checks of all of the employees at the different stations?'

'It's in progress. There are a lot of staff, especially in Newcastle and Leeds.'

'The Super has been in touch with the RF. The use of chloroform, the random selection of the victim, and the fact the murder took place on an older train, has led them to believe this is the work of the serial killer they've been looking for in connection with twelve murders across the country over the last two years. They've sent us their files, as have the forces where the other murders took place. The RF is also going to send two officers to assist us.'

A massive groan echoed around the room.

'Typical of them wanting to take over,' Frank said. He could always be relied on to say what everyone else was thinking.

'Well, they're not coming just yet, so we'll get on with solving this before they arrive. But remember, when they do arrive, we'll extend them the same courtesy we do all of our visitors.' Whitney couldn't believe the words coming out of her mouth, especially as she knew she'd find it difficult to work alongside them.

'Do we know who's coming?' Doug asked. 'I've got a friend who works there.'

'No idea. Okay, carry on with what you're doing. George and I are going to go through the files from the previous murders, that have been sent from the other forces and the RF, to see if anything stands out which could assist us.'

Whitney took George back to her office. The files were piled up on her desk.

'How did you get everything so quickly?' George asked.

'The files were emailed in, and I had one of the admin staff print everything out for us. I figured we could go through them while waiting for the witness statements.'

There was a knock at the door and Matt popped his head in. 'I'm just about to interview a Mrs Zena Bratt who was on the train the entire journey, sitting in the second to last carriage. Do you want to come with?'

'Good idea,' Whitney said.

'Do you need me as well?' George asked.

'No. You stay here and go through the files. Your time's better spent looking into the previous cases.'

Whitney and Matt left the office and made their way to the interview room, where the woman had been left.

'Good morning, Mrs Bratt,' Whitney said as they opened the door. 'I'm Detective Chief Inspector Walker. You've already met DS Price. Thank you for coming in to see us.'

'When I heard about it on the news, I got in touch straight away. I can't believe this all happened while I was on the train.' The woman pressed her hand to her chest.

'Can you tell me, in detail, about the journey you took?' Whitney asked.

'I'd been to see my sister who lives in Newcastle. She hasn't been well recently and suffers from angina. She lives on her own and needed some help. Her children live overseas, so I'm the only one.'

'How long were you with her?' Whitney asked.

'Two weeks. I wanted to stay longer, but my husband asked me to come back home. He was fed up of having to fend for himself.'

'And you caught the eight-thirty train from Newcastle on Sunday,' Whitney confirmed.

'Yes, I did.'

'How did you pay for your ticket?'

'I paid with cash, on the day. I didn't book in advance because Sunday is always quiet, and I knew there'd be plenty of room on the train.'

'What time did you arrive at the station?'

'I was there by seven-forty-five. A taxi picked me up from my sister's house at seven-fifteen, and the journey took half an hour.'

'Where did you go once you arrived?'

'To wait for the train,' the woman said, frowning.

'Did you go into the waiting room, or did you stay on the platform?' Whitney elaborated.

'I sat on a bench in the waiting room for half an hour and then went onto the platform.'

'While you were in the waiting room, who else was there?' Whitney asked.

'I was the only one in there first of all, and then, after about fifteen minutes, a couple came in, followed by another woman and a man, both on their own.'

'Did you notice anything unusual about any of them?' Whitney asked.

'No. They sat quietly.'

'Would you recognise them again?'

The woman was silent for a few seconds. 'I'm not sure. Possibly not, apart from the woman who was part of the couple. I remember she was wearing a straw hat, which had big flowers on the side.'

'When you went outside to sit on the platform, how many people were there?'

'By that time, it was quite busy. Other trains were coming into the station. Maybe around fifteen people were on my platform. Across the other side I could see a few people waiting, too.'

'Did you see anything out of the ordinary? Or anyone acting suspiciously?' Whitney was asking these detailed questions to lead her gently to the actual journey, hoping it would prompt something.

'No. I'm sorry. Nothing.' Mrs Bratt slowly shook her head.

'That's fine. You're doing really well. We appreciate your help. Could you take me through when you got onto the train?'

'I got on about halfway down the platform. I never like to go in the first two carriages, as they're usually the busiest, and it can be noisy. I walked through the train until I came to the next to last carriage. I sat on one of the seats pointing in the direction we were heading. I can't travel with my back facing the way we're going, as it gives me motion sickness.'

'Was anyone else in the carriage with you?'

'There was another woman, and just as the train was due to leave, a man came hurrying through and sat down a few rows in front of me on the right-hand side.'

Could this be the killer?

'Can you describe him for me?'

'He was in his thirties and was wearing jeans and a dark grey hoodie. He had on a dark baseball hat and he wore sunglasses, which I thought strange, as it wasn't sunny and it was first thing in the morning, but I just thought he had a hangover or a headache.'

'Did he stay seated all the time?' Whitney asked.

'He got up and went out of the carriage. The one which linked with the last one. I assumed he was going to the toilet. He wasn't gone long. Maybe five minutes.'

Was he casing the last carriage? Had he earmarked Hugo as his target?

'Did he look at you at all?' Whitney wondered if she would have been the victim if there hadn't been another person in the carriage.

'Not that I know of, but I was reading.'

'Did anyone else get into the carriage?'

'Two people got on at Leeds. A young girl in her twenties, and an older woman. They weren't together.'

With so many people in the carriage, he clearly wouldn't have done anything there. Far too risky.

'The next stop, Coventry. What did you notice?'

'The man in the hoodie got off.'

Damn.

'Did you actually see him leave the train and go onto the platform?' Whitney clarified.

'No. He walked out of the carriage, and I assumed he'd left. I wasn't really paying much attention at that point.'

'Which door did he leave out of?'

'He went to the back of the carriage again.'

'The one connecting with the end carriage?' she asked, just to confirm.

Her heart pumped in her chest. This could be the lead they were looking for. The man may have gone into the toilet to keep out of the way, and then gone into the end carriage once the ticket collector had gone through. Except it didn't make sense. Hugo didn't get on the train until Coventry, so the suspect wouldn't have known about him. She would have to check Stanley Crabtree's account to see if anyone else had been in the end carriage at that time. The killer might have had somebody else in his sights, but when they got off and Hugo got on, he moved to a different victim.

'Yes,' Mrs Bratt replied. 'There's an exit to get off the train there.'

'Did anyone get on at Coventry and come into your carriage?'

'A young boy walked through, in the direction of the last carriage. Oh.' She slammed her hand across her mouth. 'He was the victim, wasn't he? It said on the news a fourteen-year-old boy had died.' The woman's eyes widened and filled with tears.

'We can't confirm anything at the moment. Did anyone else get on?' Whitney asked gently, passing her a tissue from the box at the end of the table.

'No. Not at Coventry.' She shook her head.

'What about when the train reached Banbury?'

'I don't know. That poor boy. He was so young. I know you're not meant to tell me, but it was him, wasn't it?'

'I understand this is hard, but if you could please think back to when the train was in Banbury,' Whitney said, ignoring the woman's question.

Mrs Bratt wiped her eyes with the tissue and sniffed. 'Nobody got on there. Well, not in my carriage. I don't think anyone got off, either, but I can't be sure.'

Whitney doubted the woman could give them any more useful information, and she needed to get back to the incident room to arrange for the CCTV footage from Coventry to be checked, to ascertain if this man got off the train.

'You've been very helpful, Mrs Bratt. We really appreciate you coming in. Can I arrange for someone to get you a cup of tea?' she offered.

'No, thank you. If we've finished, I'd like to go. My husband's waiting for me in reception. He'll be getting anxious if I'm much longer.'

'If you do think of anything else, no matter how insignificant it seems, please contact us straight away. You have our number. DS Price will show you out.'

When she got back to her office, George was pouring over the files. She looked up and smiled.

'How was the interview?' she asked.

'Good. We might have something. I've asked Frank to check footage to see if the man she described actually got off the train at Coventry. If not, he could've been hiding in the toilets waiting for a potential victim.'

'Excellent. I've gone through the files and started to put together a profile we can work with. There are certainly some similarities between the cases, and it does give an indication of the type of person we're dealing with. The other forces should have made the same links, but nothing in the files is leading me to believe they did.'

'Maybe that's because they don't have someone like

you working with them. Or, even if they did, they wouldn't be up to your standard.'

'I'm sure that's not the case.'

'What's with the modesty all of a sudden? You know you do a good job. That's why we work so well together. Take it as a compliment.'

'I will. Thank you. But it could be they haven't given us all of the information from their investigation. Or maybe they didn't share files with each other, so no one has the full picture.'

'The RF would have all the documentation. But it certainly wouldn't surprise me if they haven't sent us everything. We won't know until they arrive.'

'Let's go back to the incident room, and I can run through everything with you and speak to the team. Even if we don't have all the information, I'm sure you'll be interested in what I've got to say from what I've learned so far,' George said.

They left Whitney's office and went back into the incident room.

'Listen up, everyone,' Whitney said. 'George is going to tell us what she's found from going through the existing case files.' She nodded at the psychologist to start.

'From what I've read, there's no pattern to the choice of victim. Chloroform has always been used before the stabbing. There have been no notes admitting guilt, or making demands, or explaining the reason behind the murders,' George said.

'But is it likely the offender would send a note if the murders are indiscriminate?' Doug asked.

'It depends on the motive behind what they're doing. Are they looking for attention? Do they enjoy killing? My hunch, and you know how much I hate hunches, is there's some reason behind this. They don't appear to be in it for the thrill of the murder, or why else would they use the chloroform to ease the pain?'

'That's what we've got to find out. Was there anything else you noted from going through the files?' Whitney asked.

'Yes. Although the murders took place on different train operator lines, they are all part of a wider group called Transwide. The operators targeted are: Pathway Trains, Coastal Rail, Link Railways, and ours, which is Central Group.'

'If it's a vendetta against Transwide, what have the previous investigations turned up?' Whitney asked.

'The information in the files is sketchy,' George said. 'I can see one interview with the Chief Operating Officer, but nothing helpful was recorded. If these are revenge killings, the perpetrator could certainly be a disgruntled ex-employee or customer.'

'Ellie, look into Transwide. Find out how many rail operators they own and how they're all linked. Anything you can find. If they are integral to these murders, I want to know about it,' Whitney said.

'Yes, guv.'

'If we can solve a case the RF have failed to, I'll be very happy.'

Not to mention, if they didn't find the killer soon, someone else would die.

Chapter Ten

Wednesday, 12 June

How are you feeling today, Transwide?

Concerned?

Worried?

Are your profits plummeting?

Of course they are. And by the time I've finished with you, no one will ever want to ride on your trains again.

Remember, everything I do is down to you.

All this loss of life. The devastation caused. The blame is at your feet.

You destroy lives, and I destroy lives. We're the same, you and me. Except we're not. I'm cleverer than you.

For two years I've been carrying out these murders, and no one has been able to catch me. What I do is unpredictable. Yes, you know when I've chosen an area there will be four murders, and the first and last will be exactly two weeks apart. But that's all I'll allow you to know. Call it a little teaser.

You don't know how I make my choices. My choice of train. My choice of victim. My choice of station. And that's why I won't be caught. By the time the police get their shit together, I've moved on and left no evidence.

I wasn't always cruel. You made me like this. You destroyed my life, and now I'm going to destroy yours.

So, what are you going to do? Stop running trains in an area during the two-week period? It could work. And then, guess what? I'll extend the time between murders. I'll keep doing it until you stop every one of your rail operators from running trains at all. A perfect plan.

You wrecked my family, and nothing will ever compensate for that. I won't allow you to do it to anyone else.

No one should suffer like we did.

No one should have their world turned upside down for it never to be the same again. You ruin so many lives, but you don't care. People think you can't be held responsible because you're a company and not a real person. But you're real to me. Decisions are made by actual people, and these people wreck lives.

I've already chosen my next train route. My ticket's been bought, and I've made my preparations.

I'm never going to stop.

Not until you've been destroyed forever.

Chapter Eleven

Thursday, 12 June

The phone ringing on her bedside table caused George to wake up with a start. She glanced at the clock. It was already eight. Crap. She'd slept in. She'd been out again with Ross the previous night to a real ale bar and had rather a lot to drink. Her head was thumping.

She reached for her phone. 'Hello.' Her mouth was dry, and the word barely came out.

'George?'

'Yes.'

'It didn't sound like you. It's Whitney. There's been another murder. Can you meet me at the station?'

Another murder? The station. Why?

'Don't you want to go to the scene?' she mumbled.

'The *railway* station not the police station. Are you okay?'

'I think so. I'll be with you once I've got up.'

'You're still in bed?' The officer's incredulous tone was unmistakeable.

'I had a late night.' She rubbed her temples, but it didn't have much effect.

'Did you go out with Ross on another date?'

George yawned and stretched out. She had no energy to deal with an inquisitive Whitney at the moment. 'If you want me there, leave me alone to get dressed. I'll be with you as soon as I can.'

She ended the call and headed into the shower, turning it to cold. Her whole body spasmed as the water hit it, but she forced herself to stay under for as long as she could. After getting ready, she grabbed a couple of headache tablets and a glass of water. Was the alcohol still in her system?

After arriving at the station, she walked into the building and out onto the platform, where a cordon had been put up around one of the trains. She caught sight of Whitney standing with Matt Price and went over to them.

'You look rough,' Whitney said once she'd reached them.

'Thank you.' She rolled her eyes towards the sky, then wished she hadn't, as it hurt her head. 'Tell me what happened.'

'The victim is a woman in her fifties, travelling on her own. A passenger who got on at Lenchester raised the alarm. We've emptied the train, and everyone on there is currently in the waiting room. Sue and Doug are taking their statements, and Matt's about to join them.'

'I'm off now,' Matt said as he walked away from them.

'Were there are a lot of people on the train?' George asked.

'Quite a few, because it was going to London. It started

in Coventry, and this was the second stop. Banbury being the first.'

'A bit risky for the murderer with so many people around,' she said.

'Yes, but he's clearly got it down to a fine art.'

'He certainly has. Have you spoken to the passenger who found the victim?'

'Briefly. But she was very distressed and came over all faint. I've left her in the station manager's office. We need to give her time to recover before speaking to her properly,' Whitney said.

'Have you seen the body?'

'Not yet. I let Claire go on board first. She's been there a while, long enough to do the preliminaries. I'm sure she won't mind us going in now. Well, she might, knowing Claire.' Whitney stared at her. 'Are you sure you're okay? You're very pale.'

'I'm fine. I've just got a slight hangover,' she admitted.

'What? Since when have you ever got that wasted?'

'Since I went to a pub that served real ale.'

'Were you with Ross?'

'Yes. And that's all I'm telling you. I'll go and sign the log.'

She left Whitney and walked over to where a uniformed officer was standing at the entrance to the scene.

After signing, she skirted around the cordon and onto the train, following Whitney. Again, it was one of the older trains with no CCTV. The murderer obviously knew which trains to target.

'We should check the types of trains used in all the other murders. If ours are anything to go by, he chooses older trains. The ones giving him the best opportunity of not being caught on camera,' she said.

'Yes, I'd been thinking that, too,' Whitney agreed.

They made their way through the train until reaching one of the connecting doors to the carriage where Claire was working. They walked through and could see the victim sitting at a table. Her body was twisted over, and her head was leaning towards the window.

'Hello, Claire,' they both said as the pathologist glanced up and acknowledged them with a nod.

'We meet again. This is getting to be a habit,' Claire said.

'The same as the last one?' Whitney asked.

'There are similarities, and that's all I'm saying until I get her on the table,' the pathologist said.

'And the chloroform?' George asked.

'I haven't got close enough to smell. I'll do that back at the lab. In the meantime, let me continue, so we can move the body and find out more.'

George glanced around the murder site. 'Did you say this was the first stop?' she asked.

'Second. Why?' Whitney replied.

'Look under the table on the floor. A ticket.'

'Let me photograph it first,' Claire said, stepping in front of them.

Once the photo had been taken, Whitney pulled on some disposable gloves, leaned down, and picked it up. 'It's got today's date on it, and the journey was from Coventry to Lenchester.'

'The murderer could have dropped it,' George said.

'He could, but how likely would that be when you consider he's never left any evidence before?' Whitney said.

'True. It could be the victim's. Or dropped from a random traveller,' she suggested.

'Although we shouldn't dismiss the possibility it belonged to the killer,' Whitney said. 'Regular travellers will most likely pay online, using a railcard, and not have a physical ticket.'

'Good point. I doubt the killer would buy his ticket online; the virtual paper trail would be too incriminating,' George said.

'We certainly have to consider it a lead.' Whitney dropped the ticket into an evidence bag. 'I'll get forensics on to it as soon as we get back. See if we can find some prints. Claire, have you finished photographing the victim's handbag? I want to look inside it for any identification.'

'Yes.'

Whitney picked up the black leather handbag and moved to one side. George followed. Inside was a blue wallet-purse, and from one of the pockets she pulled out a driving license. George peered over Whitney's shoulder to look at it. The photo matched the victim, whose name was Lena Kirk.

'We need to find out her contact details, so we can get in touch with the family.' Whitney pulled her phone from her pocket and keyed in a number.

'Hello, Ellie. It's me. The second victim is Lena Kirk, date of birth ten, four, sixty-eight. I need her details a-sap. She's likely from Coventry or Banbury. We'll be back in the office later.'

Whitney ended the call. 'Let's go and see Annie Houghton, the woman who found the body.'

They left the train and went to the manager's office. Whitney knocked and opened the door. Sitting with a uniformed officer was a woman in her thirties, wearing a business suit.

'Do you feel up to talking to us, now?' Whitney asked gently.

Annie nodded. 'Yes, I'm feeling a little better.' She took a sip of water from the cup in her hand.

'You can go, now,' Whitney said to the officer.

'Yes, guv.'

'This is Dr Cavendish,' Whitney said as they both sat opposite the woman. 'Please could you go through exactly what happened, starting from when you got onto the train.'

'I was running late and hopped onto the first carriage I came to. I walked through the train, looking for a seat with a table so I could do some work. I work in London, so manage to get quite a lot done while travelling. I put my laptop on the table and glanced at the woman sitting opposite. I thought she was asleep, at first, as lots of people doze off on the morning trains. But then I looked again and could see blood around her chest area, and her eyes were slightly open … looking vacant. I grabbed my laptop and ran off the train, calling for help.'

'Was there anybody else in the carriage?'

'Not in that section, but further up there were a few. The train doesn't start getting busy until we get to Rugby, and even then, it doesn't get full like the fast commuter train. That's why I prefer it.'

'Did you notice anyone getting off the train as you were getting on?' Whitney asked.

'No, I'm sorry, I didn't. I was too busy finding somewhere to sit.'

'What about after you found the body and alerted the staff at the station? Did you notice anything strange then?' Whitney asked.

'No. Everything's a blur. I was so intent on calling for help.'

'We'd like you to make a written statement. I have some officers taking them in the waiting room.'

'Can I do it straight away? I have to get to work for an important meeting.'

Would she be in a fit state to attend a meeting, once the

enormity of the situation hit her later? George doubted it.

'That shouldn't be a problem. Come with me and I'll introduce you to my detective sergeant.'

'Will I be able to catch the next train to London?'

'I'll be speaking to the station manager about keeping part of the station open,' Whitney said.

George followed as Whitney escorted the woman into the waiting area and called Matt over.

'Please could you interview Annie Houghton immediately, and take her statement. She found the victim.'

'Yes, guv.'

After leaving Matt with the woman, they found the station manager, and Whitney agreed for all incoming trains to stop at platform four, which was on the other side of the bridge and away from the crime scene.

'You look as though you could do with a cup of coffee,' Whitney said once they were alone.

George nodded. 'That might help. I've taken tablets, but it still feels like the drums of death are going off in my head.'

'The what?' Whitney frowned.

'Drums of death. They're often played at funerals, especially in Africa,' she explained.

'Only you could come up with something like that when hungover.' Whitney grinned.

'I can't take your humour this morning,' she said, grimacing.

'Well, that'll teach you to get wasted on a workday.' A smug expression crossed Whitney's face.

George couldn't be bothered to retaliate. 'Where to now?' she asked.

'I'll meet you back at the office. I need forensics to take a look at the ticket, as it's the only lead we've got, then we'll visit Transwide.'

Chapter Twelve

Thursday, 12 June

All the way back to the station Whitney smiled, thinking about George and her hangover. She definitely wanted to meet this Ross chap. Anyone who could make the uptight, focused, forensic psychologist get shit-faced on real ale, especially during the week, had to be someone special.

They met up outside the station and walked in together, stopping at the vending machine on the way to the incident room, so George could get herself something to eat and drink.

'This is a whole new side to you,' Whitney quipped.

'Give it a rest, Whitney. I didn't have time for breakfast, as you called me in early. That's all.'

'Well, I like it,' she said, choosing to ignore George's hostile tone, as she understood what she was going through, having nursed many drink-induced headaches over the years.

They walked into the incident room, and Whitney handed the evidence bag with the ticket in it to one of the officers. 'Take this to forensics. I need it back as soon as possible.'

'Yes, guv.'

She then made her way over to Frank who was staring at the computer screen.

'Frank, get in touch with the railway station. We need CCTV footage from this morning. Check who got off the train at Lenchester, and see if you can match it to anybody that got off on the day of the previous murder. Also, get in touch with both Coventry and Banbury and check their CCTV, too.'

'Not too much to do, then.' He shook his head.

'We have two dead bodies, and we're likely to get two more if the pattern is anything to go by. So, yes. There's going to be a lot of work. Think of the overtime money.' Whitney was unable to hide her frustration with the older officer, who had a tendency to be lazy if she let him. That aside, he was one of the most loyal members of her team, and she'd miss him when he retired in a couple of years.

'Well, you can tell the missus if I've got to work late tonight. She's arranged some fancy dinner party with our new neighbours, and I promised to be home by seven.'

'Why would she arrange something during the week when she knows there's a possibility you'll be late?' Whitney asked.

'How the hell do I know? I'm sure she had some reason.' He shrugged.

'Let's see where we've got to by six-thirty, and then we'll make a decision.'

Whitney knew from experience, if she didn't offer some hope, Frank would be moaning all day and his concentration would be shot. Providing he worked hard and went through all the information they had, there was every chance she'd let him go home in time for his guests' arrival.

'Ellie, what have you got on Transwide?' she asked the officer who was walking past.

'Head office is in Coventry. They own eleven rail operators throughout the UK.'

'Text me their details and arrange for me to see someone high up and with clout, straight away. We'll be there in an hour.'

She walked over to the board where George was standing, staring into space.

'Come on, let's get with it,' she cajoled the doctor.

'I'm fine. I was just waiting for you,' George said.

She wrote the victim's name on board. 'Two victims, and two more to follow within the next ten days. And our only link is Transwide, which is where we're going, now.'

The journey to Coventry only took forty-five minutes, as it was mainly motorway, and soon they were pulling into the Transwide car park. The tall, impressive building was modern, clad with concrete panels, and had stainless-steel windows.

'How do you fancy working in a place like this?' Whitney said.

'Not for me. I much prefer the Victorian buildings at the university. They've got so much more character. This is cold and uninspiring,' the doctor replied.

'Yes, I know what you mean. I'm dreading when they finally finish our brand-new station and we have to move. I much prefer where we are, despite the fact that we freeze our wotsits off during the winter.'

They parked in the visitors' section of the car park and headed into the building through a large revolving door. They walked across a marble floor and up to reception. Ellie had been in touch to confirm she'd arranged for the Chief Operating Officer to see them.

'DCI Walker and Dr Cavendish to see Judy Tucker,' she said to the young man on reception.

'Please take a seat, and I'll let her office know you're here.' He gestured to the seating area, where there were several black leather couches and a low glass coffee table, with a variety of magazines on it.

As they sat, they could hear him phone through and announce their arrival.George picked up one of the magazines and flicked through it while Whitney looked around. If their head office was anything to go by, Transwide was an extremely profitable company.

'Leave the talking to me,' she said.

'Seriously, you still think you have to tell me? This is the third case we've worked on, and there has never yet been an interview where you've allowed me to take the lead,' George said.

'I just wanted to make sure you remembered,' she said. 'But feel free to ask a question if you think I've missed something.'

'What's got into you, being so generous? I'm very impressed,' George said, arching an eyebrow.

She was just about to reply when someone approached them.

'DCI Walker?' the woman said.

'Yes.'

'I'm Ms Tucker's assistant. Please come with me, and I'll take you to her office.'

They followed the woman to the lift, and took it to the twentieth floor, labelled Operations. After stepping out, they entered a huge open-plan office, which they walked through until reaching a large corner office, with glass windows the entire width and depth of two walls. As they walked in, a woman in her fifties stood up. She was as tall as George and had dark hair scraped back into a chignon.

She was elegantly dressed, in a navy trouser suit with a white shirt underneath, and a gold necklace and matching earrings.

'Good morning, I'm Judy Tucker.'

Whitney showed her warrant card. 'I'm DCI Walker and this is Dr Cavendish, from Lenchester CID.'

'Please sit down. Would you like a coffee?

'That would be lovely,' Whitney said.

'Iris, please organise coffee for three. Take a seat,' Judy said, gesturing to the seats in front of her desk.

'Thank you,' Whitney said.

'How can I help?'

'We're investigating the murders taking place on various train lines belonging to Transwide. The latest target is Lenchester. You may have heard about the first murder, which happened last Sunday. The second was this morning.'

'Will this ever end?' She shook her head. 'It's an awful situation and has troubled the company greatly. I wasn't involved in previous discussions with the police, as I've only been here for three months. My predecessor worked on it.'

'Is there any chance they're available to talk to?' Whitney asked.

'No. Unfortunately he was tragically killed in a skiing accident. It was dreadful. He left behind a wife and three small children.'

'I'm sorry to hear that. We're not sure how much information you provided to the other forces investigating, but one avenue we're considering is that the killer is someone who has a grudge against the company. We'd like to know about any customers who have sent you threatening letters or have made threats on social media. It could also be a disgruntled employee. Do you know of any?'

'That's easier said than done. We employ over fifty-five

thousand people, either directly in our head office or in one of the eleven rail operators we own. As far as customers are concerned, I'm afraid threats go with the territory,' Judy said.

'Do you keep copies of any threats?' Whitney asked.

'Anything serious we pass onto the police. There will be a record of them in the system. I can ask one of my HR managers to access them for you.'

'What about records on disgruntled employees?'

'Again, a company our size is bound to have employees who are unhappy, especially any who have been sacked or made redundant.'

'The murders have been taking place over a period of two years, so it will be related to something which happened before then. Can you think of anything that might have prompted someone to want to get back at Transwide?'

'Let me call Iris. She's been here longer than me.'

Before she had time to contact her assistant, the door opened and she came in holding a tray of coffee, which she placed on the desk.

'Thank you, Iris. While you're here, can you think back to over two years ago, to someone who might have had a grudge against the company, possibly a past employee?'

'In 2014 we did make a thousand people redundant,' Iris said. 'It caused a lot of anxiety and the union got involved, but the redundancies still went ahead.'

'I'd like a list of those employees,' Whitney said.

'I thought the murders didn't start until 2017. How could this be relevant?' Judy asked.

'We don't know if it is, but it's a line of enquiry we need to undertake,' Whitney said.

'We have the Data Protection Act to consider,' Judy said.

Whitney sucked in a breath. It was always the first thing thrown at them whenever they asked for information. It was so frustrating.

'We could get a warrant for the information, but that would set the enquiry back. The next murder is due to take place soon. We'd much rather you cooperated with us on this. I'm sure you wouldn't want the guilt of knowing a murder could've been prevented if only you'd assisted.'

The woman paled. 'I need to clear it with our HR Director, but she's on leave at the moment. I'll endeavour to contact her.'

'Iris, were these redundancies focused on a particular occupational area, or from all levels in the company?' George asked.

'They were mainly drivers, conductors, and ground staff. The more automated the services became, the fewer staff we needed. We were unable to deploy most of them because their skills weren't transferable,' Iris said.

'Thank you.'

Iris left the office, and Judy handed out the coffee. Whitney sniffed hers and nodded appreciatively. None of the cheap stuff they had back at work.

'Are you sure there's a chance it could be one of these employees?' Judy asked.

'Aside from them leaving several years ago, they'd certainly have good working knowledge of the train system,' George said.

'Do drivers tend to stick to the same train lines, or do you move them around?' Whitney asked.

'Each rail operator employs their own staff, and driver logistics are undertaken at grass roots level. Our work with each individual operator is mainly in respect of their HR requirements.'

'Are the procedures regarding employment and deployment similar between operators?' George asked.

'They all work under the same guidelines, as laid down by us. Within our office here, we have a team dedicated to each of the operators. These are overseen by our HR Director.'

Whitney finished her coffee and placed her cup and saucer on the tray. 'We need the list of employees as soon as possible.'

'Leave it with me. Despite what you might think, we do want to help. These killings have impacted greatly on our bottom line, as fewer people are taking the train.'

Whitney stared open-mouthed at her lack of sensitivity. 'Not to mention, lives of innocent people have been lost,' she said, turning to leave without a backwards glance.

Chapter Thirteen

Thursday, 12 June

After stopping for a late lunch on the way back from Transwide, they went to the incident room to check on progress. They'd no sooner dropped their bags in Whitney's office and gone back to speak to the team, when the door to the incident room opened, and Jamieson walked in, closely followed by two men she didn't recognise. Whitney's stomach plummeted. The expensive suits could only mean one thing: the RF.

She walked over to them. 'Good afternoon, sir.'

'Good afternoon, Walker.' He turned to the two men standing beside him. 'This is DCI Walker. She's SIO on the case. This is DI Terry Gardner and DS Vic Rowe from the Regional Force. They've come to give us their expertise on the case.'

She nodded at them, taking in their outfits. Hardly what detectives wore in her station. Gardner appeared to be in his forties, was slim, and had dark cropped hair with grey flecks. His eyes were too close together, and she could tell straight away he was going to prove difficult. Vic was younger, maybe early thirties, with fair hair and hazel eyes. She could imagine some of the younger members of her team finding him attractive. He seemed a bit too smarmy for her.

Of course, her assessment had nothing to do with her resentment for them being there. She was being totally objective.

'Good to meet you,' Gardner said.

'Likewise,' she said, shaking his outstretched hand.

'Now you're acquainted, I'll leave you to it,' Jamieson said. 'I'll arrange the press conference for later this afternoon. I don't need to tell you this case needs solving PDQ. Two murders are more than enough. You've got to stop the next two from happening.'

Her boss turned and left the room. Once the door had closed behind him, Whitney faced the two officers. 'You might have come from the RF, but just remember, this is my case. I'm SIO, and what I say goes. Are we clear?'

The two officers exchanged a glance. 'We're here to help.' Gardner smiled, but it didn't reach his eyes.

'Okay. You can have those two desks in the corner.' Whitney pointed to the far side the room. 'First, I'll introduce you to the forensic psychologist we use.'

They walked over to the board where George was standing.

'This is Dr George Cavendish from Lenchester University, and she works with us from time to time. George this is DI Terry Gardner and DS Vic Rowe. They're from the Regional Force.'

'Did you use a forensic psychologist on the other murders?' George asked.

Whitney smiled to herself. Typical of George to dispense with any pleasantries and get straight down to it.

'We use everyone available to us, and *we* only use the best,' Gardner said.

George visibly bristled. They'd better watch themselves if they didn't want to get on her wrong side. Implying she wasn't the best wasn't the smart way forward. As well as being inaccurate. Although, Whitney wouldn't mind seeing her put the two officers in their place.

'And you're familiar with the best forensic psychologists, are you?' George said, an icy tone to her voice.

'We do our research before working with experts in any field,' Gardner said.

'Interesting,' George replied. 'I'm very keen to know who you've used in the past, and in particular their research output and capabilities in the field.'

'Well, I can't tell you that without checking. But I can assure you they are top notch,' Gardner said.

'*Top notch.* Not a term I'm familiar with when discussing academic credibility. I prefer to—'

'We don't need to discuss this now,' Whitney said, enjoying the exchange, but interrupting before it went any further. 'We've gone through your files, and there isn't much in there we haven't already ascertained for ourselves, after only two murders.'

'We're dealing with a highly organised and clever individual,' Vic said.

'From what we've seen, all the murders were similar, ours included,' Whitney said.

'Yes. Chloroform and stabbing. No deviation,' Gardner said.

'Presumably you went through the CCTV footage from all the sites?' Whitney asked.

'Yes. Our team found nothing,' Vic said.

'The trains our two victims were on had no CCTV. As

older trains were chosen for Lenchester, I assume it was the same for the other murders,' Whitney said.

'Yes,' Gardner said.

'Indicating the murderer has more than a passing knowledge of trains. Have you investigated local rail enthusiast clubs in the different areas?' Whitney asked.

Gardner looked at Rowe. 'Have you?'

'I'll need to check, guv.'

'There's nothing in the files indicating you have.' She wrote on the board *knowledge of trains*.

'Have you investigated all the employees from the three rail operators targeted?' Whitney asked.

'Obviously.' Gardner rolled his eyes.

'Well, as there's nothing in the files, I wanted to check,' she responded.

'We didn't find a suspect among them,' Rowe said.

'Good to know,' she said.

'What about Transwide?' She wasn't going to tell that they'd been to visit.

'Transwide are a pain in the arse,' Gardner said.

'In what way?'

'Trying to interfere in the investigation.'

'How?' Whitney asked.

'Wanting us to make clear the murders weren't related to them.'

'But they clearly are, as all the rail operators targeted are owned by them.'

'They consider it to be a coincidence. They believe we should focus our investigation elsewhere, as the bad publicity is causing them harm.'

'Did you look into the possibility it's a disgruntled customer or ex-employee?'

'Of course.' Gardner glared at her.

'But there's nothing in the files,' she said.

'Because we found nothing,' Rowe said.

This was getting boringly repetitive. She forced herself to not respond, as they were going around in circles. Either they were extremely inept at their job, or they were deliberately keeping information from them. Well, that could cut both ways.

'Why are you using an old-fashioned board?' Gardner asked, nodding at it.

'Why wouldn't we?' she said, surprised he'd mentioned it.

'We've been using SmartBoards for the last two years. Before that we had interactive boards. Don't you have any up-to-date equipment here?' He gave a caustic laugh.

Whitney tensed. 'It doesn't matter what we use, providing we solve the crime. And our records speak for themselves.'

'It's like being stuck in the eighties. You'll be telling me next you still use overhead projectors.'

Whitney's fists clenched by her side. So, this was what it was going to be like. Their constant belittling. Fucking Jamieson. She could swing for him. There was no need for those arsewipes to be part of her investigation.

'We're getting away from the point. Now you're here, how do you think you can help?'

'We need to see the evidence you have. Has the pathologist's report come in yet?'

'I have the report from our first victim on my desk. I'll email it to you,' she said.

'We'd like to see the crime scenes.'

'That can be arranged. Would you like to go now?'

'Yes.'

'I'll get one of my officers to take you.'

'Aren't you coming with? So we can discuss it,' Gardner asked.

'No. I have things to do which need my immediate attention.' She called over one of her team. 'Take DI Gardner and DS Rowe to the railway station and show them the crime scenes.'

Once they'd left the office, she turned to George. 'What's the point of sending them here? Have they told us anything we don't already know? No, they haven't. And as for their total dismissal of Transwide, it makes no sense. As far as I can tell, they're going to be as much help to us as a chocolate teapot. Also, did you get the feeling they were holding out on us?'

'Yes, I did. In my opinion, they only wanted to know what we've got and weren't prepared to talk about their own findings. They definitely have their own agenda, and we need to be cognisant of that. I noticed you didn't mention the ticket we found.'

'I wasn't prepared to let them take over on that front. But before we investigate further, I need to arrange for the family of the second victim to be informed.' She walked over to Ellie's desk, and George followed. 'Do you have contact details for the second victim?'

'Yes. She lived in Coventry. I've got her address. I'll text it to you.'

'Thanks. I'll get in touch with the Coventry police and ask them to visit her family. They'll also need to arrange for someone to make a formal identification of the body.'

They walked away from the officer's desk.

'Don't you want to see the family yourself?' George asked.

'Not at the moment. We already know from the previous murders the victims are indiscriminately chosen.'

'We're assuming they're indiscriminate, as we haven't yet found a pattern. It doesn't mean there isn't one,' George said.

'Maybe. But I'm better off staying here and working through what we know for certain.'

'Guv,' Ellie called out from her desk. 'I've just heard back from forensics. They found a print on the train ticket. They ran it through the database and came back with a name. It's a Patrick Logan. He's got a record for breaking and entering, and petty burglary, and he's been in and out of prison. He lives at 20 Lower West Street, Banbury.'

'Good work. Come on, George, let's make a house call.'

Chapter Fourteen

Thursday, 12 June

'Shall we take your car or mine?' Whitney asked when they got into the station car park.

'Let's go in yours,' George said.

Normally she'd be happy to drive anywhere, especially as her car was much more comfortable than Whitney's. But she was still feeling less than one hundred per cent so was happy to let someone else take the wheel.

'You must be feeling bad,' Whitney quipped.

'I've felt better,' she acknowledged as they got into the car.

She thought back to the previous night when she'd been out with Ross. It had been an enjoyable evening, and she was relaxed in his company. Well, as relaxed as she could be. What she liked about him was he didn't force her to engage in conversation and seemed to respect the fact she was a little reticent in other people's company.

He was happy to talk, especially about his work, which she found absorbing, and she was keen to see some of his pieces in real life. She didn't know much about sculptures, but she did enjoy art and had seen many of the major works.

She'd googled Ross and was surprised to learn he'd got quite a following. Not that she didn't think he was talented, but he was self-effacing when discussing his work, which belied his true ability. She liked that about him. He was a member of the UK Sculpture Society, and his work was quite renowned.

He was very easy to be with and told ridiculously stupid jokes, some of which he had to explain to her. And even if, in part, she'd only agreed to go out with him because of her father, she was really pleased she had. She didn't imagine anything serious happening between them; she wasn't interested in a long-term relationship. She was happy to be on her own. But that wouldn't stop her from going out with him again. She had Whitney to thank for making her more laid back about the relationship. She certainly wouldn't have behaved like this pre-Walker.

'Earth to George. Earth to George. Can you hear me?'

Whitney's words cut into George's thoughts. 'Of course I can.'

'Are you sure about that? I've been talking to you, and you were ignoring me.'

'No, I wasn't. I heard you.'

'What did I say?' Whitney challenged.

'You asked if I could hear you.'

'What did I say before that? You don't know, do you?'

'You must have said it very quietly.' George cringed at her pathetic response.

'Yeah, right. I'd put money on you being distracted because you were thinking about your date last night.'

'What makes you say that?'

'Nothing much, apart from your eyes glazing over and you obviously being miles away.'

George shifted awkwardly in the seat. 'Glazed eyes is total nonsense. Maybe I was thinking about last night, but you make me sound like some lovesick teenager and you know that's not me.'

'Tell me about him. You've kept it so secret I hardly know anything. Other than the fact he somehow got you to go out on a work night, twice, and get pissed, which is so not you.'

'He's thirty-six, a couple of years older than me. And he's a sculptor, of figurative realism.'

'Which is?'

'Realistic figures. Often larger but incredibly lifelike. He sculpts animals and humans.'

'What does he look like? Is he tall? Is he handsome? Tell me something more interesting.'

'He's taller than me, and he looks okay,' George said.

'Looks okay. What does that mean? What colour are his eyes?'

'Blue. But I hardly think that matters. I've only been out with him a couple of times. It's nothing serious.'

'I'm glad if he makes you happy, especially after that shit you were living with before.'

'What do you think of the two guys from the Regional Force?' George asked, changing the subject, as she'd had enough of talking about herself and Ross.

'Did you notice what they wearing? Even I could tell they were expensive suits. More like they were guests at a wedding than police officers. And don't get me started on the way they put down our resources.'

'I did notice they were smartly dressed. Is that what they're all like there?'

'To be honest, I haven't met many of them, so I don't know. Unless it's just an act on their behalf to try to intimidate us.'

'They might help us solve the case. It can be useful to have a fresh perspective.'

'Don't count on it. And it's our perspective that's fresh, not theirs. I think they wanted to come so they can take the kudos once we've cracked it. Let's face it, they haven't managed to solve it, so far,' Whitney said.

'From what I've read, the Regional Force has resourcing issues and are having to restructure. That can't have helped their investigation.'

'Resources are tight for everyone. Which is why we don't have money for the most up-to-date equipment to do our job. Maybe if they'd not spent up large on all those SmartBoards, whatever they are, they wouldn't be in such dire straits.'

'Would you ever consider moving there? Could it be classed as a good promotion prospect?' George asked.

'You must be joking. I'm happy here. I like the Lenchester police force, warts and all. Right. We're almost here.' Whitney turned left into Lower West Street.

After parking the car in the road, they walked up to the terraced house. It was a newer one, dating from the eighties. The sort designed for the London overspill. Small brick-built boxes with cladding.

'Whoever designed these did an appalling job,' George said.

'I agree. They're ugly and poorly built. I've known places like this where dogs have actually chewed through the dividing walls. They were a cheap option to house many people, without a thought for what they would be like thirty years down the track. Luckily, we don't have too many of these areas in Lenchester.'

They walked up to the door, and Whitney rang the bell. After a few moments, a woman answered.

'Yes,' she said, staring at them both.

'Does Patrick Logan live here?'

'Who wants to know?'

'DCI Walker, Lenchester CID,' Whitney said, showing her warrant card.

'What do you want, this time? Why can't you lot leave him alone? He's done nothing.'

'We need to speak to him about his train journey this morning.'

'He's in bed. He's been working nights.'

'Where does he work?'

'Smithfield Distribution, in Coventry. He does the nightshift.'

'We need to speak to him about an incident that happened on his train. Please wake him up.'

'He won't be happy. He's only just gone to bed.'

'Then he won't be in too deep a sleep,' Whitney said.

The woman opened the door and let them in. 'Wait here.'

They watched her jog up the stairs and go into the first room on the left. Although she closed the door behind her, they could hear anger in the man's voice as she woke him. After a couple of minutes, she came back down, with him following close behind. He was wearing boxers and a T-shirt, and his hair was all messed up. He was a small man, around five foot six, and very skinny.

'What do you want?' He glared at them both.

'We'd like to talk to you about your train journey this morning. Is there anywhere we can sit down?' Whitney said.

A guilty expression fleetingly crossed his face. What was he hiding?

'We can go into the lounge.' He opened the door on the left.

They followed him into a small room, overpowered by

a large dark green leather three-piece suite, focused on the biggest television screen George had seen. It had to be at least seventy-two inches.

'Were you on the train from Coventry to London this morning?' Whitney asked after they were all seated.

'Yes. I was coming home from work.'

'Do you always catch that train?'

'No. Sometimes I get a lift home with a bloke I work with. He's on holiday at the moment, so I have to catch the train this week.'

'Do you have your ticket?'

'Somewhere. Maybe in my jacket pocket.'

'Get it for me,' Whitney said.

He let out an annoyed grunt and left the room. After a few minutes, he came back and handed the ticket to Whitney.

'This was for yesterday, not today,' Whitney said.

'That's the only one I can find.' He dropped back down onto the chair.

'We found a ticket on the floor of the train this morning, which has your fingerprints on it. It's from today.'

'So, why did you ask me to find my ticket? What the fuck's that all about?'

'We found the ticket near a woman who'd been murdered on the train.'

Logan paled. 'I didn't do it. I didn't do anything.'

'Where were you sitting on the train?' Whitney asked.

'Near the back.' He glanced in George's direction, and when she made eye contact, he dropped his gaze. He couldn't be more suspicious if he tried.

'Was anyone sitting near you?' Whitney asked.

'No.'

'So, how did your ticket end up on the floor of the middle carriage?'

'I must've dropped it.' He shrugged.

'When?'

'Getting off the train.' He leaned back and folded his arms.

'Why didn't you get off from your own carriage?' Whitney asked.

'I didn't want to,' he replied.

'That makes no sense,' Whitney said. 'Did anyone see you walking through?'

'How do I know?'

'Can you tell me your movements on Sunday during the day between eight and two?' Whitney asked.

'Why?' he growled.

'Answer the question,' Whitney snapped.

'I was at home,' he muttered unconvincingly.

'Can anyone vouch for you?'

'No.' He shook his head. 'Dennie was away for the weekend.'

'And you were at home all the time?'

'Yes. I've already told you. Why do you want to know?' Logan sounded agitated.

'We're investigating two murders, both of which happened on trains.'

'And you think I did them?'

'Your ticket was found near one of the victims, and you still haven't given us a reason why.'

He looked away. Guilt etched across his face. 'Were you doing something you shouldn't have?' George asked.

'I want immunity if I tell you what I know.'

'What do you mean immunity? This isn't some TV show. Either you tell us what you know, or we'll take you in for questioning,' Whitney said.

'All right, I did see a woman sitting on her own when I passed through. But she was asleep. Her laptop was on the seat next to her, so I picked it up and carried on walking. She didn't notice.'

'She didn't notice because she was probably dead,' Whitney said.

'She didn't look dead. I thought she was asleep.'

'Did you actually look at her?'

'A bit. She wasn't looking at me, so I took the laptop.'

'Is that why you always walk through the train? To see if there's anything you can steal?' Whitney asked.

'I'm not admitting anything. I only told you about this one time, so you know what I was doing there, and why my ticket was on the floor. It must have slipped out of my hand.'

'How did you get through the ticket barrier without it?'

'It's easy. Most of the time there's no one around and you can walk through the disabled access.'

'We need the laptop.'

'Are you going to charge me with stealing it?'

'Just get it for me,' Whitney said.

He left the room and came back within thirty seconds, holding a blue case. Whitney took it from him.

'Is this the only thing you took from passengers today?'

'Yes.'

'Get dressed. You're coming with us.'

The man scowled at them. 'You said if I cooperated you wouldn't bring me in for questioning.'

'I didn't say that.'

'Are you charging me?'

'We'll discuss it at the station.'

'Why can't we do it here? I didn't do anything to that woman. I didn't see anyone else hanging around. The train wasn't very busy. Why do I have to go with you?'

'You're coming to the station with us, now. If you don't

do it voluntarily, I will arrest you. Your choice.' Whitney stood, and George followed.

'What about my sleep? I've got work again later.'

'You should've thought of that before you stole the laptop. The sooner you get dressed and come with us, the sooner you'll be back in your bed.'

'Can I take my car?'

'No. Dennie can follow behind and take you home once we've finished.'

He stormed out of the room and stomped up the stairs.

'What do you think?' George asked in a low voice.

'He doesn't have an alibi for the first murder. We need a search warrant to look through this place and I don't want him, or anyone else, getting rid of anything incriminating before we get one.'

'What about Dennie?'

'That's why I suggested she follow us to the station.'

'It seems a bit of a longshot. In his job he's hardly able to travel the country. How could he commit the other murders?' George said.

'We'll know more once we've completed a background check on him. And right now, he's the only lead we have.'

Logan reappeared, dressed in sweatshirt and jeans. He followed them out to the car and sat in the back. Periodically, he'd moan about being tired and exhausted, and why it was pointless for him to be taken in. He hadn't done anything, and he thought they were picking on him because he'd got a police record.

They arrived at the station and left Logan in one of the interview rooms. Whitney asked a uniformed officer to wait outside the door to make sure he didn't try to leave.

They went into the incident room so Whitney could request the search warrant and arrange for the forensics team to be on standby. She also wanted to check whether any new information had come in.

Matt was sitting at his desk, and she walked over to him.

'We've brought in someone who was on the train this morning and stole the victim's laptop. Ask Frank to check out the CCTV footage of people getting off at Banbury so we can see which carriage he came from. The train wasn't busy, so it should be pretty obvious.'

'Yes, guv,' Matt said.

'How's it going with the rest of the CCTV search?'

'We're still working on it, but there is something I want to speak to you about.' He glanced over to where the RF officers were talking to other members of the team.

'Let's go to my office. You come, too, George.'

They reached her room, and she closed the door behind them.

'I don't trust those two,' Matt said.

'Why? What's happened?' she asked.

'They've been snooping around, asking questions. Wanting to see everyone's notes.'

'They need to get up to speed with the investigation.'

'They wanted to know where you'd gone, and when I wouldn't tell them, they got very insistent.'

'Don't worry about it. You did the right thing. Anyway, I need you to look into Logan. He doesn't have an alibi for Sunday, and we know he was in the vicinity of the second victim because he stole the laptop. Look at all the previous murders, and ask Ellie to check his alibis for those as well.'

Her phone rang. 'Walker.'

'Your search warrant has been approved,' the officer said.

'Thank you.' She ended the call. 'The warrant's come through for Logan's house. Change of plan. Matt, I want you to go with forensics to his house. In the meantime, I'm going to interview him.'

They went back into the incident room, and she stopped at Ellie's desk.

'Do you have a list of all the murders? Times and dates?'

'I can print it off for you,' the officer said.

'How's the background check on Logan coming along?'

'As I said previously, he's been in and out of prison, mainly for burglary. I'll get you the dates. He's had a variety of jobs but doesn't seem to stay very long. He's been working at Smithfield for the last three months.'

'Thanks.'

'Do you want me in with you or observing from outside?' George asked as they left the incident room.

'We'll do this one together. There's no one else available, and it's far better to have two people there.'

When they got back to the interview room, Logan was sitting with his arms folded, an angry expression on his face. He jumped up.

'Where have you been? And why wasn't I allowed to leave the room? I wanted to go out for a smoke, and the copper on the door wouldn't let me.'

'Sit down, Mr Logan. You can have a cigarette once we've finished.' Whitney prepared the recording equipment. 'Interview with Mr Patrick Logan, in the presence of DCI Walker and Dr Cavendish. Mr Logan, please confirm you're here voluntarily to help with our enquiries, and you understand you're not under caution.'

'Yes,' he replied.

'We understand you've only been with your current employer for three months. Is that correct?'

'Yes.'

'Where were you working before?'

'At a warehouse in Banbury.'

'How long were you there?'

'I don't see why you need to know all this.'

'Please answer the question.'

'I was only there for a few weeks.'

Whitney opened the folder she'd placed on the table. She glanced at the list of dates of the other murders and chose one which was earlier in the year. 'Please can you tell me what you were doing on Monday eighteenth of February?'

'You've got to be kidding. How am I meant to remember that far back?'

'Were you working in January?'

He was quiet for a moment. 'No, I'd just come out of prison.'

'You mentioned earlier that you use the train as a place to find items to steal.'

'I didn't say that. The laptop was just sitting there, so I took it. I don't stalk trains looking for things to nick.'

'That's not the impression you gave us earlier,' she said, arching an eyebrow. 'Going back to today on the train. You said you walked through and came across what you thought to be a sleeping woman. Take me through your journey, from leaving your seat to when you took the laptop. I want to know everything you saw. Every person you walked past.'

'I was sitting in my carriage, and once we'd gone past the industrial estate leading into Banbury, which meant it would only be another few minutes before we reached the station, I stood up and put my rucksack on my back. I then walked through the carriage.'

'Who was in your carriage?'

'A woman on her own. She was reading a book.'

'Next carriage?'

'There were three men and two women. The two women sat together talking, and the men were all on their own.'

'What did they look like?'

'Like people going to work. One man was wearing a workers' jacket.'

'High visibility?' Whitney asked.

'Yes.'

'Next carriage?'

'The woman. I walked past and noticed her sleeping. I saw the laptop on the seat next to her. I looked round. No one could see me, so I took it. Once the train reached Banbury, I got off.'

There was a knock on the door, and Ellie walked in. 'Can I have a moment, guv?'

'Interview suspended.' Whitney stopped the recording and left the room, with George following. She closed the door behind them.

'What is it?' she asked Ellie.

'I've been running a check on Patrick Logan against all the other murders. He was in prison for six of them. He was released midway through the last set.'

'Thanks, Ellie. I'm not surprised it isn't him. Our perp's been clever enough not to be caught all this time, and Logan doesn't appear to have a lot between the ears.'

They went back into the interview room.

'Patrick Logan, I'm arresting you for the theft of a laptop. You do not have to say anything, but it may harm your defence if you do not mention when questioned something which you later rely on in court. Anything you do say may be given in evidence. Do you understand?'

'I offered to help, so you said you weren't going to charge me.'

'I said no such thing. We currently have a forensics team going through your house, and if we retrieve other stolen items they will be added to the charge.'

'You can't do that. You have no right.'

'We have a search warrant.'

'You won't find anything.'

'I'll get an officer to process the charge, and then you're free to go.'

Whitney and George left the interview room.

'So, we're still no further,' Whitney moaned. 'With two more murders on the cards before the end of next week.'

Chapter Fifteen

Friday, 14 June

Whitney stared at the large Edwardian building that had been her mum's home for the last few months. She'd popped out from work for a quick visit. She'd have liked to spend more time with her mum, but it wasn't possible at the moment. She turned the brass handle and pushed open one of the white double doors, walking into a huge sterile vestibule with a high ceiling and bare walls, all of which had several cracks.

The entire place was in need of a coat of paint and some interior design flair. But that didn't mean the standard of care wasn't good. She'd done the research after her mum's social worker had recommended it, and it was rated highly. It wasn't a large nursing home, with only twenty residents, all with their own rooms and en suites. Her mum seemed happy there, though sometimes it was hard to tell with the dementia.

She walked over to the reception desk where an older woman was focused on a computer screen.

'I've come to see my mother, Mrs Walker.' She smiled at the woman while signing the visitor's logbook.

When her mum had first moved in, she'd spent a lot of her time in her room, saying she preferred her own company, but that was because she'd been a little nervous about joining in with the activities. It was different now, and Whitney expected to find her with the others who lived there.

'Most of the residents are in the day room.'

'Thanks,' she said as she turned and headed down the corridor.

The day room was painted a soft yellow, and there was artwork hanging on the walls. The floral carpet was a bit worn, as were the selection of easy chairs and sofas, but there was a comfortable atmosphere. Her mum was sitting on the far side of the room. The TV was on, but she didn't appear to be watching. She wandered over and tapped her gently on the arm.

'Hello, Mum.'

'Whitney. I didn't expect to see you today.' Her eyes crinkled at the corners.

She leaned down and pulled her mum into a hug. 'I thought I'd surprise you,' she said, releasing her and scrutinising her face.

Same old mum. Nothing had changed. Although, after visiting the other day, Tiffany had said her granny seemed more confused than the last time she'd seen her.

'Sit down.' Her mum tapped the arm of the empty chair beside her. Whitney pulled it around slightly so they were facing each other.

'I bought you something.' She pulled out of her bag the bar of dark chocolate she'd bought on the way there and handed it to her.

'Mmm. My favourite.' Her mum took the bar from her

and stared at it, turning it over in her hands like it was something precious. 'Would you like some?'

'Why don't you save it for later?' she suggested.

'Good idea. I'll take it to my room when you go. Then I won't have to share.'

'Do they expect you to share everything?' She frowned. She couldn't imagine that would be the case.

'The carers don't. But you see the lady playing cards over there? The one with dyed black hair?'

Whitney looked in the direction her mum was pointing and saw a woman hunched over a table, with her back to them, playing cards with three others.

'Yes.'

'That's Miss Winter. If she sees you eating something nice, she demands half.'

A bully? Here? That was ridiculous. Maybe she should have a word with one of the carers. Her mum's happiness was paramount.

'Just tell her no. You don't have to take any nonsense.' Her mum had always been able to stand up for herself. It was where Whitney got her no-nonsense streak from.

'I can't do that,' she whispered. 'She might put a spell on me. She's a witch, you know.'

What?

'How do you know?' What else could she say?

'You only have to look at her. And—' She lifted her hand to the side of her mouth to hide what she was saying from others. 'Mrs Green told me she'd seen a broomstick behind the door of her room.'

Whitney's breath caught in the back of her throat. Her mum had never spoken like that before. She wasn't sure how to deal with it.

'Then take the chocolate upstairs, like you suggested.

It's probably for the best. Tell me what else you've been doing.'

Her mum picked up the black handbag, which was at her feet, and put the chocolate in there. 'Yesterday we had a concert. Some children from a local school.'

'That's nice. What did they sing?'

'Songs from the shows. They weren't as good as you at that age.'

Whitney grinned. 'You're biased.'

Singing was Whitney's passion. She'd loved it from an early age and had put it down to being named after her mum's favourite singer, Whitney Houston. As a teenager, she'd wanted to take it up professionally. But all that changed when she'd got pregnant at seventeen and had her daughter. Not that she regretted it. Tiffany was her life, and Whitney couldn't be prouder of her. She was studying engineering at Lenchester University. The first in their family to go.

She still loved singing and that was why she'd joined the local Rock Choir. Except she often had to miss rehearsals. That was the trouble with her job. It interfered with everything. But she couldn't imagine doing anything else. Despite her family responsibilities, she made it work. It was a little easier now Tiffany no longer needed her so much and her mum and brother were being looked after.

'I miss Rob,' her mum said.

'I know. We'll arrange a time to go and see him.'

'Can we go now? Shall I get my coat?' her mum asked, her face bright.

'Sorry, Mum. I can't. This is a fleeting visit. I'm really busy at work.'

'You're always busy. What is it this time? Another murder?'

'How do you know?'

'I can tell. It's the way you become all serious and anxious.'

Tears pricked her eyes, but she quickly blinked them away before her mum noticed. It was like listening to her mum how she used to be. She'd always had an uncanny knack of knowing exactly how Whitney was feeling at any given time.

'Well, you're right. But don't tell anyone. I'm not allowed to discuss my investigations.'

'Your secret's safe with me.' Her mum tapped the side of her nose. 'We don't want the witch to hear about it. She might put a spell on you, to stop you from finding out who did it. Especially if she knows I've got some chocolate and won't give her any.'

Whitney's heart wrenched. The fucking disease. It was unbearable to watch what it was doing to her mum.

'Thanks, Mum. I've got to go now. I'll arrange a time for us to visit Rob. It will be soon. I promise.'

She kissed her mum on the cheek and headed out of there. Thank goodness she had her work to throw herself into.

Chapter Sixteen

Friday, 14 June

Whitney tried to push all thoughts of her mum and brother to the back of her mind as she walked into the incident room. It was mid-afternoon and the majority of her officers had returned.

George was sitting at one of the desks, peering at a computer screen, and she wandered over.

'Are you okay?' George asked as she looked up.

Whitney tried to speak, but couldn't, and shook her head.

'Let's go to your office.' George led her through and closed the door.

'It's Mum,' Whitney said, unable to stop the tears from falling down her cheeks. She'd managed to contain it so far, until she was actually asked, and then the floodgates opened.

'What's happened?'

'Nothing more than we should expect,' Whitney said, sniffing. 'It's just the way she can suddenly be back to her old self, and then the next sentence she sounds away with the fairies and says the most ridiculous things.'

'It's hard to deal with, but what you have to remember is she doesn't seem to be suffering.'

'You're right. I think it's also because I feel guilty for neglecting her. I've been so busy it's hard to find time to visit her and Rob. But that's going to change, or I couldn't live with myself.' Leaning across the desk, she pulled out a tissue from the box and wiped her eyes.

'She understands that sometimes your job has to take priority. She's always known that.'

Whitney glanced at George. How had she suddenly become so insightful when it came to human emotions? 'True. Come on, let's go back out. We don't have time to waste.' She sucked in a calming breath; she had to stay focused.

'Okay,' George said.

'Listen up, everyone,' Whitney said when they were back in there. 'I want to go through where we are.' She stood by the board. 'So far, we have two murders, Hugo Holmes-Reed and Lena Kirk. The only connection is they were on a train going to, or through, Lenchester. We know from what's happened in other areas, there are likely to be two more murders before the end of next week. Ellie, what have you discovered about the rail operators, aside from them being part of Transwide?'

'Nothing new, yet. All sets of murders have been on different train lines. The line running through Lenchester is Central Group. The other murders took place on Coastal Rail, Pathway Trains, and Link Railway.'

'Terry,' Whitney said to the older officer from the RF. 'You researched the different rail operators. What conclusions did you come up with?'

Gardner walked over to Whitney, stood by the board,

and turned to face the rest of the team. 'DCI Walker hasn't yet officially introduced me. It's good to meet you all. I'm DI Terry Gardner and over there is DS Vic Rowe.' He pointed to where the other officer was standing. 'We're here from the Regional Force to help you with the case. As you know, there have already been twelve other murders over the last two years. Four in Glasgow, four in Liverpool, and four in Bristol. So, any information you have, please run past me and we can see how it fits with the rest. We're going to catch this murdering bastard.'

Whitney seethed. What was his game, trying to interfere like that? Acting like he was in charge. So what if she hadn't remembered to introduce them. She was the SIO. All she wanted was his input regarding the rail operators.

'Thank you, DI Gardner. Back to what I was asking, what can you tell us about the rail operators?'

'The main link is Transwide, but we investigated the company and didn't come up with anything significant.'

'What about the redundancies in 2014? Did you speak to any employees who were let go?' she asked.

Gardner frowned. 'Redundancies?'

'Yes. A thousand of them.'

'Vic?'

'I'll have to check, but 2014 is three years before the murders started,' Rowe said.

Whitney exchanged glances with George. Were they for real?

'We don't have time to look into something which occurred five years ago,' Gardner said. 'We've got two more murders coming up.'

'Yes, murders we're going to prevent, as we don't intend to sit back and wait.' She'd sooner hunt the killer than sit pontificating over his expected next move.

'That wasn't what I meant,' Gardner said.

'So, what do you suggest we do?' Whitney asked, trying to keep the facetious tone from her voice but not succeeding.

'We need to take a note of all possible trains coming through Lenchester over the next ten days and try to ascertain which are the most likely ones for the murderer to target.'

Whitney knew it was a good idea, and it was what they were going to be doing, anyway. 'Agreed. Tell me about the previous murders. Were any of them committed during rush hour?'

'All were at different times of the day, but never when the trains were very busy.'

'Our second murder took place on a train that could've been busier than it was. It was one going to London first thing in the morning.'

'He must have done his research,' George said. 'Those first few stops are always quiet, according to Logan.'

'Who's Logan?' Gardner asked.

'Someone we brought in for questioning. He isn't our guy, but he did steal something from the victim,' Whitney said.

'You should have told me. There have been other instances when items were stolen from the victims.'

What? Why weren't they aware of that? It would have made a difference to their interview with Logan, even though they now knew he wasn't in the frame.

'That information wasn't in the files you gave us.'

'We didn't think you needed to know.'

She couldn't stand there and let that pass. She wanted answers.

'I think we'll take this discussion to my office,' she said quietly. 'Okay, team, carry on with what you're doing. I'll be back shortly.' She marched into her office with Gardner following. She closed the door.

'What else haven't you told me?' she demanded.

'You have our files, which contain everything you need to know, apart from the fact items were stolen from victims.'

'And you didn't think it was important enough to tell us. What is it with you? You're just here to pick our brains. So we can solve the crime, and you can take the kudos. Let me tell you, that isn't going to happen. We'll be solving it, and my team, who are the best, will rightly take the credit.'

She stared up at him. He wasn't going to intimidate her, despite being a head taller. She was the higher-ranking officer, and he needed to respect that.

'We kept quiet about the items being stolen in case of copycats.'

'That doesn't wash. I'm SIO. You should've told me. I'm not happy about this. I didn't want to bring you in in the first place, and I'm being proved right. All you're doing is putting yourself before the case.'

'You know now.' He folded his arms and locked eyes with her.

'Do you have a list of items that were stolen?'

'I'll get it to you. There were a variety of things taken, ranging from items of clothing, like gloves and scarves, to make-up or trinkets from handbags.'

'No purses or wallets? Anything of value?'

'No. Just trinkets.'

'So, the fact we arrested the guy with a laptop doesn't actually coincide with the other items taken.'

'Not unless the murderer has changed his MO. Why didn't you tell me you'd found someone of interest?'

'I didn't feel it was necessary. A ticket was found on the train, and we discovered who it belonged to. I don't have to share everything with you, the same as you believe you don't have to share everything with me.'

'You need our expertise on this case, so instead of giving us the cold shoulder, maybe you should listen to what we have to say and include us,' Gardner said.

'I'll include you when I think it's necessary. In the meantime, what do you and your partner intend to do to assist us? Are you prepared to sit down and scroll through mountains of CCTV footage, like the rest of the team?'

'I'm a DI. I don't involve myself in that.'

'What do you "involve yourself in"?' She held up her hands and did quote marks with her fingers.

'Do you have the pathology report on the first victim? You were going to email it to me.'

'I'll forward it to you shortly. What about Rowe? Will he look through the CCTV footage with the others?' She walked around her desk and made a note on a scrap of paper to send him the report.

'Yes. When is the pathologist likely to have something on the second murder?' Gardner asked.

'When she's ready.'

'So, you allow her to set the pace, do you? If it was my case, I'd make sure she operated in accordance with our timelines.' He shook his head, and it took all Whitney's will power not to slap the disdainful look off his face.

'That's not the way things work here. We have a very good relationship with the pathologist.'

If she wasn't so intent on stopping him from taking over, she'd send him to Claire for some of her treatment. That would soon sort out his 'work to our timelines' nonsense.

'As do we, as long as it doesn't hinder the investigation. But in your case, it seems like the tail is wagging the dog, and not the other way around.'

'That's your opinion and not mine. Go back to the incident room. I've got something to do.'

She walked out from behind her desk and opened the door for him to leave, slamming it behind him. This wasn't going to work, and she intended to do something about it.

Chapter Seventeen

Friday, 14 June

Whitney knocked on Jamieson's door and waited impatiently, moving from foot to foot. She could hear him on the phone, as usual, but it didn't sound like a work call. After five minutes, she knocked again and heard him end the call.

'Come in,' his voice boomed out.

She opened the door and marched in, standing in front of his desk with her hands on her hips.

'If you've come about the press conference, it's arranged for five, this afternoon.'

It had totally slipped her mind.

'No, I'm not here about that. It's something else.'

'What?'

'This can't carry on. Bringing in the Regional Force was totally ridiculous. All they've done is annoy everyone and withhold evidence. How can that be cooperation? I told you it was a mistake, and I stand by my view. I think you should send them back. We don't need them.'

'Sit down and tell me exactly what happened.'

He was being remarkably calm, which was totally unlike him. It was unnerving.

'We brought a man in for questioning after discovering he was at the scene of the second murder and had no alibi at the time of the first. Also, he stole a laptop from the second victim. When Gardner found out about our man, he informed me that the murderer had stolen something from each victim, and when I asked why the information wasn't in the files, he said he'd deliberately omitted it.'

'Did he give a reason why?'

That was immaterial. It shouldn't matter what the reason was.

'He said he wanted to prevent a copycat, but that's not good enough. We can't have them withholding information. How are we expected to do our job properly if we don't know the full facts?'

'It makes sense to me,' he said.

'I disagree. It's acceptable to keep certain facts from the media, but it doesn't make sense to keep them from your colleagues.'

'You have the information now. What did Gardner say about the man we have in custody?'

'He doesn't know anything about him, other than I mentioned the laptop had been stolen.'

'So, you kept something from him. Something which could affect the investigation?'

'We were pursuing a line of enquiry. I didn't believe it necessary to include him at that stage.'

'Let me get this straight. You withheld information from him, in exactly the same way he withheld it from you. Have I got that right?'

'No, that's not what I'm telling you. I'm SIO, and the highest-ranking officer on the case, so it's up to me to decide what he knows. He should do as I say. He's also trying to ingratiate himself with the team and making out he's in charge of the case.'

She could have kicked herself. She sounded like a petty schoolgirl.

'And what do you suggest I do?'

Whitney frowned. It wasn't like him to ask her advice.

'We have the files, or partial files, so I suggest you send Gardner and Rowe back to their station. We don't need them, and if it turns out we need any assistance, we can get in touch by phone. But like I've said, so far they've done nothing to help. Not only have they omitted information from the files, there's been no proper investigation into Transwide, the company who owns all the rail operators targeted. If I hadn't been to visit them, we wouldn't have known about the mass redundancies they made a few years before the murders started.'

'A few years? I hardly call that relevant.'

'We don't know for sure. Also, Gardner isn't prepared to do anything in terms of going through CCTV footage or any of the other mundane investigative work that needs to be done. He just wants to swan around. The pair of them are getting in the way, and I don't need them here.'

Jamieson leaned back in his chair, his hands behind his head. His manner was relaxed and difficult to read. Was he going to side with her, for a change?'

'I'm not going to send them back, as I think they can help with the investigation. It's just a matter of you accepting they're here and making use of them in an appropriate way. We don't expect DIs to do the work of a constable.'

'When it comes to necessary grunt work, there's no hierarchy in my team. We all muck in.'

'Well, it's not going to work that way now. The RF is a prestigious force, and it's not going to do us any harm to have links with them. Links we could maybe exploit sometime in the future.'

Now she understood. He was thinking of himself. If a position came up at the RF, he believed he'd have more chance if he already had a good relationship with them.

'I'm still not happy about having to work with them.'

'I can always take you off the case as SIO and give the role to Gardner.'

He couldn't be serious.

'Fine, if you want to see the federation rep, sir. You can't bring in someone from an outside force and make them SIO. It doesn't work that way.'

'Don't push it, Walker. I expect you to work with Gardner. Put your differences behind you and concentrate on what's more important. Making sure we put an end to these murders. Do you understand?'

She drew in a breath. 'Yes, sir.'

'Good. I don't want to hear any more complaints from you. Get back to work. You have a job to do. I'll handle the press conference myself.' He dismissed her with a nod of his head and started reading something on his desk.

She stormed out of his office and down the corridor.

How could anyone be so insufferable beat her. Just when she thought they'd begun to get on a little better, he acted like a total arse. It was times like these she wished she smoked.

She stopped at the ladies' on her way back to the incident room, and splashed water on her face. By the time she had returned, she was relatively calm.

'Listen up, everyone,' she said. 'We've got to try to work out potential trains our guy could target next, and once we've done that, we'll put officers on them. Sue, contact the victims' families and find out what was taken, as we now know the killer has always stolen something from each of them.' She looked for George and saw her standing close to Ellie. 'George, with me in my office.'

The psychologist nodded, her face set hard.

'What's that all about? I don't appreciate being ordered around,' George said once they were alone.

'Sorry, I only did it so Gardner didn't think we were discussing anything to do with the case without him.'

'What do you want to talk about?'

'I went to see Jamieson and asked him to take Gardner and Rowe off the case, but he refused. I wanted someone to vent to.'

'That's fine, but if they're not going, we need to work with them and make use of what they've got, rather than spending all of our time being antagonistic towards them,' George said.

'Whose side are you on?'

'I'm on the side of solving the murder. Look at it this way, they're here and we can make use of two extra bodies. Instead of wasting time looking at how we can work without them, let's use their knowledge. Remember they've got experience of the case that we haven't.'

'So they can take credit for solving it?'

'What's more important, preventing another murder or having someone pat you on the back for doing a good job? You've really got to pull your head in, otherwise it's going to end badly,' George said.

'Why are you always so rational?'

'You know me. It's the way I am. Come on, let's go back and work with them. We can still show we're better than they are.'

'You're right. From now on I'll be nice to them. Well, maybe not nice, but I will include them, and we'll get this job done.'

They returned to the incident room and went over to

the two desks on the far side, where Gardner and Rowe were sitting. Whitney glanced around to make sure there was no one close enough to hear what she had to say. She wasn't ready for that yet.

'We need a truce,' she said. 'We're not going to solve this unless we work together.'

'Agreed,' Gardner said.

'Which means not withholding any information, on both of our parts.'

'Deal,' Gardner added.

'Good. We need to identify potential trains.'

'Both of our murders were on trains going north to south,' George said. 'In the previous murders was there any pattern regarding which direction the trains came from?'

'Vic?' Gardner looked at his sergeant.

'I'm not sure. I'll check it out.'

'Good, that's a start,' Whitney said.

She and George left them to it and went to the board, where she put up a map of all the different train routes coming into Lenchester or passing through.

'We've got eight days' worth of trains to consider. How on earth are we going to work it out?' she asked George.

'We can eliminate some of the days. None of the murders have taken place on consecutive days. There were at least four days between them. Also, the last murder has always been two weeks after the first. Our first murder was on the ninth, which means the last will be on the twenty-third. Therefore, we can exclude the twenty-second, twenty-first, and twentieth. The second murder was on the thirteenth, so we can exclude the fourteenth, fifteenth and sixteenth. Now we're left with the seventeenth to the nine-teenth, a possible three days when the third murder could occur. A bit more manageable,' George said.

'Attention everyone,' Whitney said. 'We can narrow our search down to trains on three days. I want you to look at timetables in and out of Lenchester from the seventeenth to the nineteenth. We know the kills are at a time when the trains are fairly quiet, and typically on those without CCTV. This means we can discount the fast commuter trains from London, Leeds, and other big cities. We'll split it up by days. Matt and Vic, you can take the seventeenth, Frank and Sue, the eighteenth, Ellie the nineteenth, and Doug, you pick up the slack from our other lines of enquiry. Any questions?'

'Can I work on it tomorrow?' Frank asked. 'It's the wife's birthday and we're going out for a meal.'

There was always something going on in the detective's life. How did he manage it?

'Okay, Frank. Just make sure you're in first thing, with no hangover. Where are we with passengers coming forward after the first murder?'

'Everyone who bought a ticket using a credit card has been accounted for,' Doug said. 'Five tickets were paid for using cash, but we've only tracked down one. A woman who'd seen it on the news and came forward.'

'There'll be a press conference shortly for the second murder, so that might prompt people to come forward for both murders. Ellie, contact the railway stations for credit card details of passengers on today's train and pass the information to Doug. Somebody must have seen something. Terry, did you find any leads from passengers on the previous murders?' she asked the DI.

'No, that was one of the problems. We took statements from many passengers and didn't find similarities between them. It was like the murderer was invisible.'

'Did you compare witness testimonies between targeted

areas and not just between murders in the same area?' George asked.

'Not as far as I'm aware,' Gardner said.

Their incompetence surrounding basic police work was astounding. Their remit was to take an overall view of the bigger picture. Comparing targeted areas should have been done, at the very least.

'What are you getting at, George?' Whitney asked.

'Suppose the murderer disguised himself. He could have had four different disguises that he'd use on the trains, to stop himself from being recognised. He could well use the same disguises in different areas. It would certainly be a useful exercise to compare witness testimonies between areas, to see if we can find a pattern.'

'Do we have all the witness testimonies in the files?' Whitney asked.

'I'm not sure,' Gardner said.

'You check, and if they're not there, arrange to get them, and then you and Vic can work on comparing them.' She glanced at her watch. 'Let's meet again in the morning. Someone needs to stay late to answer the phone, as there will be calls following the press conference. The rest of you, I want fresh tomorrow. We're going to work out where the next murder will take place and nail this son of a bitch before he knows what's hit him.'

Chapter Eighteen

Monday, 17 June

George shivered. Despite it being June, it was still cold first thing in the morning. They'd spent the last few days looking through train timetables and trains, and had come up with a list of possibilities for where the next murder could take place. Officers had been deployed on all the trains, and George, Whitney, and Terry were positioned at Lenchester station in order to go through every train that came through before allowing the passengers to leave. Whitney, who'd managed to curtail her annoyance at the Regional Force officers, had also arranged for the British Transport Police to patrol the platforms on each of the routes. That meant the team could be utilised more effectively on the actual trains.

George walked into the station building where Whitney and Terry were standing. The first train they were going to inspect was due in fifteen minutes.

'Right, let's get ourselves in position,' Whitney said once George had reached them. 'Just to recap, we've identified five possible trains. Two are arriving shortly, one later in the morning, and another two this afternoon.'

'Do they know not to let the passengers off?' George asked.

'Yes. The drivers have been instructed to keep the doors locked until we give permission for them to be opened.'

'That makes our lives easier,' George said.

'As long as they do as they've been told,' Terry said.

'They should do,' Whitney said. 'The first train is coming from Birmingham and stops at platform three, so we'll need to go over the bridge. Doug and a uniformed officer have been on there for the entire journey.'

They walked over and waited for the train. Once it arrived, they boarded through the cab, where the driver was seated, and walked into the train from there. Doug was at the entrance of the first carriage, waiting for them.

'Everything's all clear, guv,' he said. 'We continually patrolled the carriages, making a note of all the passengers. Nothing seemed out of the ordinary.'

'Good. We'll walk through and make sure everyone's still alive, and then we'll let them off.'

They went from carriage to carriage and, as Doug had said, all the passengers seemed alert. Several of them were waiting for the doors to open.

'Why can't we get out?' one of the female passengers asked.

Whitney held out her warrant card. 'Once we've checked the train, you'll be free to go.'

'Has there been another murder?'

'We're just undertaking a routine inspection,' Whitney said.

'I'm going to be late for work,' the woman said.

'Well, the sooner you let me continue, the sooner you'll be able to get off the train.'

Once they'd reached and checked the last carriage, Whitney used her radio to contact the officer she'd left with the driver. 'Okay, open the doors,' she said.

The doors opened and the passengers, of which there were only around twenty, got off.

'We'll stay here, as the next train on our list is due in ten minutes, coming from Leeds and terminating at this station. It then becomes the fast train to London,' Whitney said as they all stepped onto the platform.

'I'm wondering whether we should have had plain-clothes officers, and not uniform, on the trains,' Terry said.

'Is that what you did, on potential targets?' she asked.

'We did put plainclothes officers on some trains, but it was harder for us because initially we didn't have sufficient information to work out exactly which ones to focus on. Once we were on the third set of murders, we looked at identifying particular trains, but didn't manage to isolate particular days like you did.'

George glanced at Whitney, noticing the hint of a smile as her lips turned up slightly at the edges.

'The public will feel less nervous about using the trains if they see a police presence on there,' Whitney said.

'But if the killer sees them it might put him off from acting,' Terry said.

'Are you saying we want him to kill someone so we can catch him in the act?' Whitney asked.

'Of course not. I don't want another person dead, but how else are we going to identify him?'

'The killer's cocky. Confident. Thinks he's untouch-able,' George said. 'He's got away with murdering so far, and he won't stop until he's forced to do so. I have no doubt that he'll attempt a murder, even with the police presence.'

'I couldn't agree more,' Whitney said. 'The killer has already got away with fourteen murders and avoided being caught. We have nothing to lose by policing the trains we've identified. Here comes the next one.' She pointed at the train coming into the station.

The carriages came to a standstill. Once again, the doors remained shut and they were let on board by the driver. They were met by Whitney's officers, who had nothing to report. Everyone was alive and well, and after surveying the whole train, the doors were opened and the passengers allowed off.

'The next one isn't for a couple of hours, on platform one,' George said. 'Coming from the south. It's the Milton Keynes train. What do you want to do in the interim?'

'I need to go back to the station. My boss wants an update on what we're doing, and I've got some other paperwork to get on with. I'll meet you back here later,' Terry said as he turned and walked away.

'What shall we do?' George asked.

'First, let's grab some coffee,' Whitney said, rubbing her hands.

They walked back over the bridge, into the café, and ordered their drinks.

George took a sip and screwed up her nose. 'This is awful.'

'We can't always have your good quality shit. At least it's a caffeine hit,' Whitney said.

They sat at one of the tables. 'How are you feeling now the truce with Terry and Vic has been in force for three days?' George asked.

'I'm dealing with it. At least they're being helpful, although I'm not impressed with their investigative skills. I think we've got way better-quality officers here. Don't you agree?'

'I think their problem is they've gone stale. They've had twelve murders and been unable to solve them. My guess is they've mentally put it in the *too hard* basket and are paying lip-service to the investigation. We've come in with fresh eyes and have the benefit of the previous murders to assist us in looking for patterns. Even though at first glance it appears there aren't any, that's a pattern in itself. If you understand what I mean.'

'Not really. I think you're doing your usual *George* stuff. But haven't we already worked out a pattern in the time-frames and come to the conclusion the murderer must disguise himself? Plus, the murderer always uses a knife and chloroform.'

'I was meaning in terms of trains, and the victims. But yes, you're right, there are patterns, and we can use them to solve the case. And we're fairly confident we can pick the trains on which these murders are going to take place,' she said.

'But, as Terry said, if the murderer sees police walking up and down the train it might stop him from acting,' Whitney said.

'I think he'll still try, but even if he doesn't, we've got to be prepared for it to happen.'

'True,' Whitney agreed.

After a few minutes, George looked at her watch. 'Do you mind if I pop into the centre for an hour? My favourite shop's having a sale, and I want to buy something to wear for my brother's wedding.'

'Would you like me to come and help you choose?'

Did she? She'd never been shopping with another woman before. 'Your decision. But won't you get in trouble for going shopping during an operation?'

'We'll call it our lunch break. Plus, it's not like we're going to bump into Jamieson in a women's dress shop.'

'Okay, let's go.'

They drove into the city centre and stopped outside the small shop.

'I've never been here before,' Whitney said. 'It looks expensive.'

'That's why I like to buy in the sale.' It wasn't strictly true. She had enough money to shop there whenever she wanted, but she didn't want to show off in front of Whitney.

'Where's the wedding being held?'

'Westminster Abbey, and the reception is at the Imperial War Museum.'

'You've got to be kidding me. I thought only the royals got married there.'

'The bride's father is a senior civil servant and has been awarded the Order of the Bath, which means the family is entitled to use the Abbey.'

'Wow. No wonder you wanted something really fancy and came here.'

They looked through the rails, and George pulled out a calf length navy dress, which was fitted at the waist and had a skirt that was draped to create an asymmetric line. 'What do you think?'

'It's beautiful, but don't you want something with a bit more colour, as it's a wedding?' Whitney pulled out a floral print with flared sleeves and skirt. 'This would look amazing.'

'I don't wear fussy, pretty things.'

'There's always a first time for everything. Try it on.'

George took both dresses into the changing room. She tried the navy one first. It was elegant and felt right.

'How are you getting on?' Whitney called from outside.

'Fine. I'm wearing the navy dress.'

'Come out and show me.'

George opened the door and walked out. 'Do you like it?'

'Give us a twirl.'

George slowly turned around. 'I think this is the one.'

'It's lovely, but I still want you to try the other one.'

'Why?'

'You can't choose something to wear for such a fancy occasion after only trying on one dress. That's crazy. You have to try on lots.'

'No, I don't. I dislike shopping, and if I find something straight away then I buy it. I fail to see the point in going from shop to shop once something suitable has been found. It's a complete waste of time.'

'I'm only asking you to try one more. Anyway, how much is it? Let me have a look at the label.' George reached in and pulled out the label from inside the dress. Whitney took it from her. 'Bloody hell. Have you seen the price?'

'Yes, but it will never date, and I want something nice for the wedding.'

'How much is the other one?' Whitney walked into the dressing room and took a look. 'I think I'm going to faint. I can't believe people pay this much for clothes.'

George felt a little embarrassed. It was what her family expected her to wear. 'I know they're expensive, but I have no choice.'

'Are you going to put on the other one?'

'Okay, if it gets you off my back.' She let out a frustrated sigh before heading back to the fitting room.

After trying the dress on, she stared at herself in the mirror. Soft floaty fabric with bold flowers. She'd never worn anything like it before and didn't know what to think. She opened the door and walked out.

Whitney's eyes widened. 'I don't care what you say, you have to buy it. You look absolutely stunning.'

The assistant came over. 'Beautiful,' she said.

'She doesn't think so,' Whitney said, shaking her head.

'I'm hardly beautiful.' She knew exactly what she was like. Her height, and the way she carried herself, made people wary. She had an interesting face but would never call herself beautiful, no matter what she wore, especially when compared with the bride, who was petite and exceptionally pretty.

'Are you going to buy it? I'm sure Ross will agree how fabulous it is,' Whitney said.

'He's not going to see it.'

'Aren't you taking him to the wedding?' Whitney frowned.

'I haven't asked him.'

'Do you want to take him?'

Did she? She wasn't sure. It would certainly cause a stir amongst the family, but was she prepared for that? Not to mention it wouldn't be fair to him, as her family could be intimidating at the best of times. Then again, he hadn't let her father get the better of him when they were at the restaurant.

'I'll think about it. He might not want to come.'

'Who wouldn't want to go to a wedding at Westminster Abbey?'

'It's not going to be as incredible as you think,' she said.

'Back to the dress. Yes?'

'I know you love this one, but I don't have any shoes to go with it.' She stared at herself in the mirror and had to admit that now she'd got used to seeing herself in it, she liked it.

'We have a fabulous pair of leather sandals which would be absolutely perfect,' the shop assistant said. 'What size are you?'

'Forty-two European.'

The assistant disappeared, then came back with a pair of open-toed silver patent sandals with a two-inch heel and a gold multi strap.

'Gorgeous,' Whitney said.

George slipped them on. They fitted perfectly. She was beginning to warm to this new look. 'Okay, I'll have them.'

Back in the changing room, she got dressed in her day clothes, black trousers with a pale blue shirt and black jacket over the top. She felt comfortable in her 'uniform'.

After paying, they headed back to the railway station.

'Twenty minutes to go,' Whitney said once they'd arrived. 'Let's wait on the platform for the train.'

When they arrived, Terry was already pacing up and down.

'Where have you been?' he asked.

'Important police work,' Whitney said. She exchanged a glance with George and grinned.

The train from Milton Keynes was a few minutes early. They were greeted by Vic and a uniformed officer.

'Nothing's happened on here,' Vic said. 'We've walked up and down the train several times. There were only two stops, Northampton and Rugby.'

'Let's walk through, and then the passengers can get off,' Whitney said.

They went through the first carriage, where several people stood by the door, and a further three were seated. It was similar in the next two carriages. When they got to the fourth, there was one person waiting by the central door, and as they walked through to the end of the carriage, they saw an elderly man leaning forward in his seat.

Whitney went over to him. 'Sir, are you okay?' There was no answer. 'Sir,' she repeated. She shook him gently by the shoulder, and he fell to the side.

He was dead.

Chapter Nineteen

Monday, 17 June

Whitney turned to face Vic, whose face was devoid of colour. 'Well?'

'Fuck,' he said, unable to make eye contact with her.

'Is that all you can say?' She didn't even try to hide the anger she was feeling. 'When was the last time as you saw this man alive?'

'I think he got on at Milton Keynes,' the officer said.

'You think?' Whitney snapped. 'What do you mean by *you think*?'

'We were at the front of the train.'

'But the stop after Milton Keynes is Northampton, and it's nearly twenty minutes away. How can you not get through the entire train in twenty minutes?'

'We were talking.'

'Talking? To whom?' She couldn't believe he'd been so slack.

'DC Carver and I were chatting with the conductor, so we were only halfway through the train by the time it reached the first stop. After that we walked right through and back again several times.'

'Did you see who got off at Northampton?'

'Not exactly.' He shook his head.

'Or who got on?'

'I think there were about ten people who got on in various carriages, but I'm not sure. I took a look out of the window as we drew into the station.'

'Did you see this man?' Whitney said nodding at the deceased.

'He was asleep when we walked through the first time.'

'How do you know?'

'I heard him snoring.'

'So, we know he was still alive at Northampton, but that's all. I want everyone taken off the train and escorted to the waiting room. No one is allowed to leave until my officers have spoken to them. Can you manage that?'

'Steady on,' Terry said. 'It wasn't intentional.'

'I'm not saying it was. But if he'd done his job properly, maybe this man would still be alive.'

'The last time I saw him, he was alive,' Vic said, uncertainty showing in his voice.

'He must have been dead one of the times you walked past. I'm assuming you just thought he was still asleep and didn't double check. Am I right?'

Vic nodded. 'Yes.'

'Start at the front of the train and escort them one carriage at a time. Take the passenger waiting at the door of this carriage with you. Terry, you go with Vic and give him a hand. I'm going to arrange for the pathologist and scenes of crime officers. We need a cordon up. Terry, can you ask uniform to do that?'

She left the train with George and made the calls. Claire arrived within five minutes of being notified.

'Thanks for getting here so quickly,' she said to the pathologist as she approached.

'You were lucky. I've just been to see the coroner, and it's only a few minutes away.'

Whitney led her onto the train to where the body was. George followed.

'As you can see, we've got another one. I nudged him gently on the shoulder. Nothing else has been touched.'

Whitney stared at the elderly man and shook her head. Another victim. Another distraught family. It had to have happened between Northampton and Rugby, where she'd bet the murderer had got off. No way would he still be on the train. He was too clever for that.

'Okay, move out of the way and let me get on with my job.' The pathologist pulled on her coveralls and gloves, then unpacked her camera.

George and Whitney took a step back while Claire examined the body and took photographs.

'I take it we have the same stab wound as before,' Whitney asked.

'I'll know more when I get back to the lab, but I'm not discounting it,' Claire replied.

It was probably the most they'd get out of her.

'Let's take a quick look around the carriage, in case there's anything of note,' she said to George.

'Shouldn't we wait for SOCO?' George asked.

'We're only looking, not touching,' Whitney said.

When they couldn't find anything, they returned to the murder site.

'We need some identification. Is there anything?' she asked Claire.

'There's a wallet in his jacket pocket. Let me photograph it, and then you can take a look.'

Whitney pulled on some disposable gloves. When

Claire had finished, she handed over the wallet, which contained a photograph of two young children, a driving license, a senior railcard, a credit card, and a small amount of cash.

'The victim's name is Neil Thomas.' She pulled out her phone and called Ellie.'We've got another body. His name is Neil Thomas. I'll text you his driving license number. I need family details. He got on the train at either Milton Keynes or Northampton, but we don't know if it was his inbound or outbound journey.'

'Yes, we do,' Claire called out.

'Hang on, Ellie. What have you found?' she asked the pathologist.

'His ticket was in his pocket. It's a Milton Keynes to Lenchester return.'

'Thanks. Ellie, he got on at Milton Keynes and has a return ticket, so my guess is he lives around there.'

'Thanks, guv. I'll get onto finding his details straight away.'

Whitney ended the call and put the phone back into her pocket, furious the murderer had got the better of them so easily.

'I wonder what he took from the body?' George said.

'He's only wearing one glove. It could be that,' Claire said.

Whitney and George exchanged a glance. Claire's sudden helpfulness was extremely disconcerting.

'A watch was taken from the first victim and a bracelet from the second. So he's sticking to his pattern. I need to call back the officers who were on the other trains. We'll have a briefing after lunch.'

'Do you need me until then?' George asked.

'Why, do you want to look for a bag now you've got the shopping bug?' Whitney arched an eyebrow.

'No. I wanted to sneak a cigarette.'

'Can it wait a while longer?'

'Of course.'

Whitney turned to the pathologist. 'When can we expect to hear from you, Claire?'

She stopped what she was doing and lowered her camera. 'You really need to ask, after all this time?'

'So, this afternoon, then,' Whitney said. 'We'll leave you to it. George, we'll go to the waiting room to see how they're getting on with interviews.'

'How did you get on with your funding application, Claire?' George asked.

'Still haven't heard, which isn't a good thing.'

'These things can take a while,' George said.

'Come on, let's leave her to get on,' Whitney said impatiently.

They stepped off the train and onto the platform.

'Well, that was weird,' Whitney said.

'What was?' George said.

'That Claire was okay with you asking a question unrelated to the case.'

'Yes, you're right. I hadn't thought about it. Also, she volunteered information about the victim, which isn't how she usually acts,' George said.

'It's a total mystery,' Whitney said.

'Agreed.'

They walked into the waiting room, where there were around twenty people, some sitting and others pacing impatiently. Five officers were taking statements. They headed over to Vic.

'How's it going?' Whitney asked, forcing herself to act normally towards the officer.

'We've two reports of a man walking through the train, heading towards the toilet. He was wearing dark trousers, a casual jacket, and a baseball cap. They both said he had mid-brown curly hair, but they did give conflicting ages. One said in his thirties and other said fifties. He got off at Rugby.'

'That's given us something to work with. We'll need the CCTV footage from Rugby.'

'Although, if he's disguised, it might not help us much,' George said.

'We'll be able to see if he left the station or hopped on another train from there,' Whitney said.

'Agreed. Plus, we can compare the statements with those from our other murders, and also with those from previous murders. We might find a link with disguises, if he used one,' George said.

'Yes.' She turned to Vic. 'I want you to stay until SOCO arrives. We'll have a briefing in the office at one this afternoon. Make sure everyone knows.'

'Yes, guv.'

They left and made their way to the exit. 'You're still annoyed with him, aren't you?' George said.

'I can't help it. If he'd been doing his job properly, this murder might have been avoided. But I can't let it interfere with the investigation. I get that he's trying his hardest to put things right, but even so.'

'Sometimes we have to learn by our mistakes. He won't do it again.'

'It still frustrates me that because they're part of the RF they think they're better than us, even though we've proved, on several occasions, they're not.'

'Let it go.'

'I'm trying, but it's not easy.'

'Are you going to tell Jamieson what happened?' George asked.

'Not yet. It would serve no purpose. Our primary

concern is to capture the murderer before he strikes again. Once he moves onto a different area, solving the case will be much harder. Especially as he takes a few months off before starting again.'

'Which is an interesting feature of this series of murders. With many serial killers, the time between murders decreases. They become addicted to the high they get from committing the actual murder and want to replicate it.'

'But we suspect this isn't the case with our perp, because of the chloroform,' Whitney said.

'Agreed. As we've discussed, it's more about revenge than any deep-seated desire to harm others and promote personal self-gratification.'

'We need to focus our investigation on anyone who might have the need or desire for revenge,' Whitney said.

'And the question is, who are they seeking revenge against?' George said.

'My money's on Transwide. Frank's chased them twice for the list of redundancies, and both times they've fobbed him off. We also need to find out about the other threats they've received. It looks like I'm going to have to weigh in and get it sorted. We'll discuss it at the briefing this afternoon.' Her phone rang, and glancing at the screen she saw it was from the home where Rob was living. 'I'd better get this. Whitney Walker.'

'Hello, it's Gwen. Do you have time to call in to see us today? We're having some issues with Rob.'

'What's happened?' The words caught in the back of her throat. Ever since her brother had moved in, she'd worried something might go wrong.

'Three times now he's left the house without our knowledge. Luckily, each time we managed to find him quickly and bring him back.'

Shit. She had to deal with this pronto.

'Okay. I'll be with you shortly.'

'What's wrong?' George asked.

'It's Rob. He keeps doing a bunk from the place he's living. I need to go and see them, to find out what's happening. I should be back in the office for the briefing at one. If I'm not, can you start it off?'

'Of course. You go. I'm sure you'll get everything sorted out.'

Chapter Twenty

Monday, 17 June

Whitney rang the bell to the home where Rob now lived. It was a large modern detached house in pleasant surroundings. Her brother had seemed happy when she'd last visited a few weeks ago. Was it really that long? She was annoyed with herself for not going more often.

'Hi, Gwen,' she said when the carer answered.

'Thanks for coming in, Whitney. Let's go through to the office for a chat. Can I get you a coffee?'

Could she ever. She was gasping.

'Yes, please.'

She followed Gwen into the kitchen and waited while she made them both a hot drink, then they went into the office.

'Tell me what happened,' Whitney asked.

'Like I said on the phone, he's been disappearing.'

'What does he say when you ask him why?'

'He won't tell us. He's being very stubborn.'

She groaned to herself. It was a family trait.

'Yes, he can be like that. But there must be a reason. Do you think he's unhappy here?'

'Not at all, which is why his behaviour is so baffling. He fits in well and has made friends. He also enjoys going to the day centre. If anything, he settled in a lot quicker than others have in the past.'

'So, why is he disappearing?'

'Maybe he'll tell you,' Gwen said.

'Is he here?'

'Yes, we kept him back from the day centre today, as we were hoping you could come in to see him.'

'Where is he at the moment?'

'He's in the lounge playing computer games.'

'Okay, I'll have a chat and see what I can find out, then come back and see you after. I don't want him to know you've called me in. I'll pretend it's a normal visit.'

Whitney left the office and headed down the corridor to the lounge, a large square room with doors leading out into the garden.

'Hello, Rob,' she said as she walked in.

'Whitney.' A beaming smile lit up his face.

'How are you?'

'I'm already at level thirty-two of this game you bought me,' he said proudly.

'That's brilliant. Well done. What else have you been doing?'

'I've been going to the day centre to see my friends.'

'That sounds lovely. Have you been anywhere else?' She knew from experience, you had to take it slowly. He'd tell her what she wanted to know, but it was always one step at a time.

'I went to see Mum, but before I could get there, they found me and made me come back.'

So that was the reason. Relief, mixed with guilt,

flooded through her. He wasn't unhappy, which had been her biggest worry. She should've realised how much he'd be missing their mum. It had been quite a while since she'd taken him to see her. This whole problem was all her fault. She'd put it right straight away. It would have to be a quick visit, but they could at least spend half an hour together.

'Well, you know you can't go out on your own, in case you get lost. Go upstairs and get your jacket. I'm going to take you to see Mum now.'

'Really?' He jumped up from the chair.

'Yes, really.'

While he went to get ready, she spoke to Gwen and explained where they were going. 'I don't think he'll disappear again, now we're seeing Mum. I'll also make sure to schedule more regular visits for him.'

'That sounds perfect,' the carer replied.

Once Rob returned from his room, they went out to her car and drove straight to the care home where their mum lived. They signed in at reception and went to the day room to find her.

'Mum,' Rob called when he saw her sitting in the corner in front of the television. He ran over and flung his arms around her neck.

'Hello, you two,' her mum said after Rob released her from the hug. 'What are you doing here? It's nearly lunchtime.'

'We've come to say hello. Rob's missing you.'

'I don't think there'll be enough lunch for you,' her mum said.

'That's okay, we don't want to stay. It's just a fleeting visit. I have to get back to work.'

Rob sat next to their mum and Whitney sat opposite. She listened to the two of them chatting. It grieved her that they couldn't live together, but it wasn't possible. The main thing was they were both in lovely places, with caring staff. Their family home had to be sold to finance her mum's care but, luckily, Rob's was state funded. She promised herself she'd make sure they saw each other every week from now on, even if it was only for a short time.

'I'm sorry, Mum, but we've got to leave now,' Whitney said after half an hour.

'I want to stay,' Rob said.

'Not today. How about I buy you a burger on the way back?'

'Can I have a double decker?'

Whitney felt guilty for using his favourite treat to get him to come with her, but it saved a long argument and she didn't want him upset.

'You can have whatever you want. Say goodbye to Mum and we'll go. We'll stop off at the drive-through and then I'll take you home, as I've got to get back to work.'

'Are you catching criminals?' Rob asked.

'I hope so.'

'Do you have someone bad you're going after at the moment?'

'Yes. And we're going to catch him very soon.'

Chapter Twenty-One

Monday, 17 June

Whitney took Rob home, and made sure he was settled. Just as she was leaving, her phone beeped, indicating a message. It was from Matt.

You're needed back here. Jamieson on warpath.

She tensed. Was he expecting a briefing on the latest murder already? Typical. She'd only been gone a short time. She drove to the station and hurried to the incident room. It was only one-twenty, so she wasn't too late for the one o'clock briefing she'd arranged, not that Jamieson knew about it … unless someone had told him.

She pushed open the door, expecting to hear the usual noise of her team chatting, but it was remarkably quiet. What the hell was going on? They were all sitting at their desks, with their heads down, working. It was totally weird. She walked further into the room and did a double take.

Standing by the board with Terry, Vic, and George was her old nemesis. Dickhead Douglas. Aka DCI Grant Douglas. She hadn't seen him for a few years, but despite the hair loss and even-further-expanded waistline, there was no mistaking him.

He'd made her life a misery and put paid to her promotion when she wanted to go from sergeant to inspector. And all because she turned him down when he came on to her when she was new in the job and he was a sergeant.

The last she'd heard was he'd transferred to the Met.

Well, she wasn't going to let him get the better of her. She was older and wiser since their paths last crossed, and she certainly wasn't prepared to take any nonsense from him.

She walked over to them, and when he turned and saw her, he gave an obnoxious, supercilious smile.

'Walker,' he said.

'What brings you here?' she asked.

'Checking up on my officers.'

She looked at Terry. 'You didn't tell me DCI Douglas was your boss.'

'It's Detective Superintendent now,' Douglas said, a smirk on his face.

Crap.

'Is there anything we can help you with, sir?' She kept her hands firmly by her sides, despite the urge to slap the stupid smile off his face.

'First of all, where have you been? I was told the briefing was to start at one, and it's already twenty minutes late. No one knew where you were.'

'I had something to deal with which took longer than expected.'

'Personal or work-related?' he demanded.

If she told him it was work, he'd be within his rights to find out what it was. So, she might as well tell him the truth.

'A family issue.'

'Some things never change.' He rolled his eyes towards the ceiling.

She glanced at the other three, who stood staring at them, bemused expressions on their faces.

'Shall we take this discussion to my office?' she said.

'Good idea. You're late anyway. A few more minutes won't make any difference. I'm sure your slipshod team won't mind.'

She marched to her office, with him following. Once in there she slammed the door shut.

'I don't appreciate you undermining my authority by talking to me like that in front of my team,' she said, not giving him chance to speak.

'And I don't appreciate being kept waiting when I'm here for a briefing that I'd been told was starting twenty minutes ago.'

'Why are you here? It doesn't concern you.'

'My officers are involved, therefore it does. We've been on this investigation for two years, and I want to know if we're any closer to solving it.'

'So your force can take the credit, I suppose. Even though any progress we make is undoubtedly down to my officers.'

'You're treading on dangerous ground here, Walker. You might have crawled your way up to DCI, which certainly wouldn't have happened on my watch, but remember, I'm your superior officer and what I say goes. If I want to come to your briefing, I will, and you have nothing to say about it, other than *yes sir*. Do you understand?'

Before she had time to answer, the door opened and Jamieson walked in, closing it behind him. That was all she needed, the pair of them ganging up on her.

'Detective Superintendent Tom Jamieson,' he said, holding out his hand to Douglas.

'Detective Superintendent Grant Douglas,' he replied as he shook the outstretched hand.

'I couldn't help hearing the conversation as I approached Walker's office. Your voice carries somewhat, Grant.'

'I'm not happy with Walker's attitude, and I let my feelings be known.'

'Yes, you certainly did. I understand you used to work here. Was that behind your decision to interfere with the investigation?'

'I have every right to be here,' Douglas said.

'You should have come to see me first,' Jamieson said, an icy tone to his voice. 'These are *my* officers, and this is *my* investigation. I invited your men to assist, but that doesn't give you carte blanche to waltz in here whenever you feel like it and take over. You've clearly got personal feelings about Walker which go above and beyond her work on this case. It's not appropriate, or advisable, for you to cast aspersions on her ability to do the job. She is one of our most able DCIs.'

Whitney clamped her jaw shut. Had she stepped into an alternate universe? Jamieson was sticking up for her. It was beyond ridiculous.

'I may have stepped over the line in this instance,' Douglas said. 'But that doesn't change the fact that a briefing was arranged for one o'clock and Walker was out dealing with family issues, not returning until twenty minutes after it was due to start. Since I've known her, she's always had to deal with *issues* relating to her family. I don't believe she should've been promoted. She's not prepared to make the commitment required.'

'That's absolute bollocks,' Whitney blurted out, no

longer able to contain herself. 'Would you like me to tell the Super the real reason why you've always had it in for me?' She glared in his direction, willing him to let her explain.

'It's all in your imagination,' he said.

'That will do,' Jamieson said. 'Grant, I'd like a private word with Walker. I think we're finished here. You're not required at the briefing, and if you'd like to know more about the investigation, we can talk in my office. I'll be back there shortly. Ask one of the officers in the incident room for directions.'

Douglas stormed out of the office.

'Thank you, sir,' Whitney said.

'Don't thank me. He was right, you shouldn't have been late. We've already had a discussion about being able to lead an investigation at the same time as having personal commitments to deal with.'

'I don't believe this. I'm in here seven days a week. I work as hard, if not harder, than any member of my team. I literally popped out for an hour. Everyone has family issues that crop up, you included, sir. It has not affected my work. Douglas just wanted to put the boot in.'

'What did happen between the two of you to cause such friction?'

It surprised her that he wanted to know. 'When I was a young DC, he made a pass at me, and I told him where to get off. He swore after that he'd make my life difficult. And he did.'

'But despite that, you've done well.'

'You know me. If I want something, nothing will stop me. I'm prepared to stick up for myself. Thank you for not letting Douglas get away with it.'

'You're part of my team, and I don't like people interfering. But that doesn't mean I'm happy about you not being here when you should have been.'

'I'd better get back, then, sir. I understand you wanted to speak to me about something.'

'Yes. We have to sort out the press conference. I want you with me this time. Announcing murder number three isn't good, especially as we had officers on the train. We need to have something we can tell the public.'

'I'll put something together.'

'We'll arrange it for four o'clock. Be at my office by three-thirty, and we'll go through what you've got. In the meantime, I'll have a conversation with Detective Superintendent Douglas and make sure he doesn't poke his nose in our investigation again.'

He turned and left her office. She wasn't sure what had just happened. He'd stuck up for her and said how good she was at her job, and then bawled her out for not being there. The man was a total mystery.

She returned to the incident room, which was back to being as noisy as usual. George was still standing by the board with Terry and Vic.

'So, you have some history with our illustrious leader,' Terry said, a smirk on his face.

'We go back a long way,' Whitney said. 'Twenty years to be exact. I'd no idea he was on your force. The last I heard he was at the Met.'

'He joined after a promotion a few years ago.'

'Lucky you,' Whitney said.

'What did Jamieson say? We saw him going in,' George said.

'Well, believe it or not, he actually stuck up for me.'

'So he should,' George said.

'True. But once Douglas left, I got bawled out for being

late. He's right, I shouldn't have missed the start of the briefing. Did you talk to the team, George?'

'I didn't have time. Douglas arrived at ten to one. He said he was here for the meeting, so I felt it inappropriate to start without you.'

'How did he even know about it?'

'That was down to me,' Terry said. 'He turned up, wanting to know how we were getting on. Once I told him you were in charge, he decided to attend. I think he was just passing through Lenchester and decided to call in to see us. Our DCI is on sick leave, so Douglas has been taking more of an interest in what we're doing.'

'So, he only came because he knew it was me. How fucking typical.'

'What did happen between you?' Terry asked.

'It was when I was a DC, and he was a sergeant. Let's just say he didn't get what he wanted.'

'Why doesn't that surprise me?' Terry laughed.

Whitney laughed with him. She was beginning to warm to the officer. Maybe she'd misjudged him.

'I paid for it, though. He stopped my promotion from sergeant to inspector. It wasn't until he left for the Met that I got it.'

'And here was me thinking women were the ones who bore grudges,' George said.

'Are you serious?'

'According to research, men are better able to put things to the side, whereas women are more likely to bear a grudge against someone who has wronged them.'

'Well, Dickhead Douglas is clearly the exception. Anyway, we need to get on and see where we go from here. If that arsewipe thinks he's going to get under my skin, he's got another think coming.'

Chapter Twenty-Two

Monday, 17 June

George watched as Whitney jumped on the desk in front of the board. It was one of her tactics when she wanted to garner everyone's attention and was unable to do it by speech alone.

'Listen up, everyone,' Whitney called out over the din. 'With three murders down and one to go, we've got to do something to prevent the fourth one from happening. Dr Cavendish believes the motive behind the killings is one of revenge and not personal gratification. I'm going to hand over to her so she can update you on her profile. Then we'll need to decide exactly how we're going to tackle the next stage of the investigation. This is crucial if we're to prevent the last murder, because once the offender moves on, it's going to be difficult for us to solve, as our colleagues from the RF have discovered.'

Whitney jumped down and nodded at George to continue. She stepped forward.

'The murderer is clever, knowledgeable, and well organised. He knows about trains, timetables, and the number of passengers likely to be on them at any one time. Which tells us what?' she asked, employing her usual tactic of getting everyone involved.

'He's a train spotter,' Frank said, grinning at everyone.

'Not the time for one of your jokes, Frank,' Whitney said. 'We've got a ticking clock here, and we need to pull out all the stops to find him.'

'Sorry, guv.'

George thought Whitney was being unnecessarily harsh, as Frank meant no harm. He was an interesting specimen, and she'd love to sit down with him and a battery of psychometric tests. Despite continually playing the fool, his loyalty to Whitney was second to none.

'He has some connection with the railway and may well have worked there,' Doug said.

'That's a possibility. But has he worked at all the rail operators targeted so far?'

'Did you do a cross check of employees between rail operators from the previous murders to see if anyone had worked at more than one?' Whitney asked Terry.

'Yes. And we didn't come across anyone. But we did limit our search to those working in the targeted areas, as there were tens of thousands of employees, and we didn't have the time to investigate all of them.'

Yet again, their ham-fisted attempt at research surprised her. A more productive way of slicing the data would be to eliminate based on age and gender and then examine who was left. This could all have been done very quickly using a basic data analysis program. Unless they were like Whitney and weren't IT literate.

'He could have worked at Transwide,' Doug said.

'In my opinion it's not likely. The murderer has the sort of knowledge administrative staff in a head office are unlikely to have. I believe it's far more possible he worked at ground level in some capacity,' George said.

'That aside, he must have spent time in each area he chose, researching the individual train lines, deciding which were the best stations to get on and off at,' Whitney said.

'Yes,' George agreed. 'His actions are methodical and not done on the spur of the moment. He clearly researches his targets thoroughly. It would also explain why he focused on specific areas on each train line. To research into every town or city on a train line would be a huge undertaking.

'If he spent time in each targeted area, we should check accommodation providers close to the stations, as he could've stayed overnight during his reconnaissance.'

'Agreed. Let's start with Lenchester and contact all accommodation providers close to the railway station. We want to know all visitors staying in the two months leading up to the murders,' George said.

'Then we'll move onto the other areas, if there's time,' Whitney added. 'Though obviously Lenchester takes priority.'

'Another thing we need to consider is the actual murder. The offender is very proficient with a knife and knows exactly the right way to kill someone with minimum force. The knife is held on its side and passed through the ribcage until it connects with the heart or lungs. What does that tell us about him?' She glanced around at the officers looking in her direction. Sometimes she forgot she wasn't in class lecturing.

'Did he kill in exactly the same way from day one?' Matt asked.

'Yes. All the murders have been identical,' Terry said.

'Which means he's not learning on-the-job, so to

speak,' Matt replied. 'He must've had prior experience using a knife.'

'More than just using a knife. Most likely in actual killing.' George nodded in agreement.

'He might have been in the forces,' Frank said.

'But he also might have been a surgeon, a vet, a butcher, or a hunter,' Whitney said.

'Could he have learned from killing animals?' Sue asked.

'That's a possibility, although it would be different when faced with a human,' George said.

'He could've learned how to do it on the Internet,' Vic said.

'Learned the theory, yes. But I suspect if he hadn't put it into practice until the very first murder, there would have been some hesitation marks. Were there, Terry?'

'As far as I remember, the first murders were just as clean as the later ones. I'll check the pathologist's report to confirm.'

'In that case, we should narrow it down to either forces or surgeon,' George said.

'Okay, let's put up "possible ex-forces or surgeon" on the board,' Whitney said. 'Anything else to add, George? What about age and personality type?'

'Bearing in mind the dexterity shown and that we believe the offender to be trained in either combat or surgery, I'd put him at over thirty. Also, he's either a loner, able to come and go as he pleases without any questions asked, or his job takes him around the country and absence from his family isn't seen as out of the ordinary.'

'So, he could be a family man but might not be. And he could be a loner but might not be. That's not giving us much,' Terry said.

'Profiling isn't an exact science. It gives us information

to use alongside other avenues of investigation. You've worked with forensic psychologists before, you should know this.' She gave him one of her patronising looks, the sort she usually kept for those who challenged her research findings without good grounds.

Terry's mouth opened as if he was about to speak, then he closed it, clearly thinking better of it.

'Thank you, George. Anything else?' Whitney said.

'No, other than stressing we need to focus the investigation on accommodation close to Lenchester railway station and look into ex-forces or medical staff who have a connection with one of the rail operators or Transwide,' George said.

'We also need to identify the possible trains for the fourth murder. We've got four more days if it's going to take place on Sunday. Is that still likely, George?'

'There's no reason for him to change.'

'Apart from the fact he would've known we had police officers on the train when he committed the third murder, so that might make him worried enough to change his MO. In the previous investigations, were any of the officers you had on trains actually on the one targeted, Terry?' Whitney asked.

'No. We hadn't worked everything out in the same way you have. We didn't make the connections.'

George glanced at Whitney. Was he admitting to not undertaking the investigation as well as he could?

'Well, we've made them now, which is the main thing,' Whitney said. 'Right, does everyone know what they're doing? Any questions? I've got to put together some information for the press conference and then see the Super. George, I could do with your input.'

There were no questions, so they went to her office.

'What do you need me for?' George asked.

'I want to ask your advice.' Whitney's face was like stone.

Whatever the problem, it was clearly serious.

'Of course.'

'I'd been to see Rob. That's why I was late. He's been running away from where he lives because he was missing Mum. I feel so guilty that I haven't visited often enough. When I found out, I took him straight there. It was only a quick visit, but it made me realise I've got to spend more time with both of them. I have to make the effort and take Rob to see Mum every week. It's not fair on either of them if I don't. Especially considering Mum's prognosis.'

'It's not your fault. You can't be with them all the time. You do your best, but you still have your job and Tiffany to consider.'

'You're not getting it. They're my responsibility. I don't want excuses.'

'So, what do you want from me?' George asked, unsure of what to say.

'Do you think Douglas was right that I should step down as SIO?'

'No. It's not an option. Why do you think it is?'

'Jamieson wants me to commit twenty-four-seven, and I can't. So, I should step down.'

'Whitney, you're taking it too literally. No one works twenty-four-seven on a case. It's just a figure of speech. I'm sure you can find one hour a week to take Rob to see your mother when you've got a heavy workload. When it's quieter, you can spend longer. You need to put it into perspective.'

'You make it seem so easy, but the hour each week will have to be during the day. They don't like visitors at night.'

'Don't do anything rash. After Sunday, even if we haven't solved this case, you will have more time. You've done this week's visit. I'm sure next week you'll find an hour.'

'You're making it sound like it's a chore, but it's not like that at all. I want to see both of them.'

'I didn't mean it like that,' George said, annoyed with herself for not being able to express herself properly. She sort of understood where Whitney was coming from, wanting to stand down, but she could also see the logistical side of things and believed it would work out.

'I suppose you're right. Normally, I can handle it all. It was seeing Douglas again and remembering all the shit I had to put up with when he was here. The constant looking over my shoulder, and people thinking I wasn't doing my job properly. I thought I was over it, but clearly I'm not.'

'You do realise a lot of this is in your head. Nobody would say you don't do your job properly. You need to step back and look at the reality of the situation. And stop getting all emotional over everything.'

'Easy for you to say. I can't switch my emotions on and off like that.'

'I'm not asking you to. All I'm saying is, take a look around you. You're doing a good job, as Jamieson pointed out.'

Whitney laughed. 'You could've knocked me down with a feather when he said that. You should've seen Dick-head's face. I'd love to have been in Jamieson's office when they had their chat later.'

'That's the thing with bullies like Douglas, when someone actually stands up to them, especially someone of an equal rank, they back down. I noticed your manner towards Terry and Vic has changed.'

'Yes. I admit to being a little harsh on them when they first arrived. They've been trying to solve this case for two years, unsuccessfully, which doesn't look good on their record. Not to mention they don't have time for Douglas, so that definitely goes in their favour.'

'Going back to what you asked me about stepping down, how are you feeling about it now?'

'You're right, as usual. But don't tell anyone I said that. I need to cut through the crap going on in my head and look at things logically. I just need you to talk me down every so often.' Whitney gave a wry grin.

'Glad to help.'

'Okay, what are we going to tell them at the press conference? Should we warn people not to travel by rail on Sunday?'

'If you single out Sunday, the murderer may break his routine and carry out the next kill another day. I think we're better off telling people to only travel if it's absolutely necessary.'

'That makes sense,' Whitney said nodding.

'You can tell the public we're making progress with our enquiries.'

'The usual fob off. But I'm not sure that will cut it. And it certainly won't keep Jamieson happy. I think we should tell them about the definite link between the other murders. It was obvious, but we haven't yet confirmed it.'

'Yes. And the murderer will see the news and believe we're nowhere near catching him.'

'Thanks for your help. I really appreciate it.'

'It's what I'm here for.'

'I'm off to see Jamieson shortly. What are you going to do for the rest of the day?'

'I need to go back to work. I've exam papers to mark, which can't wait, as I'm out Thursday evening, and they have to be back by Friday.'

'Another date with the sculptor?' Whitney grinned.

'Yes, we're going to the theatre.'

'And are you going to ask him about the wedding?'

'I'm not sure.' She hated being stuck in this world of indecision. It was too hard to cope with.

'I thought we'd already decided you weren't going on your own.'

'Is it fair to Ross to inflict my family on him?'

'I'm surprised you're even thinking that. You've certainly come a long way in the short time I've known you.'

'What's that meant to mean?' she asked, even though she suspected she knew the answer.

'All I mean is you putting yourself in someone else's shoes is something you've struggled with in the past, but now you seem to be doing quite well.'

'You mean I've become more empathic.'

'Whatever the technical term is, then yes.'

'I'll think about it. I might ask him but won't be offended if he says no. It's not like we're in a committed relationship.'

'You can always take me. I'd love to go to some fancy wedding at Westminster Abbey. How do you think I'd fit in with your family?'

Was she being serious? It would be interesting to take Whitney. She could just imagine the family's response.

'Umm … I'm sure they'd love you.'

'And I'm sure they wouldn't.'

'I've got a curriculum meeting tomorrow so don't know what time I'll be in, if at all. It could last for hours.'

'Don't worry. It's going to be head down, bum up for the team, so we can work out which trains he'll be targeting on Sunday. Come in whenever you can. I'll keep in touch with any developments.'

Chapter Twenty-Three

Monday, 17 June

Whitney followed Jamieson into the press conference. As usual, the room was teeming with reporters, and the cameramen were at the back. Melissa, their PR officer, took the mic first.

'Thank you for coming in. I'd like to hand you over to Detective Superintendent Jamieson.' She slid the mic over to him.

'Good afternoon. I've called you in today to inform you a body was found on the Milton Keynes to Lenchester train earlier today. We believe this murder is linked to the two other recent suspicious deaths.'

'Can you confirm this is the work of the Carriage Killer?' a reporter in the front row called out.

'We are treating it as such.'

'Could it be a copycat?' another reporter asked.

'As far as we're aware, no. But we're not excluding that avenue from our lines of enquiry.'

'In the past, there have been exactly two weeks between the first and fourth murders. Does that mean you're expecting another on Sunday?' the reporter continued.

'We are working on the assumption there will be another murder attempt, unless we catch the perpetrator in the meantime.'

'How likely is that?' the reporter continued.

'I'll hand over to DCI Walker, and she'll give you more information regarding the actual investigation.'

This was the bit she didn't like, being put on the spot. She took the mic from Jamieson.

'Thank you, sir.' She looked at the sea of faces staring back at her. 'We anticipate a fourth murder will be attempted some time on Sunday.'

'Why don't you shut the line for the day?' someone called out.

'It's not our decision to make. That would be down to the Central Group. We're asking people to only travel by train if it's absolutely necessary.'

'But after Sunday, the killer will disappear until they show up somewhere else,' the reporter continued.

'That's likely, but we can't discount the fact they may change their MO. We want everyone to keep a lookout, and if you do have plans to take the train, please travel in pairs, if at all possible. We do know the killer strikes someone on their own, with usually no other person in the carriage, but never with more than two or three people. We all have to be vigilant.' She passed the mic back to Melissa, who ended the conference.

They all left the room together, although Melissa went on ahead, while Whitney and Jamieson stopped to talk.

'I didn't agree with your comment for people not to travel by train from now on. I thought it was a bit extreme,' he said.

'We have to keep people on their toes.'

'It soon won't be our issue.'

She stared at him. He couldn't be serious. Did he have no concern for the victims, or were they just a name and number to him?

'It will always be our issue, until such time as the offender is caught.'

'What are your plans to minimise the chances of the fourth murder happening?' he asked.

'We'll be working out potential train targets and making sure we have officers on them all.'

'Officers who actually do their job this time. You were lucky the press didn't pounce on the fact we were patrolling the train when this latest murder happened.'

'Yes, sir.' He was right, and she was surprised he hadn't bawled her out over it. She'd fully expected to be blamed. 'We're also continuing to research likely suspects, using all the data we have from previous murders, to see if we can find any links between them.'

'Well, keep going. I, for one, will be glad when Sunday is over and we're not the sole focus of attention. I want us to catch the murderer, obviously. But as we're only one out of four areas where he's struck, if we don't solve the case it won't look too bad.'

Whitney stared at him, open-mouthed. Was that all he cared about? How they looked? His behaviour astounded her sometimes.

'That's not going to stop my team doing their best to catch him.'

'That's not what I meant,' he said.

Before she had time to reply, they'd reached the stairs, and he marched up them. Glad to be away from him, she carried on walking. She needed some time alone, as she'd got a resourcing report to look at, that Jamieson had asked her opinion on. The note attached to it had asked for her comments by the end of the day. It was like he'd totally forgotten her attention should be focused on formulating a strategy for stopping the murderer. Then again, after his last comments...

'Has she seen it?' Whitney overheard Terry say to Matt as she walked through the incident room towards her office.

'Has she seen what?' she demanded.

The two officers started at the sound of her voice.

'This,' Matt said, pointing to an open newspaper on the desk.

She stepped forward and leaned in to take a look.

'What the fuck?' Staring her in the face, in bold red letters were the words:

£10,000 reward for information leading to the capture of the Carriage Killer

'It's Transwide, guv. They've advertised this reward in the local paper and all over the net,' Matt said.

'Without checking with me first? You know what this means, don't you? The phones will be ringing off the hook, and we'll have to deal with anyone and everyone who thinks they can make a quick buck by coming up with some fanciful story,' she said without giving them a chance to answer. 'How could they be such idiots? Why didn't they run it past me first?' She could cheerfully strangle the lot of them.

'I did mention they were a loose cannon,' Terry said.

'Actually, no you didn't. You said they interfered in the investigation. You didn't mention how they'd attempted to sabotage it,' she snapped, immediately regretting her response, as it wasn't his fault.

'What are you going to do?' Matt asked.

She glanced at her watch. It was almost five-thirty, so pointless getting in touch with them now. 'I'll pay Judy Tucker a visit tomorrow and demand an explanation.'

Chapter Twenty-Four

Whitney sat in the Transwide reception, drumming her fingers on her leg. This was ridiculous. She'd been waiting over half an hour to speak to Judy Tucker. Matt had phoned in advance and arranged the appointment. It was frustrating enough the woman wasn't available until the afternoon, but the fact she was late wasn't acceptable.

'DCI Walker?' She looked up as the woman's assistant, Iris, stood there. 'Please will you come with me. Sorry to have kept you waiting. Judy's meeting went over time.'

She followed in silence to the COO's office. Iris opened the door, and Judy stood.

'Come in,' she said, smiling at Whitney.

'We've got a problem,' Whitney said, dispensing with any pleasantries. 'The reward.'

'I wondered if that's what you were here about,' the woman replied.

'Why didn't you discuss it with me first? If you had, we wouldn't be in such a difficult position.'

'It was a decision made by the Senior Management

Team. We can't sit back and let this continue. We have the business to think about.'

'If you'd have told me, I'd have explained that rather than moving the investigation forward, you've probably succeeded in setting it back.'

'How can that be? Has the reward generated a response?'

'Of course it has. And now we have to use officers, whose time is better spent elsewhere on the investigation, to follow up on the hundreds of calls coming in, the majority of which are freeloaders trying to get some money.'

'But that doesn't mean you won't find information which will lead you to the killer.'

'That could take days. And we don't have the time if we're going to stop the last murder that's due to happen in Lenchester. At the moment, we're close to identifying possible trains the killer will be targeting. It's our best chance of catching him. Unlike going down the rabbit hole of following up on every phone call we receive from people who have seen your reward offer.' She sat in silence, waiting for her words to have some impact.

'I understand,' the woman finally responded. 'What can we do?'

'Take down everything from the net relating to the reward and don't advertise it again in the newspapers. Can you do that?'

'I'll try. I need to speak to the Chief Executive.'

'Thank you. And while I'm here, what happened to the list of people who were made redundant in 2014?' she asked. 'My officer has contacted you several times, to no avail.' Not that they'd have time to go through all thousand names straight away.

Judy coloured slightly. 'I'll get onto it. I don't have the

information to hand. It will be with one of the managers in the HR department.'

'Here's my card. Email it directly to me as soon as you have it.' Whitney handed it to her as she stood and left the office.

~

She made it back to the station by three and, after speaking to the team to see how they were doing, she went to her office. On the desk was a message asking her to phone Claire. She called the pathologist straight away.

'It's Whitney,' she said once Claire had answered.

'I want you at the lab for my initial findings from the murder.'

'Can we do this over the phone?' She really didn't have time to spare.

'No.'

'Okay, I'll be with you shortly,' she said, realising it was pointless arguing with the woman. Especially as it wasn't like Claire to demand a face-to-face. Usually she got rid of them as quickly as she could and preferred to talk on the phone, so it had to be important.

She grabbed her bag and coat from the back of the chair and went through to the incident room. 'Terry,' she said after spotting him sitting at his desk and walking over.

'Yes?'

'You're coming with me.'

'Where are we going?'

'To see Dr Dexter, our pathologist. She has her initial findings on the latest murder.'

'Can't she email her report?' he asked, frowning.

'No. She wants to see us.'

'Okay. If you're happy for us to leave the investigation

and pander to her whims.' He shook his head as he stood and put on his jacket.

She knew exactly what he was thinking—his 'tail-wagging-the-dog' comment he'd made when he'd first arrived. She was looking forward to seeing first-hand how he'd *deal* with Claire. She smiled to herself.

'Yes, I am. So, let's go.'

When they arrived at the morgue, they walked into the building and down the corridor to the lab. Claire was sitting at her desk, scowling at the computer screen. She was wearing navy and white spotted wide-leg trousers, and a bright green and red blouse with a bow at the neck. One day she'd pluck up the courage to ask her where she bought her clothes. They were nothing like Whitney had ever seen.

'Is everything okay? You're looking puzzled.'

'Puzzled is one way of putting it. I'd say bloody furious,' Claire said.

'What's happened?'

'The funding I wanted for a new MDCT has been turned down by a committee of arsewipes who swan around like they're God, just because they hold the purse strings.'

'MCDT?'

'Multidetector computed tomography machine. But that's not what's annoyed me. The very next email I received was the staff newsletter, telling us how much they're spending on new ultrasound equipment. How come others get what they want, and I don't? Just because I'm dealing with dead people. And don't tell me we have finite levels of funding.' Claire waved her finger in Whitney's direction. 'Is he with you?' She nodded at Terry.

'This is DI Terry Gardner from the Regional Force.

He's helping us on the case. Terry, this is Dr Dexter, our pathologist.'

'Good to meet you. And sorry to hear about your funding.' Terry held out his hand, but Claire didn't shake it.

'Why are you sorry? It's nothing to do with you. Let's get on. There's no point in me being angry now. I'll save it until later, over my whisky.'

Claire put on her white lab coat and disposable gloves and headed out into the main area, where Neil Thomas's body was stretched out on the centre stainless steel table. Whitney and Terry followed. The pathologist reached up and angled the overhead light, so the upper body was lit.

Terry stepped forward and leaned in to take a look.

'What are you doing?' Claire asked.

'Looking at the body,' Terry said.

'You're in my way.' She turned to look at Whitney. 'Didn't you tell him how I operate?'

'I thought I'd leave it to you to do the honours.'

'Would someone care to explain?' Terry said, looking from Whitney to Claire.

Whitney turned her head to hide the smirk she was unable to prevent from appearing on her face. They might be getting along better now, but that didn't mean she couldn't have some fun.

'You stand where I tell you and keep out of my way. You may ask questions when I say you can. I operate on a basis of three strikes and you're out,' Claire said.

It couldn't have worked out better if Whitney had actually primed the woman herself.

Terry looked at Whitney, his brow furrowed.

'What Claire means is, if you ask more than three questions which she doesn't wish to answer then you have to leave. Is that right, Claire?' she said.

Whitney was guessing, as this was the first she'd heard of the rule.

'How do I know what questions you're prepared to answer?' Terry asked Claire.

'Strike one,' she said.

Terry glared at Claire and folded his arms.

'Okay. We all know how it goes. Can we start now, as we have to get back?' Whitney said.

'This murder's slightly different from the others,' Claire said.

'In what way?' She edged forward and stared at the body.

'The victim struggled, and when the knife was inserted it hit one of the ribs and some of the blade snapped off. I found it lodged in the lungs.' From the trolley beside her, she picked up a silver bowl. In there was a small piece of metal, about an inch in length. She lifted it out and showed it to Whitney. 'This is the end of the blade.'

'May I look?' Terry said.

'You may,' Claire replied.

'How come he struggled if he'd been given the chloroform?' Terry asked as he stepped forward and stood next to Whitney.

'The chemical possibly took a little longer to work. It doesn't always affect everyone in the same way.'

'Can you identify the knife from that small piece?' Whitney asked.

'We're looking into it. We know from the size of the tip, plus the wound width and depth, the blade used was smooth and five inches in length. See the bruising around the entry point?' Claire pointed to purple and yellow discolouration of the skin. 'This is from the rim between the blade and handle. It's typical of a hunting knife.'

'If you can find out the make and model, that would be

of great help. There are only five more days until the next murder is due to happen,' Whitney said.

'We'll do our best. There's something else.'

'What?' she said impatiently, sensing Claire was about to reveal something big.

'When the chloroform rag was placed over the mouth, the victim bit the murderer's hand.'

Whitney's heartbeat quickened. Finally, a break.

'So, you've got the murderer's DNA?' Terry said.

'Unfortunately not. He was wearing gloves. But we do know they were black leather. There are traces of leather in the victim's teeth.'

Whitney swallowed her disappointment.

'So, really we're no further on in identifying the perp?' she said.

'I didn't say that,' Claire replied, a mysterious tone to her voice. 'I've been saving the best bit until last.'

The woman was a mystery. One moment all brusque and business-like, the next wanting to play games.

'Come on, Claire. I don't have time to mess around.' She shifted anxiously from foot to foot.

'Fine. You can wait for my report if you're going to be like that.' Claire shrugged.

'Guv,' Terry warned. 'We need this information now. Remember the three strikes.'

Whitney laughed. She couldn't help it. Even Claire glanced at her and gave a little smile.

'Sorry, Claire. I didn't mean it. Will you tell me, please?'

'I found two hairs on the victim's clothes that don't belong to him. We've run them through the National DNA database.'

'And? Have you come up with a name?' she asked.

'No.'

Her heart sank. 'Oh.'

'You're not understanding. Now, you have much more to work with than you did before,' Claire said, her eyes bright.

'But how do we know the hairs are from the murderer and not from someone else?' Terry asked.

'Simple. I found a third hair in the victim's mouth, among the fibres from the cloth used to administer the chloroform. They could've easily been missed.'

'What's the chance of it being someone else's hair, already in his mouth?' Whitney asked.

'Unlikely. So, now you get the importance of what I'm telling you.'

She could kiss the woman. But of course, she wouldn't, as she valued her life.

Whitney turned to Terry. 'And that, DI Gardner, is why we work with Claire the way we do. She's the best. I don't care how many pathologists you have dancing to your tune, Claire could outshine all of them put together, with her eyes closed.'

'I get it now.' Terry nodded.

'What the hell are you going on about?' Claire asked.

'Just singing your praises, Claire. Anyway, back to the body. That's fantastic news. Thank you. Now all we've got to do is find him. Is the offender male?' she checked.

'Yes.' Claire nodded.

'We'd been working on that assumption, as you know.'

'Well, now it's confirmed,' the pathologist said.

'Anything else you're holding out on telling me?'

'No. Now go and find him.'

Chapter Twenty-Five

Thursday, 20 June

George watched Ross as he stood at the bar waiting to be served. They'd had a really nice meal, and she felt relaxed in his company. She hadn't yet decided whether to invite him to her brother's wedding. She knew Whitney thought she should, but on so many levels it could turn out to be a disaster. Not to mention it would be admitting they were actually dating, as opposed to being friends who went out occasionally.

Did that bother her? She had too much going on in her life to embark on dating again. It had been a disaster with Stephen and not something she wanted to repeat. Her work had suffered, and she'd felt out of her comfort zone. She much preferred being on her own, with no one to please but herself. She'd always enjoyed her own company and had never found herself bored or lonely.

'You're looking serious,' Ross said as he placed their glasses on the table and sat opposite her.

'I've got a lot on my mind,' she said.

'Work?'

'Not exactly.'

'Police work?'

'Not exactly.'

'You're not making this very easy. Shall I assume you don't want me to know?'

Stephen would have hounded her until she'd told him. And if she'd still refused, he'd have sulked like a child. Ross was refreshingly different.

'It's not that I don't want you to know. There's something I want to ask you, but I'm just not sure about it yet.'

'That's cool. Ask me when you're ready.' He smiled.

His reply convinced her to bite the bullet.

'My brother's getting married soon, and I wondered if you'd like to accompany me to the wedding?'

He stared at her, frowning. Asking him so soon had been a mistake. She shouldn't have listened to Whitney. It was obvious by the expression on his face he was looking for a reason to say no.

'Are you sure?'

'It doesn't matter. Forget it. I knew you wouldn't want to.' She picked up her glass and took a sip of her beer.

'It's not that. Under normal circumstances I'd have jumped at the chance. It's just—'

'Just what?' she interrupted.

'Having already met your father, what happens if he remembers I was the waiter he had a go at?'

'He probably won't recall the interaction, but I can always remind him, if you'd like me to.'

'Do you think that's a good idea? I wouldn't want to upset him at the wedding.'

'Do you want to go or not?' she demanded.

He laughed. 'That's what I like about you George. The way you're so direct and get straight to the point. If you'd like me to come with you, I'd be honoured. Where is it being held?'

Would he change his mind once she told him? Whitney had been astounded once she'd found out. How would he react? 'Westminster Abbey for the service, and the reception's at the Imperial War Museum.'

'Whoa. I'm guessing you waited until I'd said yes before telling me that.'

'You can change your mind, if you want.' She shrugged like it wasn't important, but actually it was.

'I'm joking. I won't change my mind.' He leaned forward and took her hand in his and gave it a squeeze.

'It's black tie. You can hire a tux.'

'I won't need to. I have my own. When you go to as many awards dinners as I do, it's cheaper to own one than hire all the time.'

'I'll book some accommodation for the Friday and Saturday nights. There are some excellent hotels close to the reception. My treat.'

'Why don't we go up on the Wednesday or Thursday and make a proper break of it? We'll have time to check out the Tate Modern and catch a show. What do you say?'

She bit down on her bottom lip. If he wanted to arrange a short holiday, did that mean they were officially dating, and not just friends with benefits?

How did she feel about it? Actually, not bad. Whitney would approve.

'Okay, let's do it,' she agreed.

'Text me the dates, and I'll make sure to put it in my diary.'

She glanced at her watch. 'I can't be too late this evening; I need to be at the station with Whitney first thing. We've got a busy few days ahead of us.'

'I've been following the news reports on the murders. I

assume that's what you're working on. It's a dreadful situation. There's another one expected on Sunday, isn't there?'

'Yes. Unless we can stop the murderer beforehand.'

'Do you have any leads?'

'I'm not allowed to share anything about the investigation. All I can say is we're working out possible trains he's likely to be on.'

'That's promising.'

'Don't say anything. Nobody knows.'

She could have kicked herself for telling him. Whitney would go ballistic if she knew. If it got out, it could make the killer change his plans.

'Of course I won't. You can trust me. Hopefully, working out where he'll be will mean you're able to stop him.'

'You'd have thought so, but we knew the potential trains when the third victim was killed.'

'Sounds like you could do with a break.'

'Yes. And soon.'

∼

Friday, 21 June

George set her alarm to six, and by seven-thirty, she was already at the station. She was conscious there was still so much to do, and she wanted to pull her weight. She hurried inside, through the back door, and made her way to the incident room, where several of the team were already seated at their desks. She continued to Whitney's office, hoping the detective was in. Whitney was peering at her computer screen, and when she glanced up and saw George standing there, she beckoned for her to come in.

'Bloody Excel spreadsheets. I'll never get to grips with

them. I'll have to take this home and see if Tiffany can help. She's an IT whizz.'

The mention of Tiffany's name reminded George she hadn't seen Whitney's daughter for a few weeks. They caught up in one of the university cafés fairly regularly, but as it was exam time, the young woman wasn't around.

They'd become close since Tiffany had been abducted and George was part of the rescue. After her ordeal, Tiffany had put on a brave face in front of her mother, not wanting to worry her. But she'd confided in George. She'd been seeing a counsellor, at George's insistence, and had made remarkable progress. She was almost back to her old self, but George knew they still needed to keep an eye on her, as she could easily slip back if things got difficult.

'I can help, if you'd like. I use Excel all the time.'

'Thanks for the offer, but we've more important things to do. What are you doing here? I didn't expect you until later, as I thought you were out with Ross last night.'

'I was, but I didn't stay out late because I wanted to get in here early to see you,' she said.

'So you could tell me you've fallen in love with him and couldn't wait to share it.' Whitney grinned.

'That's silly, and not what I meant.'

'Did you ask him about the wedding?'

'Yes, I did, and—'

'And is he going with you?' Whitney interrupted.

'Why are you so interested in the wedding, when we've got work to do?'

'Just humour me. Is he going with you? Yes or no?'

'Yes.'

'Awesome. Now let's go into the incident room and get moving.'

They left Whitney's office and walked over to the board. More people had arrived.

'Listen up, everyone, I have something important to tell you. We have the murderer's DNA.'

George's jaw tensed. How come Whitney hadn't told her? When did she find out?

'Well done, guv. What did he leave it on?' Matt asked.

'There were stray hairs on the victim's clothes and one in his mouth, mixed in with fibres from the cloth used to sedate him. It seems our elderly victim put up quite a fight. This murder wasn't as easy as the others. The DNA also confirmed our assumption the murderer is male.'

'Any chance he's in the database?' Matt asked.

'Unfortunately not.' Whitney's phone pinged, and she picked it up from the desk. She frowned at the screen. 'I've finally received the list of a thousand employees who were made redundant from Transwide in 2014. Ellie, I'd like you to start going through it. We'll need background checks on any red flags.'

'There are certain people you can eliminate,' George said. 'You don't need to check the women, or any who are currently under the age of twenty-nine, or over the age of sixty-five, as they're unlikely to be our perp.'

'Thanks, George. Narrowing it down should make it a bit easier,' Whitney said. 'Ellie will need help, so I want half of you to continue working on identifying the potential train targets, and the other half working on the list of people made redundant.'

'Is it really worth the effort, considering the lapse in time since Transwide let these people go and when the murders started?' Vic asked.

'Do you have any other ideas?' Whitney asked.

'No,' he said.

'If I may interrupt,' George said, resting a hand on Whitney's arm. 'The desire for revenge can fester in a person. It could be that something happened to this man which tipped the balance between *wanting* revenge and actually seeking it. It makes sense to consider this in our investigation if we have the resources to do so.'

'You heard the doctor. Let's do it,' Whitney said.

Chapter Twenty-Six

Friday, 21 June

Two more days and I'm done with Lenchester. Then I need to decide where I'm going to next. So many areas to choose from. If Transwide had cared as much about the people they employed as they did about their profits, then none of this would've happened.

But no, they allowed their greed to interfere, and we all know what happens to greedy people.

They lose out in the end.

The old bugger I killed last time proved to be difficult. I've no idea why he was resistant to being sedated, as I used the same amount of chloroform I'd done in the past. As for when he bit me, luckily, I was wearing gloves, so none of my blood seeped through. Not having my DNA means they're no closer to catching me than before.

I wish I could say committing these murders was making me feel better. But nothing I do will ever come close to getting payback for what Transwide did to me and my family. Maybe when they're out of business I might think differently, but at the moment I still feel sick when I think of how they destroy lives without caring one little bit.

Part of me wants to tell them what I'm doing. But if I do, I'll be unable to continue, and I don't want to stop until I've totally destroyed them, however long it takes.

I've got nothing else in my life, so I can devote all my time to putting an end to their despicable work practices.

It would be nice to share this with someone. Someone who understands. Sometimes I feel guilty for taking the lives of innocent people, but they died for the greater good. The greater good being not allowing giant corporations to destroy the lives of anyone who gets in their way.

The government should have stepped in and offered help, but they're just as bad. They let them get away with everything they've done. All they can see are the taxes from which they profit.

How many more deaths before they put people first and taxes second?

Chapter Twenty-Seven

Saturday, 22 June

When George arrived at the incident room, Whitney was beside the board, staring at it while running her fingers through her hair. Despite not leaving until ten the previous night, most of the team were already at their desks working. It was imperative that their efforts were focused on researching those made redundant from Transwide and identifying potential train targets. It seemed an insurmountable task, especially as tomorrow was the two-week deadline.

'Morning, Whitney. How's it going?'

'Not fast enough.'

'We'll find something today. Remember, we're already further on this time than we were when the last murder took place.'

'You're right. Listen up, everyone,' Whitney said. 'I want a rundown of where we are, and then we'll decide what we're going to do for the rest of the day.'

'I'm currently looking at credit card ticket sales from all the different rail operators on the actual murder days, including ours, and comparing them with the list of names from Transwide,' Ellie said.

'Any joy?' Whitney asked.

'Not yet. I did find a woman who was on one of the trains coming into Lenchester, but she's out of our age range, and also female.'

'She could have bought a ticket for someone else,' Frank said.

'Maybe,' George said. 'But it's unlikely she'd be involved when you consider she only bought one ticket out of many. It's just a coincidence.'

'Keep going with your research, Ellie,' Whitney said.

'We've been going through potential trains and train times,' Doug said. 'Using the same parameters as we did for the previous trains, we've come up with three possible trains. The first is the train leaving Newcastle at eight-thirty in the morning and arriving in Lenchester at one-ten.'

'The same train as our first victim was on,' George said.

'Yes. No CCTV on the train, and it's relatively quiet,' Doug said.

'Have they targeted the same train twice before, Vic?' Whitney asked the detective.

'No. But that doesn't mean he won't this time. There doesn't seem to be a pattern,' he replied.

'What about the others?' Whitney asked.

'There's one leaving London at one-thirty-five and arriving in Lenchester at two-thirty-five. The other's going from Salisbury to Birmingham and will be in Lenchester at two,' Doug said.

'So we have three potential trains, and we'll have offi-cers on all of them,' Whitney said.

'Providing the murderer sticks to his usual MO,' Frank said.

'I think it's likely,' George said. 'We know he needs a quiet train with no CCTV, so we have to assume he won't change, especially as he most likely believes this isn't going to be his last set of murders.'

'Speaking of CCTV, now we have the list of names, has anyone suspicious been identified?' Whitney asked.

'We've gone through everything we can from the CCTV footage we've received from the various stations on the Lenchester routes,' Frank said.

'Terry, did you keep a copy of footage you looked at when you were undertaking the previous investigations?' Whitney asked.

'I'll check. It should be somewhere, I hope,' Terry said.

'How many from the list fall within the age and gender range?' George asked.

'Seven hundred,' Ellie said.

'So most drivers and conductors were male,' George replied. Seven hundred was a huge sample for the team to go through.

'It looks like it,' Whitney said.

The team got back to work just as Whitney's phone rang. 'It's Jamieson. What does he want?' She answered and stepped to the side to speak to him.

George stared at the board. On there were the names of all the rail operators who'd been targeted, together with maps of all the different routes their trains took.

There had to be something. They just weren't seeing it. A pattern. There had to be a pattern. It seemed indiscriminate, but all behaviour was patterned, even if it was subconscious.

She focused all her efforts on the board.

'Think. Think,' she muttered to herself. Suddenly it hit her. 'Birmingham,' she said out loud. 'It's Birmingham.'

'What's Birmingham?'

George jumped at the sound of Whitney next to her. 'I didn't realise you were there. I thought you were talking to Jamieson.'

'I was. Tell me about Birmingham,' the detective said, sounding excited.

'The key to the puzzle. Look at the four rail operators.' She pointed at the board. 'There's one thing they all have in common.'

Whitney stood silent for a moment, facing the board. 'They all have some lines which run through Birmingham,' she finally said. 'So, what does that mean?'

'I think our murderer lives there.'

'How did you come to that conclusion?'

'He has to get to all these different places and commit the murders. If you think about it, how much simpler would it be if he could get to his target easily? Look.' She picked up a pen, and on the board drew four circles, all overlapping. In each circle she wrote the name of a rail operator, and in the overlapping piece she wrote *Birmingham*. 'This is the part that links every single operator. I know we have the Transwide link, but they own many more lines than the ones targeted. So, we also have to find a link between the actual operators he's chosen so far.'

'It makes sense,' Whitney said.

'We've discussed before how serial killers use locations familiar to them. We were just thinking Transwide, but the evidence points to our killer being familiar with Birmingham and the trains going in and out of there, too.'

'George, you're a genius,' Whitney said.

'Providing it works out,' George said, feeling uncomfortable by the lavish praise.

'Attention, everyone. We've made some progress. We believe our murderer comes from the Birmingham area. It seems that every rail operator he's been targeting has trains which go through Birmingham. If that's where he lives, he's going to be much more familiar with these particular operators, and he'll feel comfortable targeting them. Ellie, I want you to contact the two Birmingham stations, New Street and Birmingham International, and ask for the credit card details of anyone buying tickets over the last two weeks.'

'What about the other murders?' the officer asked.

'Ideally, we'd check those, too, but at the moment ours are the priority. If you do have time, look at the previous four.'

'Onto it now, guv,' Ellie said.

'The offender could have bought his ticket from Birmingham to wherever he got onto the Lenchester train and paid cash for the next part of the journey. We need CCTV footage from the Birmingham stations, and that needs to be compared with the footage we have.'

'Leave that with me,' Frank said.

'You'll need help. I want everyone pitching in with Frank, apart from Sue. You help Ellie.'

'Yes, guv.'

'What do you want me to do?' George asked.

'Claire's latest report has arrived. We'll grab a coffee and come back here to go through it.'

Thirty minutes later, while they were in Whitney's office, Ellie knocked on the door and rushed in.

'I think I've got something, guv. Norman Thackeray, who was made redundant by Transwide, lives in Birmingham and he bought tickets for trains on all three days of our murders.'

'Where did he go?' Whitney asked.

'On the ninth he went from Birmingham to Newcastle. He also went from Birmingham to Coventry on the thirteenth, and from Birmingham to Wolverton, the stop before Milton Keynes, on the seventeenth.'

'And from there he would've paid cash for his next ticket. Well planned,' George said.

'What about his return journey to Birmingham? Have you looked into that?' Whitney asked.

'I'll get onto it.'

'First of all, get me his contact details.'

'Already have them, guv,' Ellie said.

'We need to interview him,' Whitney said.

'Are you going to bring him in?' George asked.

'I think we'll pay him a visit. First, we'll go into the incident room and let the team know.'

'We've got a lead,' Whitney said as they walked in. 'His name is Norman Thackeray. He lives in Birmingham and was made redundant by Transwide. We know he's been using the trains on the days of the murders.'

Cheers went up around the room.

'Early days yet. We'll continue with what we're working on. Ellie will circulate Thackeray's details. We need a full background check on him, and once she has his photo, you can check against CCTV footage to see if he's on there. If we arrest him and prevent the fourth murder, the drinks are on me.'

George smiled to herself, excited by the fact they could be solving the crime and preventing further deaths.

'Terry, I want you to come with George and me,' Whitney said.

'Don't you think that's overkill?' the officer said.

'No. We don't know what we're going into. Although George's profile points to him possibly being a loner, we don't know for certain, so I'm not going to risk it. You can also take a look around the house while we're there.'

'Okay.'

'Can we go in your car, George, as it's more comfortable?' Whitney asked.

She was more than happy to do the driving, especially as it was a longer run, and as much as she liked Whitney, neither her car, nor her driving, were the best.

'My pleasure.'

'Don't forget to put in an expenses claim, as we keep going out in your car.'

'I won't,' George said. 'Come on, let's get this guy.'

Chapter Twenty-Eight

Saturday, 22 June

The three of them went downstairs to the car park and got into George's top-of-the-range Land Rover.

'Nice,' Terry said. 'No wonder you wanted to travel in this.'

'Certainly beats my old Ford,' Whitney said.

'I agree,' George said, giving a wry grin.

She pulled out of the station onto the road leading to Birmingham. Unfortunately, they hit the traffic, as it was still rush hour. The journey was stop-start until they got onto the motorway, and then it was clearer.

'Tell me how you became involved in working with the police,' Terry asked George.

'I started towards the end of last year, when one of my students was murdered. I offered to help on the case,' George said.

'Had you done any police work before?'

'No. All my work had been academic,' she said.

'And I refused her offer, by the way,' Whitney said.

'Why?'

'I didn't want it. And even when we did work together it wasn't plain sailing. But we eventually got over that,' Whitney said.

'You have a good relationship, now,' Terry said. 'We bring people in to help on cases, but we don't have one particular person. It just depends on who's available.'

'We're very lucky to have George,' Whitney said.

'Thank you,' George said.

They continued the journey, making small talk, and soon hit the outskirts of Birmingham. Using the car's navigation system, they made their way to Barry Street where Thackeray lived. It was a row of small terraced houses. Whitney knocked on the door. After a short time, she knocked again. Finally, a slight, balding man of around fifty-five answered.

'Norman Thackeray?' Whitney asked.

'Who wants to know?'

'DCI Walker, DI Gardner, and Dr Cavendish from Lenchester CID. We'd like a word with you.' Whitney held out her warrant card for him to see.

'What about?'

'We'd like to talk inside. Please let us in.'

He opened the door. They walked in and stood in the hall.

'Well?' he asked.

'We understand you used to work for Transwide,' Whitney said.

'Yes.' He glared at them, his arms folded.

'They made you redundant.'

'Yes.' He gave a sharp nod.

'How did you feel about that?' Whitney asked.

'What do you think? I hate them. I lost my job.'

'Is there somewhere we can sit down?' Whitney asked.

He opened the door on the right and ushered them

into the small lounge, which had a two-seater grey sofa and two other chairs, all focused around the small television.

They all sat, apart from Terry who stood by the door.

'Are you working now?' Whitney asked.

'I haven't worked since they made me redundant. Thirty years I worked there, and that counted for shit. No one wants a train conductor.'

'You must have been given a redundancy payment,' Whitney said.

'That went a long time ago. Now I rely on state benefits.'

'What were your movements during the day on Sunday the ninth, Thursday the thirteenth, and Monday the seventeenth of June?'

'I don't know. Maybe here. Maybe at the pub.' He shrugged.

'Records indicate you used your credit card to purchase a rail ticket from Birmingham to Newcastle on the ninth, Birmingham to Wolverton on the thirteenth, and Birmingham to Coventry on the seventeenth. You do have a credit card, I take it?' Whitney asked.

He was quiet and looked down at his feet.

'Mr Thackeray, answer the question,' Whitney said.

'Yes, I do have a credit card. What's this about?'

'We're investigating the recent murders which took place on trains going through Lenchester.'

'The Carriage Killer. I've seen it on the news.'

'Tell me what you were doing on those trains.'

'You think I committed the murders?'

'I repeat, what were you doing on the trains from Birmingham on the dates I mentioned?' Whitney said.

'I can't remember.'

He covered his mouth with his hand while speaking. A

tell-tale sign of someone not wanting to answer a question put to them.

'Were you on the trains?'

'You said I was because of my credit card.'

'Are you saying you weren't on the trains?' Whitney asked, clearly frustrated. 'Could someone have taken your credit card?'

'I'm not saying anything. I want a solicitor.'

'Do you have a solicitor you can call?' Whitney asked.

'You can get one for me. Legal aid.'

'Well, in that case we're taking you to Lenchester police station for questioning. Is there anyone you want to contact to let them know where you are going?'

'No, I live on my own.'

'Just to confirm, you're not under arrest at the moment, but you're coming with us voluntarily in order to help with our investigation,' Whitney said.

'What if I told you I committed the murders and I'm the Carriage Killer?'

From her observation of his blink rate, George could tell he was lying. Liars blink far less than normal during a lie, then after it becomes excessive, often up to eight times faster. Thackeray's blinking fit that pattern.

'Are you admitting to the crimes?' Whitney asked.

'Yes.' he said.

'Norman Thackeray, I'm arresting you on suspicion of the murder of Hugo Holmes-Reed, Lena Kirk, and Neil Thomas. You do not have to say anything, but it may harm your defence if you do not mention when questioned something which you later rely on in court. Anything you do say may be given in evidence. Do you understand?'

'Yes.'

Whitney handcuffed him and escorted him to George's car, where he sat next to Terry. They drove in silence, but throughout the drive, George was thinking it all seemed too easy. The killer had managed to evade capture for two years and the first time he'd been interviewed he was admitting to it. But if he wasn't guilty, why would he say he was?

Unless he had an accomplice and he was doing it to waste their time and make sure the fourth murder went ahead. They'd know soon enough, once his DNA was taken and compared with samples Claire had got from the last victim.

They arrived back at the station and Thackeray was checked in. He was put into a cell until a solicitor could be called and they were able to interview him.

They went into the incident room.

'Stop what you're doing for a moment. We have arrested Norman Thackeray for the murders. He's actually admitted to them, and we'll be interviewing him once the duty solicitor has arrived,' Whitney said.

'You don't sound too excited by this, guv,' Frank said.

'One step at a time. We need to test his DNA to put him at the scene.'

'Who's going to interview him?' George asked.

'Terry and I will interview, and you can watch from outside.'

The phone on the desk rang, and Whitney picked it up.

'Walker.' She paused for a moment. 'We'll be there shortly.' She ended the call. 'The duty solicitor's here. Let's go.'

They went down to the interview room, and George positioned herself next door, so she could see what was happening. Norman Thackeray was seated, his head lowered, and hands clasped together in his lap. The duty solicitor was sitting next to him, leafing through a file.

Whitney and Terry entered the room, and she turned on the recording equipment.

'June twenty-second. DCI Whitney Walker. In the room is …' She nodded at Terry.

'DI Terry Gardner.'

'And—please state your names,' she said to Thackeray and the solicitor.

'Norman Thackeray,' the prisoner said.

'Roger Ashton, acting for the accused.'

'Mr Thackeray, you are still under caution and anything you say may be used in evidence. Do you understand?'

He nodded.

'Please answer for the tape.'

'Yes, I understand,' he said.

'When we interviewed you at your house, you admitted to carrying out murders on the ninth, thirteenth, and seventeenth of June.'

The solicitor leaned in and spoke quietly to him.

'Yes, I said that,' Thackeray said.

'And you're still pleading guilty to these offences?'

'Yes, I am.'

'He's lying,' George said to Whitney in her earpiece. 'Keep going with the questioning, and we'll find out what's behind it. I suggest you ask him to give a detailed account of the actual murders.'

Whitney gave an almost imperceptible nod.

'I'd like to start with the murder of Hugo Holmes-Reed. I want you to tell me exactly what happened and how you carried out the murder.'

Thackeray shifted awkwardly in his seat. 'Why do you want to know everything? All you need to know is I did it.'

'Where did you board the train on which you committed the murder?' Whitney asked.

'I don't remember.'

'And how did you get to the station?'

'Which station?'

'Where you boarded. How did you get there?'

'I caught the train from Birmingham.'

'You caught a train from Birmingham to …?'

'The station.'

'Mr Thackeray, do you realise you're facing a life sentence for these murders?' Whitney asked, frustration showing in her voice.

'Yes. My memory's a little hazy.'

'Ask him about the knife and how he carried out the murder,' George suggested. 'So far he's given us nothing he couldn't have ascertained from the media.'

'Mr Thackeray, what weapon did you use in the murders?'

'A knife.'

'What sort of knife?'

'A hunting knife.'

'Please describe it to me.'

'It's a fixed blade knife with a green handle.'

'How long is the blade?'

'About five inches.'

'Do you know a lot about knives?'

'Yes. I learned from my father, who used to take me hunting.'

'His version of the weapon certainly fits with Claire's account,' George said. 'So, maybe he does know something.'

'Returning to the murders, can you explain in more detail exactly how you carried them out?'

'I went on the train, found someone who was on their own, and stabbed them with a knife.'

'He'd know all this from reports of the other murders,'

George said. 'But he hasn't mentioned the chloroform or described how the victims were all stabbed between their ribs.'

'Show me exactly how you stabbed the person,' Whitney said.

'I fail to see why we need this line of questioning,' the solicitor said. 'My client has admitted to the offences; we don't need to go into any detail at this stage. Mr Thackeray, I advise you to say nothing further. Save it for when we're in court for your sentencing hearing.'

George observed how Whitney's body had tensed.

'Mr Thackeray,' Terry said. 'Do you admit to all of the murders over the last two years?'

Whitney looked in Terry's direction. He clearly didn't know about Whitney's no-asking-questions rule. George smiled to herself.

'Yes, I am,' Thackeray replied.

'Why did you commit these murders?' Terry said.

'To get back at Transwide for making me redundant.'

'Don't you think murdering innocent people was taking it a bit far?' Whitney asked.

Thackeray shrugged. 'Maybe. I don't want to talk about this anymore. You've arrested me, so do what you have to do.'

'We have the murderer's DNA on file. A sample was taken from you when you arrived, and we'll have the results soon. Is this going to make any difference to your plea?' Whitney asked.

'No. Why should it? I've told you I did it, so stop pestering me.'

'Mr Thackeray, I know you've admitted to the crimes, but I'm not convinced of your guilt.'

He scowled in Whitney's direction, his eyes flashing. 'I've told you, I'm guilty, so what more do you want? I can't give you a minute to minute replay of what happened, but that doesn't mean I didn't do it. Speak to my doctor. I suffer from memory problems. There are lots of things I can't remember.'

'He could be right. There are a number of psychological disorders that may be affecting him,' George said.

'Well, assuming you're right, and you did commit all these murders you can't remember—'

'I didn't say I couldn't remember any of it. It's just the details I forget,' Thackeray interrupted.

'It's very convenient,' Whitney snapped.

'DCI Walker, all you're doing is going around in circles. I suggest we terminate the interview,' the solicitor said.

'We'll finish when I'm ready. Even though you don't remember all the details, I'm assuming you can tell me where you keep the murder weapon.'

'It's hidden.'

'Hidden where? And don't tell me you don't remember, because this is getting tedious,' Whitney said.

'In a brown plastic hollowed-out flowerpot placed along the wall of the house, in my garden.'

'That's very detailed,' George said. 'I'm inclined to believe him. So, either he's telling the truth about his memory, or he's covering for someone and he knows about the weapon.'

'Do you live alone?' Whitney asked.

'Yes.'

'No wife or children?'

'My wife's dead, and I don't see my son.'

'Where is he?'

'I've no idea. We haven't spoken in a long time. That's all I'm saying.' He leaned back in his chair and folded his arms.

'I don't think you'll get any more from him,' George said.

'Interview suspended.' Whitney ended the recording. 'We're going to your house to retrieve the weapon. You'll be escorted back to your cell.'

She picked up the file she had on the table and left the room, with Terry following.

'Well, that was bizarre,' Whitney said as she entered the room where George was.

'He's covering for someone,' Terry said.

'Agreed,' George said.

'We'll go with forensics to his house. But first I need to go back to the incident room,' Whitney said.

When they got back, Whitney and George made a beeline for Ellie.

'What can you tell me about our suspect?' Whitney asked.

'His wife committed suicide two and a half years ago. He has a son, Ben, but I don't have an address for him. I'm still searching.'

'The wife committing suicide could have been a catalyst for the start of the murders. We need to know more,' George said.

'I'll see about accessing her medical records,' Ellie said.

'What we really need is the DNA sample to come back. Then we'll know for certain whether he's our perp,' Whitney said.

Chapter Twenty-Nine

Saturday, 22 June

Whitney returned to Thackeray's house in Birmingham with George. The suspect had given permission for her to take his key, and they were able to access the property without having to break any windows or doors.

'First, we'll go to the garden and look for the knife,' she said.

They went through the kitchen and unlocked the door which took them straight into the back. It was small and unkempt, with weeds growing through the flower beds. The thick grass hadn't been cut in a long time.

'What a mess,' George said.

'I bet your fingers are itching to get stuck into it,' Whitney said, laughing.

'They are. It might be tiny, but so much could be done with it,' George said as they both got to work.

Flowerpots were lined up all along the back of the house, and they systematically looked at each of them.

'Nothing here,' George said after picking up the last one.

'Why was he so specific? It was the only thing that sounded genuine,' Whitney said.

'Perhaps the knife was here, and he thought finding it would confirm his guilt.'

'Which means someone must have moved it. Someone he's protecting.'

'It could be his son. He was adamant he wasn't in contact with him. If anything, he was too insistent,' George said.

'He wanted to put us off pursuing that angle, which makes sense if he's covering for someone he loves,' Whitney said.

They returned inside and looked around the house. Once upstairs, they went into the first bedroom, which was bare, apart from a bed, a dressing table, and a wardrobe, which Whitney opened.

'Judging by the clothes, I'd say this is Thackeray's bedroom.'

She headed to the dressing table, on which was standing a photo of Thackeray when he was younger. To one side of him was a woman and on the other a small boy. He had his arms around them both. They were all smiling. There was another photograph of him that looked more recent, in which he was standing next to a man in an army uniform. 'Look at this photo. It must be his son.'

George walked over. 'Definitely. They look alike, although the son is taller, and it fits with our theory that the murderer possibly had a military background.'

'We need to get in touch with Ellie to find out.'

She pulled out her phone and called. 'I want you to look into Thackeray's son, Ben. He's either currently in the army or was in the past. We need to know where he is so we can bring him in for questioning.'

'Yes, guv.'

After ending the call, they went into the other bedroom. Again, not much in it, but when Whitney opened the wardrobe, she found some men's clothes which clearly belonged to someone taller than Thackeray.

'If Ben's keeping clothes here, then his dad might know more than he's letting on, regarding his son's whereabouts. I think we should get back to the station and re-interview Thackeray,' Whitney said.

'Good idea. We also need to keep focused on the fourth murder. With Ben at large, we have to assume it's going ahead.'

'Maybe we can persuade Thackeray to give him up.'

'I don't think that's likely. I suspect the whole series of murders is to do with the wife's suicide. Hopefully, we can access her medical notes. If not, Thackeray might tell us exactly what happened.'

They were back at the office within the hour, as the traffic wasn't so heavy, and Whitney went straight to the incident room.

'Attention everyone. It's pointing to our murderer being Thackeray's son, Ben. We need to find out everything we can about him. I'm going to interview Thackeray again and push him harder. It's likely the suicide of the son's mother was what set this whole thing off. Ben Thackeray is still at large, so we have to prepare for the fourth murder. We need to plan what we're going to do and how we're going to apprehend him. Ellie, were you able to access the mother's medical records?'

'Yes, guv. She'd been suffering from depression for a long time and had been on medication for it on and off over the years. The depression got worse in 2014, after the redundancies, and she gradually went downhill. She was hospitalised for a short time at the end of 2016 and when she came out, she took her own life. She slit her wrists while in the bath. Her son found her and called the ambulance, but it was too late. By the time they reached the hospital, she was dead.'

'That explains a lot. George and I are going to speak to Thackeray.'

'Do we have to get the solicitor back?' George asked as they made their way downstairs.

'I'll ask Thackeray if he'll agree to being interviewed alone. If he says no, we'll have to wait, but it's not ideal.'

They went to see the sergeant responsible for the custody suite.

'Hi, Ted. I'd like to speak to Norman Thackeray. Can you find out whether he's prepared to speak to us without his solicitor?'

'Leave it with me. I won't be long.'

The officer left the desk and walked down the corridor to the cells. He went into the third, and after only a few seconds, came out with Thackeray in handcuffs. He escorted him to one of the interview rooms, and George and Whitney followed.

Whitney prepared the recording equipment. 'Thank you for agreeing to speak to us again,' she said to Thackeray.

'I haven't got anything to tell you, but it beats sitting in the cell getting bored,' he replied.

'We want to talk to you about your son, Ben.'

'What about him?'

'When was the last time you saw him?'

'I don't remember.' He avoided looking at either of them.

'Does he keep in touch regularly?' Whitney continued.

'Sometimes he does. Sometimes he doesn't.'

'Is he still in the army?'

'He came out several years ago.'

'Why?'

'Ask him. I can't tell you.'

'I'd like to ask you about your wife. She took her life two and a half years ago.'

'I don't want to talk about it.'

'I know this is difficult, but was her spiralling depression linked to you being made redundant?'

'What do you think? I had a steady job, with a regular income and a comfortable life. We weren't rich, but we got by. Then I had no job, no prospects of getting one, and everything went downhill.'

Whitney exchanged a glance with George. This was the most the man had confided since they'd brought him in for questioning. The wound was still raw, and she understood why Transwide was being targeted. What she didn't know yet was the part he played in the murders. Was it him and his son? Just his son? Or just him? The latter being the most unlikely. The fact the murderer had such in-depth knowledge about trains led her to believe collusion was involved.

'Do you ever speak to your son about trains?'

'What do you mean?'

'Do you talk about the different types of trains, train timetables, older trains without CCTV?'

'Maybe. Why?'

'The murders were possible because the murderer had in-depth knowledge of the railway system.'

'Which I have. And I've admitted committing them, so that shouldn't be a surprise.'

'What I'm suggesting is it wasn't you who committed the murders. It was your son, based on information provided by you.'

'Don't be so bloody stupid. My son has nothing to do with it. I did the murders on my own. You're right. I have a thorough knowledge of the systems, and that's why I could do them. I wanted to get back at Transwide. Leave my son alone.'

'It doesn't work like that. We will carry on our investigation and look for your son so we can interview him. Are you sure you don't want to tell us where he is? It would be in his best interest to come forward. You say that he's innocent, in which case he won't mind talking to us.'

'I have no idea where he is. And I don't want to talk to you any more without my solicitor.'

'That's your prerogative,' Whitney said as she turned off the recording equipment and left the room with George.

'Well?' she asked.

'He was lying. I've been observing his eye movements during the questioning to give me a baseline. His deception was typical in that he looked up and to the right when you asked questions requiring him to use his imagination to come up with a story to deflect your interest in his son.'

'As we can't do anything until we find the son, and we haven't yet had the DNA results, we have to make sure we have officers on all trains that could potentially be targeted. At least knowing who we're looking for makes it easier for us to apprehend him.'

'Exactly.' George's phone rang. 'It's my mother. What does she want? She doesn't normally phone. I'd better get this. Hello, Mother.' She paused. 'Yes, that's right.' She made eye contact with Whitney and shook her head. 'I'm not prepared to discuss it now.' She paused again. 'Yes, I am with the police at the moment.' She gave an exasperated sigh. 'You can tell Father he has nothing to worry about. I'll speak to you soon.'

'What was that all about?' Whitney asked once George had finished the call.

'I mentioned to my brother I was bringing Ross to the wedding, and it's already got back to my parents.'

'And what did your mum say?'

'They want to know all about him. Where he's from, and who his parents are. My brother has already told them he's a sculptor, and they don't think he'll be a suitable escort as he might not know how to behave.'

'Your mother said all that in such a short conversation?'

'She didn't have to. It was implicit from her few words. I could also tell she'd been directed by my father.'

'Are you going to cancel taking him to the wedding?'

'Of course not. I've asked him, and I'm not going to change my mind. He knows what my parents are like, and he still said yes when I asked him.'

'You go girl. Are you sure I can't come too? We could hit them with a double whammy. The artist and the cop come face-to-face with Britain's finest.'

'I think taking Ross will be enough,' George said, laughing.

'You're reacting very well,' Whitney said. 'If I'd been on the receiving end of your mother's comments, I'd have gone ballistic and told her what I thought.'

'That's not how I operate. I like to keep things calm and controlled. What's the plan now?'

'We go to the office and prepare for tomorrow.'

Chapter Thirty

George and Whitney went back to the incident room, which was buzzing with the sound of officers talking on phones or to each other. The tension was palpable, as everyone knew they were working to a tight deadline. Everything had to be in place if they were to stand any chance of preventing the next murder. She followed Whitney to the board.

'Attention please, everyone,' Whitney said. 'Norman Thackeray isn't giving us any information, but we can assume he was working with his son, Ben, or at the very least, he knows what he's up to. Ellie, an update on Ben Thackeray.'

'He joined the army in 2004 as part of the infantry brigade. He's been deployed twice overseas. After the suicide of his mother in early 2017 he was given compassionate leave, but he didn't return. Ill-health meant he was finally retired from the force.'

'Were you able to access his medical records?'

'No, but I did speak to someone in the army's HR

section, and they implied it was on mental-health grounds.'

'We know the trail of murders started after the mother's suicide. Do we have an up-to-date photo of him?'

'Yes, I found him on social media and although he doesn't post much, there were several photos of him. I made a copy of one and it's on the desk.'

George picked it up and pinned it to the board.

'Email the photo to everyone. If he's going to be on one of the trains, we need to identify him,' Whitney said.

'Unless he uses a disguise, which is what we thought might have happened,' George said.

'He does have a scar on the side of his cheek which he wouldn't be able to disguise so easily,' Ellie said.

'Good. I want everyone to be aware of that when looking out for him. Give me the details of the trains we've picked out as potential targets again, so I can write them on the board,' Whitney said.

'There's the eight-thirty Newcastle to Lenchester train, the eleven-thirty Birmingham to London train, going via Lenchester, and the eleven-forty-five Salisbury to Birmingham train, also going through Lenchester,' Doug said.

'We'll place officers on every train, starting from where each one begins its journey.'

'Do you want uniform?' Terry asked.

'We'll have one plainclothes officer in each carriage, and two uniform patrolling the train. The murderer will be expecting us to be on there.'

'What if he decides not to commit the murder because of the huge police presence?' Vic asked.

'He didn't change his MO the last time and still succeeded,' Whitney replied.

'I suggest we try to lead him to a certain victim. Let's put an additional officer on each train in a carriage where there aren't many people, in the hope he goes after them,' George said.

She glanced around the room, wondering how the team would react to the suggestion. Being on the front line could be dangerous, but no one appeared perturbed.

'Jamieson will have to sanction using decoys,' Whitney said.

'Surely it's better being one of us, than the target being a member of the public,' George said.

'I think it's a good idea,' Terry said.

'I'll do it,' George offered.

'No. Jamieson would never approve it.'

'What about me?' Ellie asked.

George could see the indecision on Whitney's face. But allowing the young officer to take part would give them the most chance of success.

'Okay. But you'll need to be kitted out in protective clothing,' Whitney said. 'All decoys will, so if they're stabbed before we can get to them, the knife won't be able to penetrate through to the heart or lungs.'

'We need to decide who's going where,' Matt said.

'I'll go on the Birmingham to London train with Ellie. We'll get on at Birmingham and act like passengers. We don't want anyone to know who we are and what we're doing, if at all possible. Is that okay with you, Ellie?'

'Yes, guv.'

'Doug, will you be one of the targets? You can go on the Newcastle to Lenchester train.'

A look of hesitation crossed his face. He'd recently become a father, and George assumed he had those thoughts on his mind.

'Yes, guv,' he said.

'Terry and Sue will be with you, and you'll all keep in

contact via radio. You'll need to get on at Newcastle. Terry, I'll leave you to coordinate the rest of the officers.'

'No problem,' the detective said.

'On the remaining train, Matt's in charge and Frank can be the target.'

'Why me?' Frank said.

'I'll do it,' Vic said.

'Okay. Vic's the target, and Frank, you can be in one of the carriages. I'll leave you to sort it, Matt. You'll get on the train at Salisbury.'

'Yes, guv,' Matt said.

'Ideally, we need to catch the offender in the act. It's important not to arrest him too soon, to make sure we've got sufficient evidence. Obviously, we have the DNA, but we all know a good lawyer can get that dismissed in court for God knows how many reasons. It's much better if we catch him attempting the attack, and then it's irrefutable. Are there any questions?'

'What about me?' George asked.

'I don't think we need you.'

George frowned. Why was she being excluded? They'd worked well together on this case and had come up with the plan together.

'Why not? I can check the passengers and identify anyone acting suspiciously. I will notice even the smallest sign, whereas other people might not.'

'I'll have to check with Jamieson.'

So, that was the reason. That, she could accept.

'If he says yes, which train do you want me on?'

'You can come with me on the Birmingham train.'

'Good.'

'We're going to need officers on every platform for the entire journey. I'll get in touch with the transport police and they can carry out that function, the same as they did last time.'

'We need to consider the location where we think the murder will take place, so everyone is on their guard,' George said.

'The three so far have been within two stops of Lenchester,' Whitney said.

'Maybe we don't need a police presence for the entire journey, then,' Vic said.

'I disagree. Having them there might help us spot when the offender actually gets on, and then we'll know the targeted train,' Matt said.

'If they spot him,' Vic said.

'Well, they won't if they're not there. We shouldn't leave anything to chance,' Matt said.

'Agreed. We'll keep it as planned. Terry, were the previous murders all carried out within two stops of the targeted city?' Whitney asked.

'I believe so. Check that out, Vic.'

Yet again, George noted how their investigation was lacking. These were all things they should've known without having to check.

'Right, does everyone know what they're doing? Those of you going to Newcastle and Salisbury will need to leave tonight and stay over.'

The phone on the desk rang and Whitney picked it up. 'Walker.' She was silent. 'Okay, thanks.' She ended the call. 'DNA results from Thackeray have just come in. He's only a partial match to our sample, which is confirmation the murderer is most likely Ben Thackeray, his son.'

'Shall we put out an APB for Ben?' Frank asked.

'No. We want to catch him at the crime scene while he's attempting the fourth murder. I'm going to see Jamieson for approval.'

'I'm also leaving,' George said. 'Providing Jamieson agrees, what time shall I meet you tomorrow?'

'Nine in the morning at Lenchester station. We'll go together to Birmingham. I'll text to confirm,' Whitney said.

George had arranged to see Ross that evening. She'd contemplated cancelling because she didn't know how the case was going to progress, but now it seemed she had the time free.

Whitney went to Jamieson's office. As she got close, she could hear his voice booming out. He was giving someone a bollocking. She waited outside until the door opened and one of the admin staff left. She knocked and walked in.

'Yes, Walker,' he said.

'We've identified our murderer.'

'The person we have in custody?' he asked.

'No, it's his son, Ben. Thackeray confessed to the crimes to cover up for him, but we have the DNA results back and they show only a partial match. We've also identified the inciting factor for when the murders first started. It was the suicide of Ben's mother, which happened as the result of the father being made redundant from Transwide.'

'Good work, Walker. Do we have the son in custody?'

'Not yet, sir. We want him to attempt the fourth murder, so no clever barrister can get him off on a technicality. We've identified three possible trains where he could make his move, and I will deploy officers on all of them. I'd like your permission to have an undercover officer acting as a decoy on each train. We'll put them in a suitable carriage, one he's most likely to target.'

'I'm not sure it's a good idea to wait for him to strike. We'd be better putting out an APB and catching him first.'

Wasn't he listening to anything she'd just said?

'Even if we did that, we still need to be prepared for him to be on the train, as he's evaded capture so far.'

'How do you know you've got the right trains?'

'It's all based on the type of train, the train's journey, and what he's done in the past. We got the right train the last time, just missed catching him.'

'Who do you want to use as decoys?'

'DC Ellie Naylor, DC Doug Baines, and DS Vic Rowe. We'll also have a plainclothes officer in every carriage, uniform officers patrolling the train, and the transport police on the platforms. He's not going to get away this time.'

'What about Dr Cavendish? Is she involved in this?'

'I'd like permission for her to be on the train with me and DC Naylor. We could use her help identifying anyone with suspicious body language.'

'I'll agree, as long she's not going to be involved in the actual apprehension of the criminal, or as the undercover target. It's not appropriate, in terms of risk.'

'No, sir. She definitely won't be involved.'

'Good. What systems do you have in place to catch this man?'

'Officers on each train will keep in contact via radio and the decoys will be wearing vests, so even if the offender attempts to stab them, he won't succeed.'

'That's good to know. I don't want any injuries. I'm happy for you to carry on with the suggested plan. Make sure you keep me up to date with everything. I don't expect to be the last to know.'

'Yes, sir.'

Whitney went back to the incident room. 'Jamieson has

given his approval for the operation to go ahead. Ellie, you meet George and me at Lenchester station, and we'll travel to Birmingham together.'

'Yes, guv. I'm going to be fitted for my protective clothing now.'

'We'll plan which carriage you'll be in once we get there and see the layout of the train. Terry and Matt, I want you to do the same with Doug and Vic. Make sure you're in contact with me at all times.'

'Yes, guv,' both officers said at the same time.

'Before the operation, I want you all to study the photo you have of the offender and commit his face to memory. All of you going to Newcastle and Salisbury, get going now. Any questions?'

'Not a question,' Terry said. 'But a thanks from Vic and me. We wouldn't have been this far in the investigation without you. We've worked the case for over two years with little progress, but this is such an awesome team, we've managed to crack it. We're really grateful.'

'We're all in this together,' Whitney said, warmth flooding through her.

He didn't have to be so giving, especially after the way she'd treated the pair of them when they'd first arrived. Not that they didn't deserve her treatment. They'd been extremely patronising. That aside, they'd managed to break through the barriers and work together. Of course, it helped that they didn't like Dickhead Douglas and could see through his supposed professional behaviour.

'But it took your team's insight and persistence, so thank you.'

'You're welcome. We'll call it a successful joint operation. At least, we will once we've captured him.'

Chapter Thirty-One

Sunday, 23 June

George stared at herself in the mirror, wondering if the clothes she'd finally chosen for the train journey were suitable. Why had it been such a hard decision? Was she overthinking? It was a Sunday, so they weren't expecting commuters dressed for work. She imagined the passengers would mainly be people out on a day trip, or visiting family, or going shopping. So, surely the jeans, lightweight cream jumper, and dark brown leather jacket would be fine.

Nerves caught in her throat and she reached for her cigarettes. It was only seven in the morning, but it was going to be a long day.

The Newcastle train would be leaving in just over an hour, and the team would already be at the station waiting to depart. She wasn't due to meet Whitney until nine, but the officer was bound to be up and ready, so she decided to call to see if she'd like a lift. It would give her something to do.

She retrieved her phone from the kitchen table and

pressed the shortcut key for Whitney.

'Morning, George. Is everything okay?' Whitney asked.

'Would you like me to pick you up this morning, and we can go to the railway station together?'

'I'm already here. I couldn't settle at home.'

That made two of them. Even though this was the third operation George had been on, she was more nervous about this one than the other two.

'Same for me. Shall I come now?' she suggested, hoping Whitney would agree.

'Good idea. We can pace the platform together.'

'I'll be with you in about thirty minutes.'

She ended the call, picked up her bag, and drove to the railway station. When she arrived, Whitney was talking with the manager. She made a beeline for them.

'There'll be officers on the platform at all times, until this is over,' Whitney said. 'Try to operate as you normally would. We're expecting an attack today and anticipate apprehending the perpetrator before he does any harm.'

'I hope you're right,' the station manager said. 'I've already had a number of staff resign because they don't wish to work in such a threatening environment.'

'It will soon be over. He won't avoid capture, as we know who he is.' To the untrained eye, Whitney was giving off a confident air, but not to George. Whitney's nerves were evident by her eye movements and the biting down on her bottom lip.

The station manager walked away, and George approached.

'Let's go to the café,' Whitney said, her jaw tense.

Once inside, they ordered their drinks and sat down. Whitney fidgeted in her seat and drummed her fingers on the table.

'We've done as much as we can. We'll catch him.'

George tried to be reassuring but didn't know whether she'd succeeded.

Whitney looked at her watch. 'The Newcastle train is due to leave shortly. Will the murderer target the same journey the first victim made? Or will he go somewhere else? I'm waiting to hear back from Ellie to see if Thackeray's credit card has been used recently.'

'How can Ellie be at work if she's going to be with us on the train?'

'She went in early to do a bit of research. She's meeting us here later.'

Whitney's phone rang. 'Walker.' She paused. 'Good work, Ellie. We'll see you soon.' She ended the call. 'A ticket was bought using the credit card last night, going from Birmingham to Coventry, which is one of the stops of the Newcastle train.'

'Are you going to call the other two operations off and concentrate on the Newcastle train?' George asked.

'No. I'm going to let it run its course. Just because he booked a ticket, doesn't mean he'll use it. He could be doing it to throw us off.'

Whitney's phone rang again. 'Walker.' She paused a moment. 'Crap. Okay, thanks for letting me know.'

She ended the call and put her phone in her pocket. She let out a sigh.

'What is it?' George asked.

'That was Ellie. He knows we're onto him, or he's got some idea. She's found out he bought tickets for the two other trains, too. One to Rugby, which is our train, and one to Reading, the Salisbury train.'

'Damn.'

'All it means is nothing's changed from first thing this morning, so we carry on with our plan.'

'Actually, things have changed. We now know the three trains we've chosen are correct,' George said.

'Unless he pays cash on another train.'

'It's a possibility, but from his behaviour so far, I believe he'd consider having three alternatives will be sufficient. I stand by my assessment.'

'That's good to know. We're still going to catch him, whatever he decides to do. I need to let everyone know this latest update.'

Whitney called Terry and Matt and explained the situation to them.

'You know, the fact he's bought tickets has given us even more information,' George said, thoughtfully.

'What do you mean?'

'We can narrow down the timeframe and places of the murder attempt. We know that on the Newcastle train it's going to happen between Coventry and Lenchester. And we can apply the same logic to the other trains. On our train it will be between Rugby and Lenchester, and on Matt's train between Reading and Lenchester. It's going to make everyone a lot more vigilant at those particular times.'

'Yes, you're right,' Whitney said, nodding. 'This is good. Thanks for pointing it out.'

'What time are we leaving for Birmingham?'

'As soon as Ellie arrives. Shall we go in your car?' Whitney asked.

'For a change.' George arched an eyebrow.

They got to Birmingham after a fifty-minute minute drive. Ellie had sat in the back of the car and hadn't said a word all the way.

'Are you okay?' Whitney asked the young officer once they'd parked and got out of the car.

'Just a bit nervous, guv.'

'That's to be expected. And some nerves are good. It stops us from being complacent. Remember, we'll have officers in every carriage and you're wearing protective clothing, so we've got it all covered. We'll hear you via your earpiece as well. You won't be alone.'

'Yes, guv.' Ellie patted her chest. She looked a lot larger than she normally did, but it didn't look fake.

'Why don't we go to the café, so we don't look so conspicuous hanging around here?' George suggested.

'Good idea,' Whitney said.

The three of them walked into the station building and sat in the cafeteria, which wasn't very busy. Whitney went to the counter and ordered three coffees and three Danish pastries, which she took back to the table.

'I don't think I could eat or drink anything, or I might throw up,' Ellie said.

'Don't worry, it's here in case you change your mind,' Whitney said.

Whenever she was involved in major operations, Whitney was the exact opposite to Ellie. She was always hungry. It gave her something to do, so she didn't keep thinking about the outcome. Especially when she didn't have full control over it.

Ellie took a single bite of her Danish and put it down.

'Sorry, guv, I can't manage it.'

'It's fine.'

'There's a train on our platform. It might be ours,' George said. 'Shall we take a look?'

'In a minute. There's no rush,' Whitney said.

Their train wasn't due to leave for another forty minutes, so they had time to finish their coffee and pastry, after which they left the café and walked onto the platform. They headed over the bridge, which took them to the opposite side of the station, where the train was waiting. When they reached it, she could see a man sitting in the front.

'Is this the Birmingham to London train?' Whitney asked.

'Yes.'

'Are you the driver?'

'I am. Who are you?'

'DCI Walker, from Lenchester CID. We're going to be on the train. Did the station manager inform you of this?'

'No. No one tells me anything. I only work here,' he replied, shaking his head.

'This is one of three trains we're predicting might be targeted by the Carriage Killer.' She used the media nickname, as it was easier. 'I'm going to have officers in every carriage.'

'I should have been told if I'm putting myself at risk,' the driver said.

'All the victims so far have been passengers. We don't envisage this changing. We need you to carry out your normal duties. Where's the conductor?' She glanced around, but there was no other rail employee close.

'He'll be here soon.'

'I'd like to speak to him, too. Do you always drive this train?'

'If I'm on duty.'

'Okay. We're going to walk through and check the whole train. Shall we go through your cabin?'

'It's easier if I open the doors and you can go in that way.'

'Thanks. I'll let you know when we've finished. What's your name?'

'Wayne Swift.'

'And the name of the conductor?'

'Des Yates.' He pressed a button and there was clunking a noise. 'Passengers aren't allowed on yet.'

'I'll leave someone on the platform to make sure no one does.' She glanced at the bridge and saw two of her officers walking over.

Once they were close, she went over to them. 'Stay here and make sure no one gets on the train. I'll be back in a few minutes with further instructions.'

'Yes, guv,' they both replied.

She returned to George and Ellie. 'Come on, let's take a look.'

'You handled the driver well,' George said. 'It can't be easy for him to do his job when there could be a murder on here.'

'Thanks.'

They got on board and walked through every carriage. They were all in the same state of disrepair as each other: tired faded seats, and in need of updating.

'Do you think Ellie should go in the last carriage or the one before last?' George asked.

'The one before last, and you and I will sit in the end one. If we're close to the front, we should be able to see Ellie and keep an eye from a distance. There will also be a plainclothes officer in her carriage, but far enough away not to be a deterrent.'

'Should I be on the left or right side of the carriage?' Ellie asked.

'Judging by the other murders, he doesn't seem to favour a particular side. All we know is the victims were on their own. Wherever you sit, we'll make sure we can keep an eye on the area,' Whitney said.

They headed back along the train and got out at the front.

'We're out now, Wayne,' Whitney called to the driver, who was still sitting at the controls. 'You can lock the doors. Has Des arrived yet?'

'No.' He looked at his watch. 'He should've been here by now. He's never normally late.'

'I'll be waiting on the platform. Send him over when he shows up.'

'Will do.'

She made a call to the sergeant in change of the transport police, who were going to be stationed on their platform, and explained where she wanted them to be situated. She then phoned Matt.

'Guv,' he answered.

'What's happening? Have you got everything set up?'

'I've been on the train and worked out where everyone is going to be positioned. The manager said this train is never usually busy and according to ticket sales, it's even less so today. People have probably decided to keep away.'

'Make sure there's someone close enough to Vic they can see if anything goes down. But not close enough to stop it from happening. We're not going to know until it actually occurs which of the trains it's going to be because of the overlap in travel times.'

'It's all in hand. We're going to catch this bastard one way or the other.'

'Thanks. I know I can rely on you. Keep in contact. We'll text, rather than call, once each train begins its journey; we don't want the killer to get wind of the fact we're more organised than he thinks. He'll be expecting uniformed officers on the train, but he won't know about the rest of us.'

'Understood. It's all in hand. Just take care of Ellie.'

Matt and Ellie were really close, in a platonic way. He'd mentored her when she'd first arrived, and made sure the team were aware of her incredible research ability. Initially, she'd only been lent to them by another department, but Whitney fought long and hard to keep her. Without her extraordinary skills, solving cases would have been so much harder. Matt had always been Ellie's go-to person if she was struggling with anything. Whitney encouraged her to come out of her shell and always let her know how valued she was in the department.

'Nothing will happen to her; you have my word.'

'Thanks, guv. We're leaving shortly. I'll text once we get close to the stop where the killer might be getting on.'

'This whole thing should be over by the end of the day,' she said, letting out a sigh.

'And the drinks will be on you,' Matt said, giving a half-hearted laugh.

'Too right they will. We'll be celebrating big time.'

'Can't wait,' he said.

'Right, off you go. We've got a murderer to catch.'

Chapter Thirty-Two

Sunday, 23 June

Once all the officers had arrived, Whitney took them on the train and positioned them in every carriage. She instructed uniform to walk up and down the train during the journey. The killer would be expecting them, and she didn't want him to think there was anything out of the ordinary going on.

She'd left George and Ellie standing on the platform, and after she'd positioned the last officer, she headed off the train. She still hadn't spoken to the conductor, so she went back to the driver who was sitting in his seat looking at his phone.

'Still not here?' she said.

'He's phoned in sick. We're waiting for a replacement.'

'Does that mean the train's going to be delayed?'

'It looks like it.'

That was all they needed. She didn't want to frighten Thackeray off.

'How long for, do you think?'

'Difficult to say. No one wants to be working on this train because of the potential danger.'

'We're doing everything we can to make sure no one is harmed.' She let out a frustrated sigh.

'Try telling that to the people who work here. In the meantime, we've just got to wait.' He folded his arms tightly across his chest and stuck out his chin.

'Are you letting passengers on yet?'

'They can get on if they wish. It's up to you.'

'My officers are all in position. It would be best to open the doors, so everything looks normal. Although we're not expecting the suspect to get on here, I don't want to take any unnecessary risks, so let's get them aboard. There are a few people waiting on the platform.'

He opened the doors. 'An announcement will be made shortly about the delay.'

'Let me know as soon as the replacement conductor arrives. I want to talk to him before we leave.'

'Will do.'

She returned to George and Ellie. 'The train's been delayed.'

'Do we know for how long?' George asked.

'No. The conductor's phoned in sick, so they're waiting for his replacement.'

There was a ding-dong, indicating an announcement was about to happen.

For passengers travelling on the 11.30 train to London, this train has been delayed for twenty-five minutes. We are sorry for any inconvenience caused. Thank you.

'I thought they didn't know how long the delay would be,' Ellie said.

'If they said that, people will get annoyed. At least giving them a time makes it more bearable. Hopefully, the conductor will be here by then, anyway,' George said.

'I'd better get in touch with Matt and let him know,' Whitney said. She took out her phone and, glancing at the time, decided to text rather than call.

Our train's delayed. Have you left yet?

A few seconds later she received a text back from him.

Just about to. Will call you.

Whitney's phone rang and she answered it straight away. 'I thought we weren't going to speak,' she said to Matt as she stepped away from George and Ellie.

'Sorry, guv. I didn't think it would matter, as we haven't left yet. We'll be leaving shortly. I've got officers positioned as planned. I'm going to stay with the uniform guys and patrol the train. I thought if we start in the first carriage, I can check all the passengers who are on here at the moment. Then I'll scan the platforms as we arrive into different stations, to see who gets on and off.'

'Have you seen anyone who fits the description yet?'

'No, but we're not expecting him for a while, are we?'

She knew that, she just wasn't thinking straight. 'No, but you should still keep a lookout. I don't know when we're going to be leaving. The conductor called in sick.'

'Okay, guv. I'll keep in touch and let you know how the journey is progressing.'

'Thanks.'

She ended the call and returned to where Ellie and George were standing.

'With all the platforms having police on them, will that put the murderer off?' Ellie said.

'He'll be expecting it and will find somewhere to hide before he gets on his chosen train. The waiting room or the toilets. There are bound to be places he'll be able to go to keep out of the way,' George said.

'Agreed,' Whitney said.

'Do you think that's the conductor?' Ellie said, pointing to a man in uniform hurrying over the bridge.

'I hope so,' Whitney said. She waited until the man had walked down the steps and reached the front of the train before heading over to him.

'I'm DCI Walker. Are you the conductor?' she said to the small, balding man in front of her.

'Yes, I'm Charlie Jones.'

'Have you been told there'll be a police presence on the train, and the reason for it?'

'Yes. The Carriage Killer might be on here.'

Whitney frowned. Judging by the expression on his face, he was excited by the prospect.

'It's one of three trains we've identified as being possible targets, so we don't know whether it's going to happen on here or not. I want you to act normal and do your job as you usually do.'

'I understand, and I'll do my best.' He nodded.

'Can you run through your procedures?' she asked.

'Once the train starts, I go through every carriage and check tickets. Anyone who hasn't got one will have to pay me.'

'What happens when you get to the first stop?'

'I step down from the train and look to see who gets off and who gets on.'

'Then what do you do?'

'I go through the carriages again and check the tickets of the new people.'

'Do you ever miss people getting on and off?'

'Rarely. In this job you get used to remembering faces and destinations.'

'Okay. When you're doing your rounds, I don't want you scrutinising people or engaging in conversation. You're not to acknowledge me or any of my officers.'

'Wouldn't the killer think I know the police?'

'Only the ones in uniform, so you can talk to them *if necessary*.'

'How do we know he's not on here already and watching you talking to me?'

'If this is his chosen train, we're not expecting him to get on board until Rugby, two stops out of Lenchester, which is the city he's targeting at the moment.'

'How do you know?'

'We've done our research and studied his routines. But that doesn't mean we won't be on our guard for the whole journey. Like I said, all we want from you is to act like there is nothing out of the ordinary happening.'

'And this will be his last murder on our train line?'

'The pattern is four murders in one area, and then he moves on. But that's not going to happen now we've identified him and he's going to be caught.' She was about to say more, then stopped. Knowing more might stop him from doing his job as he usually would.

'Which are the other two trains he might be on?'

'You don't need to know anything else, apart from all the trains are running at similar times and there's some overlap, which makes it impossible to identify exactly which one he's going to be on.'

'Okay. We need to get this train underway.'

'Thank you for your cooperation. I know it's not easy, but we're going to catch this man.'

Whitney got off the train and walked over to George and Ellie. Just as she got there, an announcement came over the public address system saying the train was about to leave. They were now only fifteen minutes late.

'Let's get ourselves on the train. Ellie, you walk in front of us, and when we see where you sit, George and I will position ourselves.'

'Yes, guv.'

They walked through the carriages. In the first there were ten people, a mix of families, friends, and solo travellers. As they went through to the second and third, there were fewer people, until they got to the fifth and there was only one other person in there, not counting the plainclothes officer. Ellie sat in a two-seat row, by the window, on the right. There was only one double seat behind her.

Whitney and George went through the connecting doors and into the next carriage, which was empty. They sat in a double seat at the front.

'I can't actually see her,' Whitney said.

'No, but we can see if anyone comes down the aisle and approaches her,' George said.

'Good point. I'll text Matt to let him know we're leaving shortly.' She took out her phone.

Leaving now. Where are you?

After a couple of minutes, she had a reply.

We're on our way. Nothing to report.

'Right, now we sit tight and wait. So, we might as well talk about Ross.'

'Why would we want to do that?' George said, looking puzzled.

'Because this waiting is killing me, and I can't draw attention to myself by pacing up and down the train.'

'I'm not discussing him while everyone can hear,' George said. 'We're all wearing mics and earpieces.'

'We'll turn our mics to incoming only,' Whitney said as she pressed the button on hers and leaned over and did the same to George's.

'What do you want to know?' George let out a sigh.

'When am I going to meet him?'

'I don't know.'

'Have you introduced him to your friends?'

'I don't know anyone to introduce him to, apart from work colleagues, and that's not going to happen.'

'I'm sorry, I forgot you don't mix with many people.'

'I have a wide range of acquaintances, but no one I see socially.'

Whitney could relate to that. She was so busy with family and work she hadn't caught up with any of her friends in months. They probably didn't even remember who she was.

'Why don't you bring him to my concert?' she suggested.

'When is it?'

'We've got one coming up in a few weeks, in a local hall. We're also preparing for a big one in November. All the Rock Choirs in the Midlands are getting together. I've been asked to do a solo.'

'I'd definitely like to come to that one. I haven't heard you sing before.'

'I'd love you to be there.' She rarely invited people to see her perform, as she liked to keep that part of her life separate. But with George it was different.

'I can bring Tiffany with me, too.'

'You can, but there'll also be Mum and Rob.'

'No problem. I'll bring everyone.'

'What about Ross, can you get him in the car as well?'

'We're talking about over four months' time. I've no idea if I will be seeing him then.' George shrugged, but Whitney wasn't fooled. She was being fobbed off.

'Except you've already asked him to the wedding, so my guess is you think you will be.'

'How did we get back to talking about my relationship again? You're so devious.'

'Not devious, just interested. Hopefully, you'll still be seeing him. I like the change he's brought out in you.'

'I think you're talking nonsense,' George said.

The train jolted and Whitney's attention was diverted as they pulled away from the platform. They were finally on their way.

Chapter Thirty-Three

Sunday, 23 June

'Right, we're just coming into Rugby, the stop where Thackeray might be getting on,' Whitney said.

George peered out of the window as the train pulled into the station. There were fifteen people on the platform. Four men on their own. Two had their heads down and one was wearing a baseball cap. Impossible to see their faces clearly.

Witney's phone pinged. 'It's Matt. He said there's a man on his train he's keeping an eye on.'

'Has he got a scar on his face?' George asked.

'He didn't say. I'll text and ask.' Shortly after, a text arrived back. 'They can't get close enough to him, but they're on the alert. I'm going for a walk. Sitting still is driving me crazy,' Whitney said, jumping up from her seat.

'Do you think that's wise, in case he's on here?'

'I'll go through the next carriage to the toilet. It might give Ellie peace of mind if she actually sees me. Also, everyone's got their earpieces and mics on, so we'll be in contact.'

'Okay, I'll see you when you get back.'

George watched Whitney leave their carriage. Although Whitney didn't stop to speak, she briefly turned her head in Ellie's direction and gave a small nod. In her earpiece, George heard Whitney whispering, 'Are you okay,' and Ellie replying, 'Yes.'

She was distracted by her phone ringing, and when she pulled it out of her bag, she saw it was Ross. Should she answer? She supposed it wouldn't hurt.

'George here,' she said.

'Ross here,' he said.

She smiled to herself. She liked his sense of humour; it was easy and light. 'I'm working at the moment.'

'I thought there were no students in over the holidays.'

'I'm working with Whitney on a case.'

'Is it secret?'

'I'll tell you when I see you. Well, not all of it, but certainly some.'

'I'd like to meet Whitney sometime,' he said.

'Not you too.' Did they have a hotline to each other?

'What do you mean?'

'That's what she said about you.'

'In that case, we'll have to arrange something.'

'She's invited us to one of her concerts. She sings in the Rock Choir and there's a big concert in November.' Why did she mention the November date? He'd think she had long-term plans for them.

'That's a long time to wait. Why don't we fix a time for us all to go out for drink? Does she have a partner?'

'No, but we could invite her daughter, Tiffany, along.'

'Okay. I'll leave you to arrange it.'

'Did you phone for anything in particular?' she asked.

'I wanted to share my news, and you're the first person I've called. I've won an award for one of my sculptures.'

He phoned her first. Why?

'Congratulations. Tell me about it.'

'It's the Havelock Prize for Sculpture, which is awarded for significant contribution to modern sculpture. There's going to be a fancy awards dinner in London. Will you come with me?'

It was strange that she was the first person he wanted to tell, and not his family or friends. Did it mean their relationship was becoming more serious? How did she feel about that? She wasn't going to move in with him. She'd had her fingers burnt with Stephen and was nowhere near ready for commitment. But she didn't want her relationship with Ross to end. She enjoyed where they were at the moment.

'I'd be delighted to go with you.'

'We can stay in a nice hotel overnight. It's on a Saturday in six weeks' time.'

'I'll look forward to it. Thank you for inviting me. I really need to go now.'

'Very secret squirrel,' he said.

'This is serious.' Why would he make light of it? She'd explained she was working on something.

'I know. I was only joking.'

Why hadn't she realised?

'Oh. Okay.'

'Are we still on for Wednesday evening?' he asked.

'Yes, I'll be over at seven,' she said, remembering they'd arranged for him to cook her a meal.

'Bring your overnight bag and you can stay over.'

'That would be nice.'

She ended the call and stared out of the window, imagining how the meeting between Ross and Whitney would go. It would—

A sound from behind made her start. Who was there?

She turned her head and gasped.

A man with brown hair, falling in clumps around his pointed jaw, towered over her. Down the side of his face was a jagged scar.

Ben Thackeray.

Her phone fell from her hands, and her mouth went dry.

'Whitney,' she yelped into the mic, only to be met by dead air. It was off.

She reached to turn it on, but before she could his arm shot around in front of her, a cloth in his hand. Chloroform. She lifted her arm, attempting to stop him from smothering her, but he was much stronger than she was. Using every last bit of strength she could muster, she managed to turn her head and at same time switch on the mic.

'Help,' she cried as she pushed back and knocked him away. But he came back and grabbed hold of her hair. She kicked out and caught him on the leg, causing him to yell out. She tried to stand up and shove him out of the way, but he regrouped and pushed her back in the seat, while grabbing hold of her head and managing to bring his arm around to her face.

She didn't want to die.

She fought again as the cloth in his hand got closer to her face. As if in slow motion, a sickly-sweet smell enveloped her and she began to feel woozy. In the distance, she heard the carriage door open, and suddenly he was being pulled off her.

Whitney held on to Thackeray's arm, but he pulled away and took off through the open carriage door, pushing aside the two officers who'd been following as she'd come to rescue George.

Someone had pulled the emergency stop lever and the train had come to a halt just as it was coming into Banbury station. Thackeray opened the exit door, jumped, and ran along the tracks. He leapt onto the platform.

Whitney followed—no way was he getting away. 'Suspect heading along platform,' she yelled into her mic. She could see him up ahead and pushed herself forward, gradually making up ground. He turned to look at her and tripped over a suitcase belonging to a woman waiting for the train. He hauled himself up, but in those intervening seconds Whitney managed to reach him. She grabbed him from behind, pulling him on top of her, just as her officers came running off the train. She rolled him off her, leapt to her feet, then grabbed him by the arm and pulled him into a standing position. He didn't resist.

'Ben Thackeray, I'm arresting you on suspicion of the murders of Hugo Holmes-Reed, Lena Kirk, and Neil Thomas. And the attempted murder of Georgina Cavendish. You do not have to say anything, but it may harm your defence if you do not mention when questioned something which you later rely on in court. Anything you do say may be given in evidence. Do you understand?'

Whitney handcuffed his wrists and gave him to the two officers standing behind her. 'Make sure he doesn't move. We'll transport him to Lenchester as soon as we can.'

As they took him away, Whitney got back on the train and ran to find George.

George opened her eyes when she heard the carriage door

open. Whitney charged in and rushed over to her. 'Are you okay?'

'I think so, yes.' She swallowed hard. 'My head hurts and I feel a bit sick, but he didn't actually press the cloth over my nose. It was being close to the smell that's made me a bit out of it.'

'I don't want you passing out on me,' Whitney said.

'Thank goodness you got here in time. I can't believe we didn't see or hear him come into our carriage. He came at me from behind.'

'The main thing is you're okay. We'll find out more when we get him back to the station.'

'I want to be there when you speak to him.'

'Once we get back to Lenchester, we're getting you some medical attention. We don't know whether the chloroform is going to have any lasting effects. It's got to be checked out.'

'I'll be fine,' she said, her voice weak.

'It's not up for discussion. You'll be heading straight to the hospital for a check-up. If they say you're okay, then I'll allow you to watch the interview. Oh, no …'

'What?'

'Jamieson's going to go off on one, big time. He made me promise not to involve you. Those were his terms for allowing you to be here.'

'It wasn't intentional.'

'No, but we should have put you in protective clothing, just in case.'

'Don't tell him.'

'That's it. We're definitely getting you checked out. The chloroform has obviously affected you. No way would the George I know suggest we keep something like that a secret.'

'Don't be silly. I've told you nothing's wrong with me.

All I have is a slight headache, and that's not going to hurt me. Chloroform can be lethal, but not the slight amount I inhaled.' She tried to sound normal, but it was an effort. More than she was prepared to let on. If Whitney knew, she'd feel guilty, and it wasn't her fault.

'I hear you, but like I said, it's not up for discussion. I want you fit and well because we're going to have a big celebration once we've sorted out this guy.'

The furthest thing from her mind was attending a celebration, but she'd keep that thought to herself.

'Okay,' she agreed.

'I'm going to have a word with Ellie. Will you be okay on your own for a few moments?' Whitney asked.

'Yes, I'm fine. You go.'

George closed her eyes, hoping it would ease the headache. But all that happened was her mind flew back to the incident. To how close she'd been to being killed. If Whitney had been much longer, he could well have stabbed her, and she'd be dead. She hadn't even considered that a possibility when she'd asked to be on the train. Her breath caught in the back of her throat. If she'd died, she would never have seen Whitney, Tiffany, or Ross ever again.

Whitney hurried into the incident room.

'I'm sure you've all heard we've managed to capture the Carriage Killer and he's in custody downstairs. I'm going to interview him soon.'

'How's Dr Cavendish?' Matt asked.

'The hospital gave her the all clear. She was lucky all she had was a waft of chloroform and no more.'

'How is she in herself? She must have had a shock being in such a dangerous situation,' Matt said.

Guilty feelings for what had happened to George hadn't left her since the attack. She shouldn't have let her come on such a dangerous operation.

'I'll be speaking to her later. Knowing George, I'm sure she'll be fine and will take it in her stride.'

She only said that because she didn't think George would want to be discussed in this way by everyone.

The phone on the desk rang. She picked up. 'Walker.'

'Detective Superintendent Jamieson would like to see you in his office,' her boss's assistant said.

'I'll be right up.'

She hurried to Jamieson's office, gently tapped on the open door, and walked in.

'Walker, congratulations. This is a huge coup for our team. I'm going to make a big announcement during the press conference later.'

'Thank you, sir. I haven't yet interviewed the prisoner, but I'm going there next with DI Gardner. It really was a joint operation.'

'That's extremely magnanimous of you, Walker, but I know the bulk of the work was done by our team. Still, I'm happy for us to share the limelight now the murderer is off the streets. Or should I say, *off the tracks.*' He laughed at his own joke.

He clearly hadn't heard what happened with George. Should she tell him? As much as she didn't want to, it was probably best to do it now, while he was so upbeat about everything, rather than leave him to find out later.

'There is something you need to know, sir.'

'What's that?'

'When we captured Thackeray, he was attacking Dr Cavendish. She managed to hold him off, so he wasn't able to sedate her, although she did inhale some chloroform fumes. Not enough to cause any damage, though.'

'What was she doing in the killer's vicinity? I told you she wasn't to be part of the immediate operation.'

'Until I've interviewed the prisoner, I'm not sure how he got into the end carriage. I thought George would be safe there. We'd actually set up DC Ellie Naylor to be the target in the carriage next door. We were all mic'd up, so Dr Cavendish was able to call for help, and we got there in time.'

He stared at her, shaking his head. 'I'm really not happy about this, Walker. Especially after my explicit instructions. We can't afford to put Dr Cavendish in danger. She's not a police officer. She's here to assist.'

'Yes, sir. I understand. It won't happen again.'

'Make sure it doesn't. I want you with me at the press conference later. Tidy yourself up a bit before then.'

What the hell was that about? She glanced down. She did look a mess after the scuffle with the prisoner. But of course she'd make sure she was presentable to meet the press. How could he think otherwise?

'I always do, sir. I'm going to interview the prisoner, now. I'll let you know if he says anything we can use in the press conference. I'll liaise with Melissa to find out what time it's going to be, and I'll come back here thirty minutes beforehand, so we can go over it. If that's okay with you?'

'Yes, that's fine. You can go now. Well done.'

Why did she feel like a pet being praised for good behaviour?

She left the office and went back to the incident room. When she got there, she saw George and Matt talking.

'What are you doing here?'

'You said I could watch the interview if I was given the all clear. Which I have been.'

'Come with me,' she said.

They walked through the incident room and into her office. She closed the door behind them.

'There's nothing wrong with me,' George said.

'Sit down, I want to talk to you.'

'If this is about the after-effects of the chloroform then—'

'No, it's not that. I'm so sorry for what happened. I shouldn't have put you in a position where your life was in danger. I'm the police officer. Not you. I—'

'Whitney, stop. It was my choice.' George held up her hand.

'But I was in charge of the operation. I also want to talk to you about what happened.'

'I'm fine.'

'You might feel okay now, but there could be some repercussions for you mentally. You know this from your work, and what happened to Tiffany.'

George nodded slowly. 'I know. At the time I did feel my life was on the line, but you saved me.'

'What would you be saying to me if it was the other way around?' she asked, taking a different approach.

George was quiet for a moment. 'I'd suggest you talk to someone about the incident.'

'Exactly. I'd like you to see the police counsellor.'

A pensive expression crossed George's face. Was she going to agree?

'I'll go,' George said.

'Really?' Whitney couldn't hide the surprise in her voice. She'd thought it would be much harder to get George to agree.

'Yes, really. I'm not stupid. I do know what can happen. I won't see the police counsellor, though. I'll go to the woman Tiffany went to. I know she's good.'

'That's great. I'm really pleased. I've been in similar situations myself, and I know it can hit you when you're least expecting it.'

'Does that mean I can now be part of the interview with Ben Thackeray?'

'Yes, we'll collect Terry on the way.'

She opened her drawer and pulled out two earpieces and mics. She handed one to George.

'Terry? What about Matt?'

'I think Terry deserves to be in on it. I know their investigation wasn't up to scratch and they could've done better, but they've helped us. It's no skin off my nose if they want to share the credit. The main thing is we've got the perp.'

'How did Jamieson feel about that?'

'You know him so well. I think he'd rather we had all the kudos. But he'll sell it as a joint-force investigation. It could help with his promotion prospects if a job comes up at the RF.'

'True.'

'We can but hope.'

Chapter Thirty-Four

Sunday, 23 June

George, Terry, and Whitney walked down to the interview room to meet with Ben Thackeray.

'Thanks for including me, guv,' Terry said.

'You're welcome. You have background information on the other murders, and I don't. Having that knowledge will help.'

'Will Terry be allowed to ask questions?' George asked, attempting to lighten the mood and stop her from thinking about seeing the man who'd just tried to kill her.

'Maybe,' Whitney replied, smirking.

Terry looked at the pair of them, a puzzled expression on his face.

'Whitney likes to ask all the questions herself,' George said.

'That's because I rely on you to keep an eye on the interviewee's body language and anything else I might need to know. Terry doesn't have that ability. So, if there's a question you want to ask, please do so.'

Once they got there, George went into the side room so she could observe.

Her heart pounded in her chest when she first saw Ben Thackeray. But he didn't seem as threatening as when he was towering over her on the train. If anything, he seemed like a rather ineffectual man. His hands were held loosely in his lap, and he looked down. His solicitor was sitting by his side, looking at his phone.

Whitney prepared the recording equipment.

'Interview on the twenty-third of June. Present: DCI Walker.'

'DI Gardner,' Terry said.

'Please state your name for the tape,' Whitney said, looking at Thackeray, who had looked up.

'Ben Thackeray.'

'And Clive Lewis, solicitor for the accused.'

'Mr Thackeray, I'd like to remind you that you're still under caution. Do you understand?' Whitney said.

He nodded.

'Please state your answer for the tape.'

'Yes.'

'I'd like to start by asking about the three murders, and the attempted murder, you committed in Lenchester. Hugo Holmes-Reed, the fourteen-year-old boy on the train going from Newcastle to Lenchester. Please could you run through exactly what happened that day, and explain why you chose Hugo.'

'No comment.'

'What about Neil Thomas, the elderly man on the Coventry train? Tell me about his murder.'

'No comment.'

'You need to take a different approach,' George said. 'Try asking about his father.'

'Mr Thackeray, we have your father in custody, and he's going to be charged with being an accessory in the case of fifteen murders and one attempted murder.'

The prisoner lifted his head and stared directly at Whitney.

'Keep going,' George said.

'What can you tell me about your father's involvement?'

'He has nothing to do with it.'

'Our enquiries are telling us otherwise. Perhaps you could enlighten me?'

'There's nothing to say. He's not involved, and he didn't know anything about it.'

'That's not enough for us to believe you. Your father's credit card was used to purchase train tickets from Birmingham on the days of each of the murders. To be more precise, that's sixteen times his credit card was used.'

'He didn't know I was using it.'

'This was over a period of two years. How could he not know? He would have received statements for his card and paid it off.'

'I have the credit card and I pay it,' Thackeray said.

'Why don't you use your own credit card?'

'I don't have one. I have a bad credit rating. My dad got one for me. He had no idea what I was using it for.'

'He confessed to the murders.'

Thackeray's eyes widened. 'He can't have.'

'Well, he did. He's admitted to all the murders and said you had nothing to do with them. I suggest you were working together, and he took the blame to protect you.'

'He was just guessing. He didn't know it was definitely me.'

'So, you're admitting guilt.'

He shrugged. 'You caught me in the act.'

'Are you prepared to talk about it?'

'Only if you drop all the charges against my dad.'

'I can't promise anything. It will be up to the CPS, but obviously the more help you give, the more it will go in your favour.'

'It's not my favour I'm interested in. It's my dad I want to keep out of this.' Thackeray folded him arms and stared at Whitney.

'You've got him,' George said. 'I think he'll start cooperating. He's obviously very close to his father.'

'Let's just hear the truth, and I'll see what I can do,' Whitney said.

'What do you want to know?' Thackeray said.

'Why? Tell me why you murdered all those innocent people,' Terry demanded.

'Revenge. Pure and simple. I wanted to make Transwide suffer. The only way to do it was to hit them where it hurt. In the pocket. I wanted them to lose money when people stopped taking the train. They don't deserve to be in operation. They have to be stopped from causing further damage.'

'What sort of damage?' Whitney asked.

'Destroying families, that's what. They made my father redundant, and he couldn't get another job. It destroyed my mother. She couldn't cope and felt ashamed because she had to go to the food bank some weeks just to get the essentials.'

'I'm sorry to hear that,' Whitney said.

'How can you be sorry? You didn't even know her?' he said.

'That doesn't mean I can't be sympathetic to what happened,' Whitney said.

'She committed suicide thanks to those bastards. I wanted revenge. Dad didn't know what I was doing. I'm not saying he didn't suspect, but he had nothing to do with it.'

'How did you know which trains to target?'

'From when I was a young boy, I was obsessed with trains. I learned everything from Dad. When I was planning my revenge, it wasn't hard to get the information I needed out of him. We'd talk about trains all the time.'

'Where did you get the knife from?'

'I've had it for years, from when I was in the army.'

'A piece of the knife broke off into the last victim. What had you planned to use this time?'

'I bought a new hunting knife. Similar blade length and handle to the one I'd used before.'

'And the way you actually killed with the knife. Was that planned?'

'I knew the most efficient way to kill using a knife from when I was deployed overseas. I'd done it before.'

'Why didn't you just kill your victims with chloroform? Why did you choose to use the knife?' Whitney asked.

'My mum used a knife to kill herself. I thought it was fitting to do the same.'

'You took items belonging to your victims. Why?'

'So I didn't forget what I'd done. I don't keep a diary, because I'm no good at writing. It was a reminder.'

'Do you feel any guilt for taking the lives of innocent people?' Terry asked.

'I did what I had to do. I'm sorry if it caused any suffering.'

'And you think that's an excuse, do you?' Terry snapped.

'I'm not making excuses. I'm stating facts.'

Terry thumped the table and stood up. He leaned forward. 'Try telling that to the families of your victims,' he shouted.

Whitney placed her hand on the detective's arm and pulled him back. 'Enough,' she said quietly.

Terry sat with his arms folded tightly across his chest.

'Back to your collection of mementoes. Where are they?' she asked.

'At the room I'm renting.'

'Where is that? We don't have a record of where you're living.'

'I live a couple of miles from Dad. I pay by cash, so no one knows.'

'Does your father know where you live?'

'I've told you. He doesn't know anything. Stop trying to get him involved.'

'Please give me your address so we can retrieve them.'

'18 Wickes Street, Birmingham.'

'I want to ask you about today. How did you get on the train and into the last carriage?'

'I thought you were onto me, especially after you'd been questioning my father.'

'How did you know we had?' Whitney asked.

'He used his one phone call to leave me a message on my mobile. So I changed things slightly. I bought three tickets from Birmingham using the credit card. But I also paid cash for another ticket. The one I actually used. '

Nausea flooded through George. He'd been on the train the whole time, and they hadn't realised.

'How did you get into the end carriage? It was empty when we were in there,' Whitney said.

'At the end of the rear carriage there's a locked door leading to a room which the conductors use sometimes. I assumed with the police on-board they wouldn't go in, so I hid there.'

'How did you get in if the door was locked?'

'I got a master key from my dad. I've had it a long time. Your officers were so useless they didn't notice me walking on when the doors were first opened. Then it was just a matter of peering out occasionally. Once we left the station, I could see there were only two people in the carriage. I recognised you from being on the telly at the press conference. I didn't recognise the other person. I waited for you to leave, and that's when I made my move.'

George dragged in a long breath. She'd been a target for the whole journey, and she hadn't even known. It could have ended up so differently. She pushed the thought away. She'd always known working with the police wouldn't be a walk in the park.

'Bloody hell,' was all she allowed herself to say.

'Going for someone who was with the police was a risk. Didn't you think about that?'

'No. All I was concerned with was the easiest way for me not to get caught. The plan was to kill the person with you and then go back to my hiding place as quickly as possible.'

'But the train would've been on lockdown as soon as we'd found the body.'

'I'd have managed to get off through the exit door at the end of the carriage in front of the conductor's room. But that doesn't matter now. You've got me.'

'Have you finished with your questioning?' the solicitor asked. 'I don't think there's any more that needs to be covered.' He closed the folder on the table and pushed his chair back as if getting ready to stand.

Whitney stared at him open-mouthed, anger coursing through her. How dare the jumped-up pathetic excuse of a solicitor think he could downplay the horrendous nature of this crime?

'That's your opinion. Not mine. We have fifteen murders to go through, and he's just tried to kill one of our own. So, this interview will continue until I say we're done. Got it?'

Chapter Thirty-Five

Monday, 24 June

Whitney pushed open the door and was hit by the sound of voices. This was the pub her colleagues used, as it was close to the station. It was always busy and full of people she knew. She walked through looking for her team. They were in the corner, standing around tall circular tables. Matt, Frank, Ellie, Doug, Sue, several others, and Terry and Vic. Pride coursed through her.

George was already there, too. She knew the psychologist wouldn't be happy, as she hated the pub for many reasons. For a start, they didn't sell real ale, but also George believed it was cold, plastic, and lacked atmosphere. The fact she was there at all meant a lot.

'Here she comes. Three cheers for the guv,' Frank called out when she was close.

Everybody whooped and shouted.

'I don't know why you're cheering me. It was a team effort,' she said.

'We couldn't have done it without you, guv,' Terry said. 'This is a fantastic day for all of us.'

'Especially as the drinks are on you,' Frank said.

'They are indeed. So, who's going to get them?' She reached into her bag, pulled out her purse, and took out two twenty-pound notes. 'This should cover it.'

'I'll go,' Doug said, taking the money from her.

'I'll help,' Ellie said.

Whitney went to stand with Terry, Vic, and George.

'I thought you would have gone back by now,' she said to Terry.

'We're going tomorrow. I didn't want to miss the celebration. I can't believe it's finally over.'

'Have you let Dickhead Douglas know yet?' she asked.

'Yes, we told him.'

'And let me guess, he wants you to take all the credit.' She shook her head.

'It was a bit late for that because your Super had done the press conference before we told him.'

'What did Douglas say about that?'

'He was annoyed. He said he should've been told first.'

'He can take that up with Jamieson.'

'You do realise we now have a new nickname for our notorious Detective Superintendent,' Terry said.

'Well, don't say it came from me,' she said, laughing.

Ellie and Doug came back with the drinks and handed them around.

'Shall we go and sit over there?' she said to George, pointing to an empty booth.

'Wouldn't you rather stay here with the rest of the team?' George said.

'They won't notice if I'm not here for a while. They're too busy congratulating themselves for a job well done.'

They headed over to the booth and sat down.

'You must be thrilled with the outcome,' George said.

'I am. But I'm more concerned with knowing how you're doing,' she said.

'I'm fine. Really.'

'Have you talked to Ross about it?'

'It only happened yesterday.'

'You haven't answered my question.'

'Yes, we spoke about it last night.'

'And did it help?'

'What's with the twenty questions?'

'Nothing. I'm just trying to find out exactly how serious this relationship is.'

'Stop pushing it, Whitney.'

'I don't know what you're talking about.' She grinned at George.

'Yes, you do.'

'I'm glad you're in a serious relationship.'

'It's not serious.'

'Of course it isn't. That's why you're taking him to your brother's wedding and were with him last night after your ordeal.'

'I'm not discussing it further. Tell me what's happening with you. Is Rob okay now?'

'We're getting there. Today I spent some time with him and Mum, and it went well.'

'Excellent. Let's hope we don't have anything else causing us problems for a while.'

'Now you've jinxed it,' Whitney said.

'There's no such thing as jinxing.'

'Well—'

'Guv, you're needed at the station,' Sue said as she came rushing over.

'Why?'

'Detective Superintendent Jamieson wants you. Something about a meeting he wants you to attend.'

Whitney stared at George and rolled her eyes. 'Jinxing's not a thing. Yeah, right.'

∼

Book 4 - George and Whitney return in *Lethal Secret* when a series of suicides, linked to the *Wellness Spirit Centre* turn out to be murder.
Tap here to buy it on Amazon

∼

GET ANOTHER BOOK FOR FREE!
To instantly receive the free novella, **The Night Shift**, featuring Whitney when she was a Detective Sergeant, ten years ago, sign up for Sally Rigby's free author newsletter at www.sallyrigby.com

DEADLY GAMES - Cavendish & Walker Book 1

A killer is playing cat and mouse....... and winning.

DCI Whitney Walker wants to save her career. Forensic psychologist, Dr Georgina Cavendish, wants to avenge the death of her student.

Sparks fly when real world policing meets academic theory, and it's not a pretty sight.

When two more bodies are discovered, Walker and Cavendish form an uneasy alliance. But are they in time to save the next victim?

Deadly Games is the first book in the Cavendish and Walker crime fiction series. If you like serial killer thrillers and psychological intrigue, then you'll love Sally Rigby's page-turning book.

Pick up *Deadly Games* today to read Cavendish & Walker's first case.

FATAL JUSTICE - Cavendish & Walker Book 2

A vigilante's on the loose, dishing out their kind of justice...

A string of mutilated bodies sees Detective Chief Inspector Whitney Walker back in action. But when she discovers the victims have all been grooming young girls, she fears a vigilante is on the loose. And while she understands the motive, no one is above the law.

Once again, she turns to forensic psychologist, Dr Georgina Cavendish, to unravel the cryptic clues. But will they be able to save the next victim from a gruesome death?

Fatal Justice is the second book in the Cavendish & Walker crime fiction series. If you like your mysteries dark, and with a twist, pick up a copy of Sally Rigby's book today.

~

LETHAL SECRET - Cavendish & Walker Book 4

Someone has a secret. A secret worth killing for....

When a series of suicides, linked to the Wellness Spirit Centre, turn out to be murder, it brings together DCI Whitney Walker and forensic psychologist Dr Georgina Cavendish for another investigation. But as they delve deeper, they come across a tangle of secrets and the very real risk that the killer will strike again.

As the clock ticks down, the only way forward is to infiltrate the centre. But the outcome is disastrous, in more ways than one.

For fans of Angela Marsons, Rachel Abbott and M A Comley, *Lethal Secret* is the fourth book in the Cavendish & Walker crime fiction series.

~

LAST BREATH - Cavendish & Walker Book 5

Has the Lenchester Strangler returned?

When a murderer leaves a familiar pink scarf as his calling card, Detective Chief Inspector Whitney Walker is forced to dig into a cold case, not sure if she's looking for a killer or a copycat.

With a growing pile of bodies, and no clues, she turns to forensic psychologist, Dr Georgina Cavendish, despite their relationship being at an all-time low.

Can they overcome the bad blood between them to solve the unsolvable?

For fans of Rachel Abbott, Angela Marsons and M A Comley, *Last Breath* is the fifth book in the Cavendish & Walker crime fiction series.

∾

FINAL VERDICT - Cavendish & Walker Book 6

The judge has spoken......everyone must die.

When a killer starts murdering lawyers in a prestigious law firm, and every lead takes them to a dead end, DCI Whitney Walker finds herself grappling for a motive.

What links these deaths, and why use a lethal injection?

Alongside forensic psychologist, Dr Georgina Cavendish, they close in on the killer, while all the time trying to not let their personal lives get in the way of the investigation.

For fans of Rachel Abbott, Mark Dawson and M A Comley, Final Verdict is the sixth in the Cavendish & Walker series. A fast paced murder mystery which will keep you guessing.

∾

RITUAL DEMISE - Cavendish & Walker Book 7

Someone is watching…. No one is safe

The once tranquil woods in a picturesque part of Lenchester have become the bloody stage to a series of ritualistic murders. With no suspects, Detective Chief Inspector Whitney Walker is once again forced to call on the services of forensic psychologist Dr Georgina Cavendish.

But this murderer isn't like any they've faced before. The murders are highly elaborate, but different in their own way, and with the clock ticking, they need to get inside the killer's head before it's too late.

For fans of Angela Marsons, Rachel Abbott and L J Ross. Ritual Demise is the seventh book in the Cavendish & Walker crime fiction series.

Acknowledgments

As usual, I'd like to thank my critique partners Amanda Ashby and Christina Phillips for being the first sets of eyes on my book. I couldn't do it without you.

Thanks also, to my editing team, Emma Mitchell and Amy Hart. Also, thanks to Stuart Bache, for yet another brilliant cover.

I'd like to mention my Advanced Reader Team, who I rely on to point out what works and what doesn't. Also, for picking up my many bloopers! Thanks to all of you.

To Zena, Judy, and Annie, who chose the names selected for the rail operators, and had a character named after them. Thanks for the great suggestions.

Finally, thanks to my family: Garry, Alicia, Marcus, Eliza and Barry, for your continued support.

About the Author

Sally Rigby was born in Northampton, in the UK. She has always had the travel bug, and after living in both Manchester and London, eventually moved overseas. From 2001 she has lived with her family in New Zealand, which she considers to be the most beautiful place in the world. During this time she also lived for five years in Australia.

Sally has a background in education and always loved crime fiction books, films and TV programmes. She has a particular fascination with the psychology of serial killers.

Sally loves to hear from her readers, so do feel free to get in touch via her website www.sallyrigby.com